MW01173373

Chasing Wolfe

Jessica P. Morgan

This is a work of fiction. All of the characters, organizations, and events portrayed in this novel are either products of the author's imagination or are used fictitiously.

Chasing Wolfe

Copyright © 2020 Jessica P. Morgan
Cover Art by Jessica P. Morgan, Knoxville, TN © 2020. All rights reserved.
Author photograph by Jessica P. Morgan.
First Printing: August 2020

ISBN: 9798671782431

Printed in the United States of America.

<u>Also by Jessica P. Morgan</u>

Take Me Home
In the Shadow of the Falls
In the Hands of Innocents
A Change in Benefits

CHAPTER 1

Folman Tennessee, Present

Never heard the strain of worn cylinders seizing and choking as her ancient Nissan tried to accelerate up the steep grade. She had agreed to meet Wolfe by the lake tonight without asking many questions. They were closing in on their three year dating anniversary, and she and her best friend Justine agreed that Wolfe would probably pop the question tonight. She had to make it on time. She couldn't go barreling into the parking lot, a trail of gravel dust flying up in her wake, and screech into a space with her curly brown hair frizzed into a cloud as she rushed to the landing-stage. How desperate would that look? She had to make up the lost time on her way.

Never slowed down as she turned onto the gravel lane leading to the parking lot by the lake and then tried to stay composed as she eased into a space at the end of the lot. She was three minutes late, but she paused to check her hair and run a hand down the length of her red dress to smooth the winkles. Passing his empty olive green Jeep, she breathed a sigh of relief that Wolfe hadn't given up on her as she made her way to the landing near the pier. Despite the world's best efforts to block her arrival, Never tried to relax and look dignified as she strolled closer to meet Wolfe on the edge of Hickory Lake where he waited with a red plastic film surrounding a clump of flowers tightly clutched between his fingers. She took her time picking her way along the boards and listened to the water lapping at the wooden supports under her feet. It really was a beautiful night to be at the lake. Sunset came early this time of year, but the last pinks and purples had not faded into the dark velvety backdrop that would showcase the stars for the rest of the night. It would be an amazing night to take engagement photos. She looked around to see if she could spot the cover the photographer would walk out from as Wolfe got down on one knee and held out a jewelry box for her approval. There was a nice cluster of bushes over Wolfe's right shoulder that would make a perfect place to shoot from. Never was sure she saw the glint of something shiny coming through the branches. Wouldn't it be a lark if he recruited Justine or Kirk from the paper to take pictures of their special moment? Justine had been trying to talk Never into a double wedding ever since her boyfriend Rory proposed in the Bahamas last April.

Wolfe didn't turn to greet her as she sauntered up to the railing beside him. He was wearing a jacket she didn't recognize and his hair looked like it hadn't seen a comb all day. His yellow dress shirt was wrinkled and she couldn't tell if it was tucked into his brown slacks. She started to reach for his hand, but realized his knuckles were turning white from clutching the flowers. The scene was nothing like she expected. Had the few minutes she was running behind upset him so much? Looking at his frazzled appearance, she hoped his explanation would soothe her and dispel the trepidation creeping up her spine. When he turned to acknowledge her, he didn't greet her with a smile or a hug. Purple half-moons hung beneath preoccupied green eyes intent on scrutinizing the space above her head. The tilt of his chin gave her a view of the new beard he had grown over the last few weeks. She studied him as the silence between them continued. He ran a hand through his hair again, disrupting the brown layers, but he still wouldn't speak. Something was very wrong. Never had interviewed gang members who were more forthcoming. The smile faded from her own lips as she crossed her arms in front of her and waited.

The words that came out were filled with regret instead of promise.

"I'm sorry Nev," he ground out in a low, labored tone. "I never meant to hurt you."

What was he talking about?

"I thought I had everything covered."

Thinking Wolfe was nervous about the proposal, she forced a smile she hoped was reassuring. It would be classic Wolfe if he wrote a speech and forgot it.

"I'm sure it will be fine," she encouraged. "Just tell me what you feel."

"It was an accident. I never meant to..."

"Meant to what?"

At her confusion, he hurried on to explain. The words spewed from his lips once he released the first sentence and he hit warp speed as he ran through the details. Wolfe wasn't trying to propose. She had it all wrong. Wolfe was confessing to something far more damning than forgetting a speech. *Could this be real?* Any minute now she expected to wake up or for someone to pop up from behind the bushes and yell surprise. Instead, Wolfe kept going.

He mentioned someone named Chasity. Wolfe used the excuse that she was young and vulnerable and he took advantage of both her and Never's trust in him. Something overcame him. That was the only way he could explain it. One thing led to another during office hours. She was one of his graduate students. He wanted to break it off, but when he finally worked up the courage she informed him things were complicated now. The only thing Never could think was: *three years.* Three years they had dated, almost to the day, and he was trying to tell her he was going to marry the girl he bent over his office desk three months ago. *And here he stands with a bundle of drugstore flowers that cost him less than a box of Plan B that could have avoided this disaster.* Never couldn't handle any more of this. She threw the flowers to the ground after he extended them in her direction and held them there with the stem of one of her red heels. Her eyes bore into his as she squared her hips and dared him to try to retrieve his offerings. She wanted him to listen to what she said next, because she wasn't in the mood to repeat it.

"You can go jump in the lake, Wolfe Strickland, and take your cheap apologies with you."

That was her closer. She turned her back on him, shaking the plastic from her shoe like the piece of trash it was, and fled for her car. She felt foolish for the care she put into her outfit and the time she spent before the mirror in the *Folman Gazette* bathroom. Thinking there might be a photographer for their surprise date, she changed into a clingy red dress and heels that produced more than one whistle when she left work. Now stalking down the boardwalk like a woman ready to set fire to everything her newly-minted ex-boyfriend owned, Never couldn't wait to get home and strip the dress off. Whether it ended up in the hamper or the dumpster was yet to be decided. The only thing she knew for certain was that it would be a long time before she ever wanted to see Wolfe Strickland's face again.

CHAPTER 2

Folman Tennessee, Present

Her usual six o'clock alarm sounded in the other room. Never rubbed her face and stumbled to the kitchen. She slammed a pod into her Keurig and powered on her phone while she waited. After turning it off last night to send a clear message that she was unavailable, Never was curious what she had missed. The first thing that popped up was a message from Justine with a video attachment. She thought it was a congratulations or a joke video about bridezillas so she didn't open it right away. She didn't want to explain how last night went so far off-course. Setting her phone aside, Never intended to wallow in her own brand of comforting self-pity for another hour. As much as she loved Justine, she wasn't sure she could endure the condescension disguised as pity from others after they found out about her non-proposal date. She wanted to hang on to the cocoon of silence in her apartment and block out the judgment of the rest of the world for a few more minutes.

Never was halfway through her first cup of

coffee when her phone dinged several times. She hadn't heard pounding on her door last night. Wolfe hadn't tried to win her back or keep her from setting fire to his house. He must have slunk back to his new babe without a second thought about her. Her messages were all from Justine. *What could be so pressing first thing on a Saturday morning? Did someone find the mayor with his mistress? Did they uncover another sex trafficking ring?* Why would Justine call at six o'clock? Her best friend knew she wasn't a morning person. And if she thought Never was with Wolfe, celebrating their engagement, she would never interrupt them so early without an unusual reason. Unlocking her screen, Never went through the motions of opening her voicemail and putting it on speakerphone as she laid it back down on the coffee table to listen. It wasn't her friend's gentle ribbing that came through the speaker. Never could almost taste the undercurrent of fear in her voice like the hazelnut creamer cutting through her coffee. Something was wrong, very wrong and Justine was worried about her. Had Wolfe contacted her last night after she had stormed off from the lake? What a jackass. He probably told Justine a sanitized version of his bullshit story and expected her to help him with the fallout. Never relaxed until the next voice came across.

"Martinez what the hell! You can't even manage to keep from being scooped on your own story? Where the hell are you?"

Her editor-in-chief didn't have to leave his name or number. She would recognize Jerry Phillips' gruff bellow anywhere. Several times it had entered her dreams. He was a hard man to escape. But what was he talking about? Never left work late to meet Wolfe because she was reworking a report Jerry wanted and her inbox was empty by 5:30 p.m.

What story had she been scooped on? She turned in the story about the town hall remodeling projects, but she couldn't confirm the rumors about a mayor's aid being fired for misappropriation of funds. Had someone else found a source? The only open investigation she was interested in at the moment was the weird after-work habits of Archibald Gordon, but she hadn't pitched it to Jerry because it hadn't panned out yet. She had watched Norton Gordon's son, "Archie", after she discovered his frequent after-hours trips downtown at night. He was ten-years her junior, single, heir to, and employed by the most prosperous business in town. It would make sense for him to enjoy the nightlife. The strange thing was Archie's choice of surroundings. He didn't bar-hop or pick up a date while he was downtown. Never could imagine many women would entertain a date with Archie despite his receding hairline and habitual limp. His job security at his father's package company could entice women to try to focus on his positive features, but he wasn't meeting any of them.

Archie haunted the city park and stared at the equipment. She had watched him, hiding in her car, as he galvanized his disabled leg into an uneven amble. He would stop and gaze at seesaws and jungle gyms as if they were difficult mathematical equations. He never approached children, but he was still there. Never kept waiting for him to pull out a package or meet with someone, but no one ever interrupted his lingering tramps through the park and quiet business district nearby. His activities intrigued Never, but she still hadn't caught him doing anything illegal.

Did someone find out about Gordon? Was this her boss's weird way of saying someone announced the engagement in the newspaper before she did? Oh my

God, how embarrassing was it going to be on Monday when she has to explain why they had to print a retraction? At thirty-seven, she was encroaching on old maid material. Would her boss send her to research dating apps for mature lovers that like to hang out in bathtubs and watch sunsets? Maybe she should take up a strange hobby? Justine would encourage her to get a cat lady for beginners kit, but Never wasn't really interested in any of that stuff. She liked her life the way it was. It was comfortable. An engagement to Wolfe would have meant changes. It was the expected path and Wolfe was more suited to her than any other man she had dated. He didn't hassle her over her erratic schedule or her writing time because he had office hours and classroom prep to take care of that went beyond his scheduled classes. They had learned to spend as much time together on the weekends and throughout the summer as they could manage and Never had supplies and clothes at his home in case she had to rush into work the next day. They pinched time for lunch meetings here or there and Never went with him to Redmond College events, often finding ways to convert them into local interest stories for the paper. Then he went and screwed everything up.

A few minutes later, Justine called again. Never gave a sigh and held the phone up to her ear.

"Where the hell are you?" was hurled at her. Justine had clearly gotten tired of waiting for the proposal story. Too bad she was going to be disappointed when she finally heard it.

"It didn't happen," she deadpanned. "There are no juicy tidbits. I'm home, alone."

"Never, when was the last time you spoke to

9

Wolfe?"

"At the lake, when the slimy bastard told me he was banging a grad student."

"Never...you didn't," Justine started then stopped.

"Didn't what? Slash his tires, spit on him, burn his house down...no."

"That's good, but honey what was the last thing that happened?"

"I really don't want to talk about it right now, and tell Jerry we will be printing a correction Monday if anyone jumped the gun on our engagement announcement."

"I don't think that was why Jerry called, Nev."

"What else could have happened between last night and now?"

"You really need to turn on your television, hon."

The tone of her voice had softened. There was a note of something in it that gave Never pause. What would everyone be so worried about?

"Alright, ruin what little pleasure I have left," she grumbled as she reached for the remote. "What channel?"

Every local station was panning shots of the lake and running "Breaking News" banners across the bottom of her television screen. The camera people were zooming in on boats in the water before zipping back to the shoreline. There were people pointing and holding up binoculars for a better look. What the hell was going on? Why would reporters be swarming the parking lot at the lake where she had been last night? Sheriff's deputies and Robertson County Search and Rescue had their boat out on the water. Did someone go missing at the lake last night? Surely they weren't looking for her on the bottom of the lake.

"What are they doing at the lake?"

"Fishermen reported a body floating in the water early this morning."

"Is that why Jerry was screaming into my message box?"

"Yes, he jarred me awake when he couldn't find you."

"Why? Landon or Ben could handle a weekend boating accident without me."

"Honey...I don't think he would be heartless enough to make you work this one."

"Then what's the big deal?"

"Landon got there first and he said Wolfe's Jeep was still in the parking lot."

Never sat in silence watching her screen for a few seconds trying to process that last bit of information.

"You don't think..." she began then stopped.

"If you're not together, how did he get home?"

"Everyone thinks Wolfe is the one who drowned in the lake?" Never asked slowly as she set down her coffee mug.

"It's a real possibility Nev."

"I'll call everyone back later," Never muttered as she disconnected and turned up the volume on her TV.

"Did he really go jump in the lake?" she asked the empty room as she waited for the local station to come back from commercial.

When she marched off in a huff last night, she never dreamed he would act on her wishes. She had said worse things when she was upset and most guys would just laugh. Now, watching the news coverage of the body being pulled from the lake, her hands trembled. Could she be responsible in some way? The grainy still shots of a body being pulled onto one of the boats looked like it was wearing the ugly jacket Wolfe had on last night. It was misshapen and darker in its wet state, but it was enough to convince her.

What was happening to her? Did she do something to piss off God in the last twenty-four hours? Things just kept getting worse. First, she was blindsided by the whole Chasity thing, and now Wolfe's body is being pulled from the lake. The people in her office would get a good laugh at her side of the story. How would she ever live this down?

Last night, after she found out she wasn't going home with Wolfe to celebrate their engagement, Never went home and changed into her pajamas to eat ice cream while her world spun out of control. She had turned off her phone after the first pint, and started a rom-com that helped her cry herself to sleep. She woke up with breath that left her wishing adequate dental hygiene had outweighed her emotional breakdown. While she was avoiding her depression in a deep, dreamless slumber, she missed calls from half the town. Three calls from work, two from other outlets, and one from the Robertson County Sheriff's Department. It was a hell of a way to wake up on a Saturday morning. And the ball kept rolling. There were lots of things she didn't want to wake up to this morning.

One thing was for sure: she wasn't able to breathe normally—much less laugh—as she watched the coverage over and over again on every network. One network reporter went to the trouble of using a regional graphic with Nashville to the south and Folman labeled beside a star marking Hickory Lake so that out-of-towners would be able to find it if they traveled north on Interstate 24.

Over and over it went. Pictures of the lake flickered before her eyes without any clear answers about whether Wolfe's was the body they pulled from the water. No outlet would confirm it for sure, but Never knew it was him. Who else could it be? No one else would wear that ugly jacket and he was upset before she arrived. Chances were he was just as upset when she left. How was she supposed to process this? Wolfe Strickland was dead and no one would be marrying him anytime soon. She should cry or scream, but all she could manage was a blind stare as she clutched the remote and gently rocked back and forth on the sofa. She knew she was being a horrible person, but the only thing she could think of was how cheated she felt. She never would get to decide if she would set his "returns" on fire in his yard or just walk up and shove the box into his chest like a stone cold bitch and walk away. Wolfe would never have to make it up to her. He would never suffer from the cold shoulders she planned to give him for the next few months when they were within 100 yards of each other. None of that would happen now. Confusion settled around her shoulders like a shawl as Never continued watching videos of the lake on a loop. One of the local first responders came up to verify small details to the press. He confirmed one death, and that the investigation was ongoing. Investigations were still in the early stages. They weren't far enough along in the process to rule it a suicide or a homicide without more evidence.

There could be a homicide investigation over Wolfe's death. If Wolfe was dead, what did that mean? Is it possible that it wasn't Wolfe walking into the lake because of his own guilt? Never sat up straight as she realized why Justine's voice had an undercurrent. She was worried about Never being alive, but she was also worried about what Never had done. If Justine was worried, and the police were already calling her, would it be long before the whole town thought she had more involvement with Wolfe's last night than a hurtful breakup on the beach? It wouldn't be much of a stretch to think she lost her temper and tried to kill him. Only an angel with the skills of an actress would be able to act graceful after an announcement like that. If something unusual did come from their investigations, Never's door would be the first one they would come to. She would be on the short list of people carrying a grudge against Redmond College's late history professor. How would she defend herself from pressures like that? She was home alone last night. No one could back up her story or vouch for her whereabouts. If Never was reporting on this story, she would be inclined to think an angry lover committed a crime of passion. How would she prove she left him without a scratch? Would she ever find anyone who believed her if her best friend had doubts about her innocence? Never couldn't say she disagreed with their logic. Who would have a better reason to kill Wolfe Strickland?

CHAPTER 3

Redmond College, Redmond Tennessee,
Three Months Earlier

Wolfe enjoyed seeing the flurry of activity when the college transitioned into its fall semester. The campus had a renewed energy that fled with summer vacation. Redmond was alive again. The narrow streets of campus were packed with moving trucks and vehicles pulling U-Haul trailers of different sizes. The fall semester brought hoards of young men and women back to the tiny settlement in the shadow of the ridge. Worried parents followed behind their arriving students and studied every possession they unpacked as though they had never seen it before. Most of the parents would leave within an hour or two of the child's arrival. A small portion, viewing it as their child's first steps into adulthood, would not come to campus at all. Wolfe enjoyed watching the changing dynamics from his office window.

He made a habit of being on campus between the end of summer semester and the weeks before fall classes were in full swing. He wasn't required to be on campus at all during those weeks, but he showed up from time to time and held office hours for his grad students and prepped for his upcoming classes. He relaxed behind his desk and watched the hopeful faces as they walked through the commons and explored their new surroundings. It reminded him of why he elected to remain in academia.

The only other things that grabbed his attention on quiet mornings in his office were the messages he received from his online treasure-hunting group. He had stumbled upon an advertisement for the site during his first year at Redmond when he felt isolated and out of his element as a full-time western civilizations professor. The group was made up of professors and history buffs like himself. He met people who still had a passion for discovery and a love of learning.

From the first encounter, Wolfe was active in the group. When clues popped up on the message boards, he couldn't resist chasing them. Today was no different. This new clue from Pierce was further away than he usually entertained, but he was free to follow his own muses for the next few days. Wolfe copied the information and booked a plane ticket for the next morning.

He liked to limit his activities to local posts during the school year so no one would notice his unusual behavior. He didn't want anyone at the college to become aware of the lengthy amount of time he spent chasing clues to find tiny prizes hidden by his friends online. This clue happened to come at just the right time, and France *was* on his bucket list, after all. One long-distance adventure would be a wonderful distraction before the semester was in full swing.

Never wouldn't perceive his absence. She had been busy day and night worrying over a piece of gossip that accused the mayor of Folman of paying for his mistress with city funds. She was sleeping in her car and eating there too. Wolfe wouldn't be able to get her to take a shower and come over until she had something concrete for her article. She would remain distracted for another week before she gave up hope.

He would have to tell Never about his hobby one day, but it could wait. She was fighting corruption and tracking down information the community wanted to know. It felt inconsequential to bother her with his strange diversion at the moment. He was confident that if she could accept cycleball, this would be fine with her. What was there to be mad at about a tiny bit of adventure? Besides, he would be back with his treasure before anyone realized he was gone. Who could resist Paris in the fall?

The crowded mess at the airport in Paris cost him an extra hour. After a series of plastic-wrapped tunnels, Wolfe found the exit he was looking for. Travelers were lined up in front of small windows to exchange currency and asking directions to the heart of the city. Beggars were blocking the metro platform like toll road attendants, taxi drivers were swarming the open areas around the exit doors shouting out to people as they emerged from the airport hallways, and a decent phone signal was nowhere to be found.

Wolfe approached a taxi driver who spoke English and followed him to a dark BMW SUV. They zipped around cars in the waiting area and listened to music Wolfe had never heard before. It was half an hour before they reached the outskirts of the sprawling structures that identified as Paris. He couldn't see the famous river Seine or the Eiffel tower. The metro raced along beside the highway and ten to twenty story buildings rose in every direction. The driver mentioned it was the slow season as they navigated easily through traffic and entered the hive-like atmosphere of the city intersections. Streets splintered in every direction as if someone said, "create your own path" and the citizens of Paris did just that. It was extraordinary compared to the open spaces and uniform building materials of the southern United States. There were no shimmering towers or hard lines in their structures. Whole neighborhoods flowed in and out of each other as they wove their way to the heart of the city.

When Wolfe did manage to get to the address he had written down for his driver, four out of five shops on the Rue du Mont-Cenis were shuttered and dark. It was a stark contrast to the thriving, bustling Paris of his imagination. There was no music, nor were people milling about on street corners as he passed by. Cafés were empty or sported a single patron nursing a coffee in a tiny white cup with a handle even a child could not get his pinkie through. Sometimes there would be a local page of advertisements or a removed hat on the table or in a chair. There were no artists brooding and walking the empty streets for inspiration, just lonely people drinking from teeny coffee cups.

Wolfe didn't find much amusement in the solitary figures, in fact, the less opportunity to run into opposition the better. The clue he wanted to investigate was on private property. Wolfe needed to remove the information stashed in the courtyard before someone questioned his familiarity with the place. He felt like a randy young buck arriving for a weekend with his mistress. Paris was his for the next twenty-four hours.

He had rented a small apartment near his objective under the guise of relaxing before his fall semester obligations crowded his schedule. Being able to see the courtyard in question from the window of his rented space was some comfort, but he had to work hard not to stand by it and constantly eye the spot marked on the map in his overnight case. The clue said something should be buried by the left leg of the bench under the lantern in the window alcove.

The prize was usually a small marker or a children's toy, but Wolfe loved the suspense more than the treasure. The group post was authored by someone known only to him as Pierce. He had several of these friends in an online chat group dubbed "CHASETE", and Wolfe gave and received many clues like this one. He had a bin full of prizes for his efforts. Most of the group posts lead to more clues or small objects. It was never anything of much value.

It seemed silly to plunk down the money for a plane ticket. It was the first time he felt compelled to hunt this far from home, but the clue intrigued him. Why, after all, would someone in his US-based group pick a courtyard in Paris? And what, he wondered; would such a sophisticated traveler hide? Wolfe was so excited he couldn't wait until dark. He felt his need draw him to the elevator. He had to walk the street and check everything out on the ground level. He donned the new jacket he had picked up at the airport and lowered his camera strap over his head. A simple tourist would be his mark and his mask. Aside from a few curious pigeons, Wolfe passed only one other living creature. A homeless woman occupied a bench at the bus stop. She held out her hand and mumbled something in French. His emotions galloped when he ran his hand over his back pocket and missed the tell-tale lump that was his wallet. When he had first reached his room, he thought he might control his excitement long enough to nap. In his haste, Wolfe left everything but his room key. When the older woman stood up and became more insistent in her request and gestured up at the bus stop sign, Wolfe suspected she wanted change for her fare. He pulled out an empty pocket to show her and shrugged. She eyed his gold watch and nice shoes, but said no more. She spat on the ground at her feet and settled back down on the bench clutching her bundles as she had before.

He was dismissed, like a schoolboy on holiday, to enjoy the views in his tiny slice of Paris. There was so much beauty in the street's inconsistency. He strolled along, stopping from time to time to take a snapshot of a building, a flower, or the diminishing sunset. Wolfe wondered if a modern city could ever compare.

Row after row of mismatched designs and slices of historical architecture were sandwiched together, broken by small alleyways and parks blanketed with as much vegetation as possible. Modern staircases shaded with young trees connected brick streets as the neighborhood climbed farther up the tallest hill in the city. The modern and the venerable existed together in harmony. Construction was everywhere, but less obstructive than in the United States. He stopped for several seconds and watched a man three stories above him work with plaster to recreate the ornate border design circling a building. It was a drastic difference from the way Americans thought about how to use space.

Street names looked like historical markers

bolted to buildings instead of on standalone posts. Apartment buildings were so tall there was neither the view nor the desire to read the billboards so popular on American highways. Instead, every large pipe on the side of a building was showcasing advertisements championed by the locals. Stickers for art, radio stations, and music events were slapped on wide plastic downspouts in every direction. Small murals or street graffiti adorned steps and handrails. One in twenty doors sported a glossy red coat of paint, and the prismatic work of a street artist featuring a multicolor salamander with small human tattoos would draw your attention to a specific delivery entrance.

This section of Paris was mostly concrete and meandering streets that seemed to be allergic to the grid system of planning, but it still managed to feel charming. Wolfe couldn't walk ten feet without passing window boxes brimming with flowering plants that accented the effects of the larger rooftop gardens floating high above him. Staircases were adorned with small, secluded garden spots. Red and black awnings popped from corner cafes and nuns passed in formal dress as they headed for their compact cars.

Every ounce of space was utilized like a debutant packing for spring break. Buildings were brimming with life and nature. Every church courtyard had a green or a flower-lined pathway shaded by small trees. It wasn't stuffed or cramped with possessions like it would be in America. Life just seems abundant here.

There it was. The sign for Saint Acacius Church hung on a wrought iron post a few feet in front of him. It was so close. The bell on the map was three feet from the black metal fence and Wolfe's excitement heightened to a crescendo only he could hear. The church was a simple white wooden structure with a brick foundation and entryway staircase. Stained glass adorned the main windows, but Wolfe couldn't take his eyes off of the landscaping. Staring though the thin metal bars, he stalked his prey. The bell sat like a large toad on the slab of concrete. Lines and patches of green from weathering and bacterial growth hugged the bronze dome. The thin hedges around it were interrupted by various flowers and climbing vines. There was no care taken to draw attention to the bell's presence from outside the border. It was easy to stroll by without noticing it.

On closer inspection, Wolfe noticed there was a plaque bolted to the concrete base detailing the journey from the previous bell tower to the place of honor it now held in the shadow of the new church built after the bombings of World War I. If he reached through the fence, Wolfe could almost touch the widest section of the dome.

The last clue on the map, a clue he had memorized, said, "hiding in a niche a few inches below the topsoil on the right corner, you will find your prize." He wanted to go inside and dig. He wanted to find what was hidden, but it was easy to be spotted by the few people still haunting the sidewalks. Wolfe squeezed the section of railing under his fingers as a reminder to himself to be patient. After dark, he would return and claim his prize.

He had his key, but Wolfe had forgotten about the lobby code to enter the building. It was stored in his phone upstairs. He tried recreating it from memory, but the light blinked red and faded. He shoved his clinched fingers in his pocket as he glared back at the machine. It was just his type of bad luck. He was in reach of his possessions and the prize that possessed him to come on this crazy trip, but he was acting as unprepared as one of his green, freshman students. Wolfe could imagine Never's face if she could see him. She always laughed when he was capable of losing things in such a short amount of time. She called it his superpower. He had done it tonight within an hour of stepping from his taxi. That had to be a record, even for him. It looked like he would be watching the last bit of light fade from the sky as he sat on the chilly front steps at the entrance to the building.

With little other choice, Wolfe lowered himself to the wide steps to wait for another person to come up the sidewalk and possibly let him in. In his exuberance, he had gone from the possibility of wandering the streets of Paris in the dark to facing the prospect of "sleeping rough" just feet below the window of his comfortable room. He would have plenty of time to berate himself for his own foolishness as he watched the shadows lengthen.

Wolfe had gotten more than a few strange looks and an offer of a few coins while he waited. He wrapped his new coat tighter than it was intended to stretch and tried to ignore the information his sore bum was sending to his brain. He didn't have his phone, and couldn't alert anyone concerning his predicament. Now all he could do was wait on the cold steps and hope someone would leave for a dinner date in the next few minutes.

Minutes stretched into over an hour. Wolfe's hands were cold and his lower body was aching from extended contact with the unyielding stone steps. He was about to give up hope on anyone moving from their apartments tonight when the light from the elevator in the lobby lit up and opened around 10 p.m. Wolfe was grateful when the caretaker noticed him huddled up against the glass door. They exchanged several comical gestures through the glass and Wolfe held up his apartment key for her to see he wasn't just lounging on her steps for his own amusement. When she shook her head, laughed and let him in, Wolfe babbled out a thank you in French and hoped she couldn't understand the English words he chastised himself with as he waited for the elevator.

After exiting the elevator into a short hallway, Wolfe opened the door to his room with a sigh and walked into the darkness. The embarrassment of his setback couldn't dull his excitement for what he had come here to do. Tonight, he would claim his prize when he went back out into the night. He would be victorious and have the object packed and ready for his early flight in the morning. Wolfe retrieved his wallet and phone from the table as he crossed the room. He would be prepared when he brought his treasure back. He couldn't be stranded outside after he found his prize.

Wolfe's fingers found the button to raise the louvered shutters separating him from the cold air and lights of Paris. Even without a moon, he could see the courtyard and the bell within it bathed in the warm glow of street and apartments lights below him. In the distance, Wolfe could make out popular American music blared through the speakers of a subpar sound system. The sound gave him comfort. It was as out of place as he was. Looking out over the rooftops, Wolfe couldn't imagine any place more different than the American south he grew up in. It was as though he had landed on a different planet. Paris was much older, teaming with life, and he was sure it held archeological secrets to rival anything modern cultures could create. In a few hours, he would unearth his own miniscule treasure from its rich soil. Could anything be more exciting?

CHAPTER 4

Folman Tennessee, Present

Never shut off the loop of images on her television. It was time to peel herself off the couch and change clothes. She had come to the decision that the best thing she could do was use her key to search Wolfe's house. She gave Wolfe three years of her life. She deserved to see what he left behind. He owed her answers. After she searched the place, Never could pick up a few of her things. She didn't want to wait for the "proper channels" to get around to giving her good thongs back. She just had to figure out a way to get there without being noticed. Stuffing her phone in her pocket and shoving her sock-clad feet into her Converse sneakers, Never was ready to roll.

    She eased open the door to the back staircase of her building and leaned in to listen. If anyone was waiting for her or loitering at the bottom, she couldn't hear them. Scooting through and stopping the door's natural swing as she disappeared behind it, Never took the steps two at a time until she reached the street. Her old Nissan was keeping guard out front in her assigned parking spot, but her longtime ride would have to sit this adventure out. She was the last one to see Wolfe alive and it wouldn't be long before someone with a badge or a camera came to find her. She didn't plan to address their questions until she could answer some of her own.

Never had one advantage everyone else didn't: a key to Wolfe's house. She had to use it while she still had time. That advantage might shed some light on his strange behavior. She wanted to be the first to rifle through his stuff. She wanted to claim her things tucked in the bathroom and in the spare drawer in his bedroom. She needed to be the first one to solve this puzzle. He owed her that much. Those things and the three pounds of Columbian coffee she left during their last weekend together. Neither Wolfe nor his cleaning lady would need the caffeine as much as she would in the coming days. Never had to get into Wolfe's house before the police and the rest of the world turned their gaze from the beach at the lake.

The key to accomplishing that was to avoid being seen. Never planned to walk two blocks to one of the busiest streets in her neighborhood and hail a cab that she could pay for in cash. Busy streets lead to less eyewitness accuracy. She had learned that the hard way as a cub reporter, talking to over three hundred witnesses after a stabbing at a high school basketball game. Everyone saw the guy fall, but no one saw anything that happened before. By the end of a night filled with interviews, Never was convinced no two people would ever describe the assailant the same way, and she was ready to pull her hair out. She was betting that no one walking Hendly Drive this time of day would notice her either. She planned to be back to her place with a big bag of laundry and a huge can of Columbian coffee by the time someone from the sheriff's office showed up to question her.

Movement by the side of the building stopped her fervent progress. She ducked behind a section of old fence to escape the view of a couple of cameramen who had walked around the side of the building to take a smoke break and chat with one of her neighbors doing the same. In something of a modified duck walk, Never made her way slowly to the alleyway connecting the backs of businesses on Fourth Street. Wiping the loose dirt from her palms, she bolted into the crowds of foot traffic heading for the small boutiques and eateries. Slowing down to match their pace, she tried to act casual and unhurried, but she could feel the lines around her mouth drawing taut. She needed to get out of sight and across town before anyone recognized her. Cutting through the parking lot at the Rusty Penny, Never ran for Hendly Drive and hoped there would be a cab waiting. She wanted to be on the return trip before the police could check the traffic cameras and see what path she took.

Things didn't go as planned. Never dispatched the two blocks in record time, but there were no cabs anywhere along the busy street. After fifteen minutes of hiding near a fruit stand, she saw one pull to the curb. Never dashed from her cover and cut off an older man's attempt to appropriate it. She didn't turn to look at him as he yelled several colorful names and shook his finger in her direction.

After giving her instructions to the driver, she kept her cap pulled down over her dark sunglasses to hide as much of her face as possible. Never slouched down in the seat for the remainder of the ride and checked all the local news feeds for updates. Most of the stations were still showing live shots of the lake and all the crews working to search the area. There were a few shots of the front of Wolfe's house, but most of them were old photographs from a realty site. The new mailbox she helped him put up in the spring and the pot of mums he won at the last faculty appreciation dinner were both missing from the coverage.

Never hoped that meant there wasn't a police presence on Wolfe's property either. Once the circus at the lake dissipated, she wouldn't be able to sneak around so easily. Robertson County Sheriff's Department, reporters, and everyday busybodies within fifty miles would be lining the road to Wolfe's property looking for information.

The driveway at Wolfe's house was long and straight. It was an open highway of concrete compared to his neighbors' properties. His yard was over an acre and the house sat back a considerable distance from the main road. The entrance rested at the end of a loop of six residences on the edge of a neighborhood abutting farm property. Wolfe would always remark on the history of the area as well as the old craftsman house's stained-glass windows and original fixtures. The placement of the farm next door and its history were things that Never could use to her advantage.

Never knew the driveway would be too exposed to the rest of the neighborhood. The sight of a yellow cab slowly going up and down the driveway of a dead man would attract cub reporters and curious neighbors. She couldn't go that way. The only hidden way in would be through the back door. To reach the back of the house, she had to hike through the wooded side of the lot and trespass across a small section of Widow

Jenkins' farm.

Never told the cab driver where to stop and hopped out. Handing an extra set of bills through the window to help him forget her strange departure, Never stepped across a drainage ditch and disappeared into the brush. It took her two minutes to reach the top of the ridge and peer down the back side of the hill that connected to Wolfe's property.

Never wasted several minutes watching for activity from behind a big oak that dominated the tree line on the ridge. Referred to as the *Hanging Tree*, the name alluded to a story about a group of drunken Confederate soldiers, she couldn't quite recall. Wolfe loved to tell her numerous local history stories when they sat on the back porch together. She could still picture him there with a coffee cup in hand looking out at the ridge.

Shaking her head clear and looking in every direction for movement, Never figured it was now or never. She raced down the hill, across the lawn, and up on the porch before skidding to a stop by the back door. The key was cool and shaky in her hand, but she managed to insert it in the lock and stumble inside. Never swung the door closed and ran her fingers down the blinds covering it before turning to take in the things around her. It was time to start her search.

The house's size made her task complicated and time-consuming. It wasn't a huge home, but spacious for a man living alone. Even with Never living there on the weekends, they both had plenty of house between them. Never needed to take as many shortcuts as she could while she was searching. She was glad Wolfe was a fanatic about keeping his doors and windows locked and covered. She was free to run from room to room without being noticed by the crowd gathering out front. She grinned as she thought about the reporters waiting outside in dismay after they found out she had scooped them yet again.

Nothing seemed any different than usual. Wolfe wasn't organized, but he was predictable in his clutter. She knew how he thought and where he kept things, but it wasn't much help. There didn't seem to be anything new since her last visit. There were no threats on the answering machine, no strange notes in the trash, or on his desk. Never didn't even find a stack of dirty clothes behind the bathroom door to rifle through.

Letting out an irritated sigh, she did a mental inventory. The only thing she knew was missing was Wolfe's cell phone and work case. Never figured they would turn up in the Jeep or the lake.

Grabbing her overnight bag and stuffing it with articles of clothing and other supplies, Never hoped she was making up for time she lost on the trip over. She snatched her coffee canister and several bags of chocolate-covered peanuts before sneaking back out the way she came. But this time as she turned from locking the door back, an unfamiliar voice told her she wasn't alone.

"Ma'am, this property belongs to Wolfe Strickland. Can you tell me why you're trespassing this morning?"

An officer she didn't recognize with "Robertson County Sheriff's Department" printed on his sand-colored uniform was blocking her retreat. It didn't look like a party she would enjoy being invited to. He kept his hand on his service revolver, but didn't attempt to pull it as he stopped her. It seemed she was going to have a conversation with authorities earlier than she intended.

"I didn't break in." Never flashed a smile hoping she could charm him as she dangled the keychain from her hand. "I have a key."

His eyes narrowed and he kept asking questions, "Who was Mr. Strickland to you?"

If she had been thinking on her feet she would have claimed to be Wolfe's cleaning lady, but Never had been through too much in the last twenty-four hours to be quick on her feet. She settled for her usual straight-forward approach.

"He was my ex-boyfriend."

"Ex?"

So much for getting out of this in a hurry.

"Yes, as of last night."

"So you're Never Martinez from the *Folman Gazette*?"

"Yes," Never nodded and hoped things would go faster.

"We have been trying to get in touch with you."

She let that comment ride.

"What's in the bag?"

33

Following the officer's hand motion, Never slid her gaze over to the strap on her shoulder.

"Personal items I left here from time to time."

"I'm afraid I am going to have to keep them for the moment."

"I don't see how my work clothes and hairspray are going to give you any leads on this case officer," Never argued as she dropped the bag in front of her feet. "Can I at least have my coffee and peanuts?"

After sliding her bag out of reach with his boot, the officer made a show of lifting the lid on the comically oversized coffee canister and checking the seal for breaks. Satisfied with the results he handed it back to her, and proceeded to mistreat the chocolate-covered peanuts until the chocolate coating was powdering the bottom of the bag.

"I believe these are safe to travel, Miss Martinez, but you'll have to come for an interview at the station this afternoon to pick up your bag."

"Great," Never gave him the biggest fake smile she could muster. "That saves me time waiting outside for a statement."

"Reeves, add Miss Martinez's name to the interview list for this afternoon," he shouted to another officer waiting at the corner of the porch. "And take her key to Mr. Strickland's house for safe keeping."

"As much as I am looking forward to our next conversation, I need to get home and start on today's article."

"We'll see you at 2," he reminded.

Giving her a satisfied grin, Deputy Henderson stepped out of her way and motioned for her to follow Reeves around the house and through the den of reporters and gawkers setting up shop at the end of the driveway. Thankfully, her wide, black sunglasses covered the red-rimmed, puffy, eyeliner-bleeding mess congregating around her eyes as cameras closed in on her escape. It hurt to think that her image would be plastered all over every media outlet in a fifty mile radius, but she wanted out of the area before the senior reporters showed up on Wolfe's doorstep.

As shutters clicked and the officer moved the crowd out of her way, Never realized she might have to walk home as well. Wolfe's subdivision wasn't exactly a hotbed of cab activity, and the one Never called earlier was long gone. Two aggressive reporters from one of her newspaper's rivals followed her down the sleepy street shouting questions and making noise for her to turn and speak with them. Never kept her back straight and the coffee canister held high as she broke into a jog. Once she was sure no one was still following her, she got out her phone and dialed for help.

Justine had picked her up a mile from Wolfe's house and reluctantly dropped her off up the street from her apartment building after a long hug and making her promise to get in touch with Jerry. Never needed to talk to her editor about adding her first-hand account of the events by the lake last night to Landon's article on Wolfe's death. She considered her to-do list as she trudged up the stairs to her apartment with her massive can of coffee, her melting chocolate candy, and the lunch Justine had insisted on buying her. Pushing her way around a gathering of reporters and camera crews, Never realized for the first time she was going to have to ask herself the questions she wasn't comfortable with.

This day just kept getting better and better. If Jerry was to get his big story about last night, she had to dredge through everything that happened before her anger and her emotional breakdown clouded her perspective. She needed to analyze her three year relationship with Wolfe like a professional. For that, she was going to require a shower and plenty of quiet time.

"Nev, honey, you had several messages while you were away," her neighbor's voice caused her to pause and look back.

"What did they want?"

"One was a nice young man at Robertson County Sheriff's Department."

"I already ran into him."

"Okay, the other two were from the *Cedar Hill Caller* and *Youngstown Howler*," she read to her with excitement. "They wanted to ask permission to quote you for their stories."

"Thank you, Mrs. Basket."

"You might want to do something with your hair and make-up before you go back out dear."

Waving her off with more fingers than she wanted to, Never turned the key and slipped inside. Locking the door and pulling all her living room blind cords for good measure, she stood for a few seconds listening to the din of people milling around beyond her vision. Unless there was a school shooting or a break in the identity of the mayor's mistress, her unwanted company would linger like an uninvited relative.

Discarding her shoes by the door, Never walked across her tiny kitchen/dining area and deposited the coffee and peanuts on the counter. She would make more coffee after her shower. The food in the take-out container wasn't in the least bit appealing at the moment. She needed time to think, and a place free of windows.

The dramatic reveal of his deception at the lake last night was bizarre. Wolfe was never impulsive with her. She wished on more than one occasion he would surprise her. She was always the one encouraging him and teasing him when he fell into the same old routines.

Maybe someone finally inspired him, but it just wasn't her? The Wolfe she thought she knew would never be interested in a fling with a grad student. He liked concentrating on improving his cycleball league when he had time to devote to things other than his work. Never couldn't entertain the idea that Wolfe would risk losing the career he worked so hard to advance, and all the advantages that went with it. Plus, Wolfe seemed to be settling down in Folman and putting down roots. Why would he throw it all away?

Nothing in the last forty-eight hours was progressing the way it should have. She wasn't engaged, Wolfe was dead, and somewhere on the Redmond College campus there could be a pregnant woman worrying over the fate of her unborn child. Never replayed his words over and over again in her mind. His anguish seemed genuine.

Never couldn't have been more confused by someone's behavior than if her workaholic boss Jerry showed up with flowers and gifted her tickets for a two week cruise. Maybe she should open with that. Who was Wolfe Aaron Strickland? It was always good to start a story from the beginning.

Wolfe was, by all accounts, a "made" man when she began dating him. He was established in his career and on his way to living a comfortable life. He was athletic, motivated, and seemed to enjoy her straightforward attitude. He was a great find for a small town workaholic like herself. In other areas of her life, she would have quizzed and dug until she knew all his dirt, but Never didn't want to beat a gift horse to death like she had in several previous relationships. With Wolfe, she took it easy. Their lives meshed in the present, and she liked having someone other than Justine to count on when she had time to socialize. But all that easy, don't-push-things attitude got her today was more questions. Who was the Wolfe Strickland she met at the lake, and why didn't she know?

In a few hours, someone at the sheriff's office would ask her the same question. Would she know then?

"A few days ago, I thought I knew. Now I don't have an answer," she told her empty apartment.

Heading for the shower, Never hoped that hot water and time would tell her what she wanted to know. After three years, she had to know something, right? She just needed the reporter in her to interrogate the girlfriend. Maybe they could have a nice chat over coffee once she scrubbed the emotions of this morning off her skin and untangled the rage from her hair.

She didn't want to face the outside world again until she had some answers and makeup at her disposal, but she would settle for having some direct questions of her own. She needed to be ready for her interview at the sheriff's office, but she wanted to be the one getting credit for the exclusive on this case. She had to work fast and find an angle only she could exploit. If Jerry demanded she share the byline with Landon, so be it. This would come down to her telling her story. It could be the hardest piece she ever attempted to write.

Never wouldn't call the relationship between her and Wolfe a power couple, but they were beyond the butterflies and passions of younger couples. They were stable, committed, working adults. God, they sounded like a PSA. They were comfortable, but they weren't gushy in their relationship.

"That is going to thrill some readers," she muttered as she switched on the water.

Never had to find her hook and she had to find it fast. She only had a few hours before she had to brave the crowd outside and make her 2 p.m. appointment at the sheriff's office. For the rest of the afternoon, her face would be popping up in news stories across the region.

CHAPTER 5

Paris, Two Months and 30 Days Earlier

It was during the early hours of the morning when Wolfe returned to the apartment with his prize. He lowered the louvered blinds before he turned on the lantern-style lamp by the bed. Looking around him to make sure he was alone, Wolfe took the wooden box out of the pocket of his coat and slid back the lid. The protection's sounds of complaint seemed to fill the quiet room around him. Sitting down on the bed, he cradled the box in his lap. He slid the lid all the way out of its thin track and shifted it to a pillow for safekeeping. The inside was lined with a tea-colored fabric and cording that could have been burgundy in its original state. Nestled in the center was a bundle of something with a curved side and a wider base. Its bulk ranged in shape between a cylinder and a cone. Details were obscured, mummified in the cobweb-like design of the deteriorating fabric. The remnants of the fabric felt and looked like handspun muslin as he ran his fingertips over it. It had been years since he had handled any fabric of this age and quality, but the memories came back as he explored his new find.

Fabric like this hadn't passed through his hands since he quit his part-time college job at Ezekias's House of Mysteries on the edge of the Little Five Points neighborhood. The fabric was part of one of his favorite memories from a lackluster summer he spent clad in a worn top hat and purple vest. Among the few genuine items the old showman had in his possession was a mummified cat wrapped in a fabric similar to the fabric in the box before him. Wolfe used to take the cat out and examine it like he worked in a real museum when his boss was out for his two hour liquid lunch break. The house cat was exquisite, but it was nothing compared to his latest find. The possibilities surrounding his new find's origins had him bubbling with excitement. Whatever was beyond this wrapper of frayed cloth belonged to him, and he couldn't wait to see it.

CHAPTER 6

Folman Tennessee, Present

By the time Never walked through the doors at the Robertson County Sheriff's Department, she was settled and her head was clear. But she still didn't like the way Sergeant Henderson, David Henderson, the older brother of the man who took her bag and ran her off this morning, was sizing her up. He could have been attractive with his dark, wavy hair and green eyes. Maybe someone she would let buy her a drink at a bar or charm her at a community fundraiser. One thing kept pricking at her senses as she surveyed him. Something wouldn't put her mind at ease with her new acquaintance. There was a cold smugness about him, like a sports jock assured he could say and do anything he pleased. She had been at college parties with his type before. Guys like him had a goal in mind and they never left until they attained it, willing partner or not. The only difference was this man had authority.

"Please take a seat Miss Martinez," he offered as she stepped into the room.

He went through the normal chitchat before he got down to business.

"How did you come to have a key to Wolfe Strickland's home?"

"He gave it to me while we were dating."

"You said were..."

She couldn't believe this sergeant was farther behind on digging into this story than she was. He had to be baiting her.

"The news said he committed suicide last night."

"Why would you go to his house?"

"I have a key and I keep things there."

"Things like what?"

"My coffee and the clothes I would like to get back."

"Why?"

She wanted to taunt him, tell him the reason a woman visits a man, make him uncomfortable with her descriptions, but there wasn't much to tell.

"I guess I'm a practical girl."

"Why was it so important for you to sneak around Wolfe Strickland's house this morning?"

Never was tired and hung over, but she was angry as well. Wolfe left her a mess to talk herself out of and she was going to tell them all his little secrets along the way.

"You want to know why? I'll tell you why..." And she proceeded to describe her trip to the lake, Wolfe's strange reveal and apology. She omitted her frantic hurry to change clothes, and how she fell asleep holding a pint of dark chocolate mint ice cream that ran down her side and woke her at 2 a.m. prompting an unexpected clean-up and curses at Wolfe for all her problems.

Sergeant Henderson sat unresponsive for several seconds looking back and forth between her and the notes he was scribbling. His expression hadn't changed much. He flipped through his file and looked through his phone as she spoke.

After she had wound to a close, he watched her for a few moments.

"Your story isn't adding up Miss Martinez," Henderson informed her with a stern tilt of his chin and the *fwhap* sound of a folder hitting the table between them.

"I can lend you my toes if that would make it easier," she told him drily as she stared straight back.

He didn't rise to her mockery. More papers rustled and he got up to leave the room for a few minutes. Never tapped her fingers along her arm under the table as she waited.

When he came back and closed the door behind him, Never couldn't read his expression. His jawline was firm, but the lines around his lips were calm. He didn't smile, but his green eyes were darker than before.

"You're still claiming he gave you the name?"

"Yes," Never insisted and kept going. "He said he was sleeping with one of his graduate students in his office and she got pregnant."

"The history department at Redmond College has no record of any Chasity in any program," Henderson told her as he pulled out a paper from his stack. "Your other woman routine might get you some sympathy in court if you pick one that exists."

She sat up straight and her brain jolted to life again. "If I pick one...you're saying the name Wolfe gave me was fake?"

"Chasity is not in the information they faxed over," he held up a paper to show her.

"That sneaky son of a bitch lied to me to keep me from finding her."

"Miss Martinez, don't you think you should drop the act now?" he said as he gave her another hard look. "No one would blame you for losing it by the lake last night."

Never despised his attitude. She was getting chafed skin from his dry, mocking tone. Anger welled up in her, but she held it in. It was a technique she had learned in an anger management class years ago. As a new reporter, she had covered the class for the "local interest" section of the *Folman Gazette*. After a few seconds, she brought her hands up to conceal her face and blew out a long breath. Never was finished justifying herself to *Sergeant Bossypants* and everyone else. She lowered her hands to her lap and tried her best to contort her features into something resembling a remorseful mask before she spoke.

"You're right." She nodded. "I lost it."

Excitement peppered his irises, but he kept a grin from reaching his lips.

"Are you ready to tell me about it?"

Never waited until she was his sole focus in the quiet room.

Lifting her hands to lay them flat on the table between them, she let it all go.

"I lost three years of trust, I lost an expected proposal, I lost respect for the man I thought I knew, and I lost control of my tongue when I got angry, but I never touched him."

The disappointment was satisfying as she watched him slump back in his chair.

"And that's all you have to say?"

"No, but you'll have to read it in the *Gazette* along with everyone else in town," she told him as she rose to her feet.

"We still have things to discuss."

"I'm sure your department and my new lawyer will be able to work it out."

With that parting shot, Never pushed her chair

under the table and headed for the door. The sergeant made no move to stop her. He promised to be in touch. She knew he didn't have enough information to hold her. She hadn't committed any crimes, but she still didn't feel safe. Her only saving grace might be that it wasn't logical to think she could force a man Wolfe's size into the lake and hold him there without help. But then...nothing in the past forty-eight hours seemed logical to her. She should be enjoying the gleam of her new engagement ring while lying in Wolfe's arms this afternoon. Or planning how she would reveal it to Justine and the other ladies at work.

Instead, she was imagining other scenarios. She didn't have to pass through the doors to her office today to know what her co-workers' pitying glances would look like. They would be voicing their theories about where things went wrong when her back was turned. She would be the center of attention, but no one would know what to say to her. It was only natural Never supposed, but she wasn't ready for those inelegant silences.

As she exited the sheriff's office, Never realized there was one place she hadn't gone back to this afternoon. Every other reporter in a fifty mile radius had been to film a spot by the side of Hickory Lake. She didn't really want to go there now. She always believed that if you wanted to tell a story right, you have to go to the source. Never was the source, and she needed to walk the boardwalk by the lake to activate her memories.

She knew from experience that witnesses were unpredictable and notoriously inaccurate. Could she remember the events as they happened? Would her judgment be clouded by anger or loss? Should she really chance another run-in with other reporters and the sheriff's department? She could go home and hide until nightfall. Everyone would be gone by then. She thought about the possibilities as she carefully navigated her way across town. Her faithful car and sidekick, Aurora, wasn't slowing down. They passed the turn into her neighborhood a few miles back. This time, Never had no romantic notions as she sped toward the lake access road. She was wearing her regular tennis shoes and snug jeans with her flannel shirt. She wanted to be comfortable while she was cooped up in an interrogation room.

Never didn't bother with her ball cap or the hoodie when she left the apartment this afternoon. They languished in the backseat of her car where she had cast them aside. Other reporters would be looking for those universal attempts made by subjects they were investigating and point her out before she could lock her car doors. Plus, the hoodie would block her vision. If anyone was coming for her, Never wanted to meet them on her terms. She had every right to be at the lake, and she wasn't giving away another scoop of this story for free. She would plant herself on the shoreline until she was confident she had everything she needed for her story. Or, if the need arose, she could run for the sanctuary of her car. Either way, her dark hair would flow free over her shoulders and her caramel eyes would send warnings to all who circled too close.

She had to park along the access road to the parking area. Everything had been roped off hours earlier to keep people away from Wolfe's Jeep and from blocking efforts at the lake itself. Never skirted the taped-off lines around the parking lot and walked around the edge of the group still gathered near the shoreline. She headed for the boardwalk and the end of the pier where she left Wolfe last night.

It was all still there. The thick layer of smooth round stones forming the bridge between the blacktop of the parking lot and the sliver of sand along the shoreline, the red plastic sheath around the flowers she had discarded and abused, and the calm dark waters of the lake greeted her as she approached the boardwalk leading to the pier deck. They were all still as she remembered them.

The red plastic around Wolfe's flowers rustled in the breeze to draw her attention. She had been angry at the cheap little bundle of flowers when he tried to hand them to her. They were unappealing and there wasn't a single rose in the sorry collection. After she struck them down, they remained here all night and most of today.

The flowers had faded. Water deprived and baking in their packaging beneath the midday sun, the sad little bundle of color took on the consistency of yard clippings. If she looked hard enough, she could make out where her heel had punctured the thin cone of plastic protection. Like a time capsule, it waited for her to return. Everything was there.

Well...everything except Wolfe. He was in a morgue or medical school nearby being photographed and prepped for autopsy. Maybe the mysterious mother-to-be would claim the body when the officials were finished with it. Never hoped that one or both of them were lying about the possibility of a baby. It would add another layer of tragedy to this sad story. As much as she despised him last night, Wolfe never struck her as a bad man. He was sloppy, he made mistakes, but he didn't take risks like she did. He wasn't excited by weekends in Las Vegas or mountain climbing adventures. His idea of an exciting weekend away was a trip to the museums in Nashville or a play at one of the theatres. Wolfe liked the stability of academia. The steady schedule of teaching and lecturing suited him. He looked good in jackets with elbow patches. Never always mused he would pass away peacefully in his office chair reading one of the multitudes of newspapers or journals he was so fond of. Affairs, babies, and suicide at the lake never made her list of possibilities.

"I guess free sex, is free sex," she mumbled as she glared out over the water.

The thing she disliked the most was the confusion she felt. How could she be so blindsided by his news and then again by his death? The anger was real. Never could justify it and rationalize it, but the confusion was irritating beyond any other emotion. Why would he decide to walk into the lake and end it all? Why would he give everything up? There wasn't just himself to think about. He would be leaving behind a child. A child he was dumping her and their three year long relationship to take responsibility for. Did he expect her to stay with him and live like a sister wife with the new woman? Wolfe would never be that naïve, would he? She would consent to being called selfish, but she would still refuse to help raise someone else's mistake. Not while the other woman was alive. She had been up front with him from the start about her disinterest in having children. Even if Wolfe had waited until after their wedding to spring his big secret, she still would have walked. He had to know that. She was just not wired that way.

Years in the foster system had taught her the hardship and sacrifice that came with the decision to have and raise children. Never had helped with the younger children and watched as the older children gave up toys before they were through with them. Once she aged out of the system, she didn't want to be responsible for another small, squirming life. The dilemma Wolfe presented her was a whole other layer of irritation.

She had no doubt he would have ended up an absentee father after all was said and done. He was the type to miss baseball games and dance recitals for work and research projects. His child would only know him by the glimpses of him as he came and went or the awards on display around his study. Now, it looked like instilling that information in his offspring would be the other woman's concern. Both women would be alone in this new future connected to Wolfe's legacy. They shared that in common.

I didn't have anyone to help me pick up the pieces after his announcement. Never thought with bitterness. She went home to an empty apartment, ate ice cream, and watched romantic comedies before she began drinking. No one handed her a mug of coffee or a pain reliever when she woke this morning. There wasn't even a text from Wolfe to make sure she made it home okay. She was on her own, and she respected capable people.

Wolfe always seemed so capable. He worked too much, perhaps, but he never seemed worn down by the path he had chosen. Like herself, he seemed energized by his work. He wanted to contribute to his field; be remembered. Never couldn't believe this was how he wanted people to remember him: a wet mass bobbing up and down on the surface of the lake.

Why would he choose this point in his life to

make this kind of mistake? Why would he destroy his career and give up his life over something like this? Many would point to a midlife crisis, but Never didn't have any facts to support that conclusion. Looking out at the boats on the water, she wondered if he contacted anyone before he took his final plunge. If he did, who would it be? He never said much about his family over the years. They were in the Florida panhandle she recalled, but Never had the feeling they weren't the type of people he would reach out to in a crisis. As long as she had known him, he didn't even offer to go visit.

Was the new woman privy to his final thoughts? Did things go from bad to worse when he reached out to her? Was she the reason he took the plunge? Whoever the mystery woman was, she didn't show up and introduce herself to reporters by the lake. Never turned to scan the few people still milling around the parking lot and the side of the lake. There was no other woman scowling out into the water with her. No hooded figures cried into tissues as they walked the pathways.

Years from now, Wolfe Jr. would want to know why his mother wasn't in his missing father's final thoughts. What would the other woman be able to tell him? There was no typical note left by the shore to tell everyone his feelings. No lines in the sand pointing the way to his reasons. He just walked away in silence.

Wolfe had to know people would talk about the quick change of the women in his life and speculate on the child's conception. Redmond College was in one of the most conservative sections of the country. Having a stain on his public profile would be unavoidable. It would follow him like a smelly cloak he couldn't seem to shed as long as he remained in any like-minded community in the south.

Never guessed if Wolfe was going to be an absent father maybe he decided it was best to be absent from the start. The problem came when she thought about Wolfe destroying or giving up his career. Never knew his career meant everything to him. It was hard to see him walking away unless he knew he would be forced from it.

Never leaned over the railing and listened to the gentle lapping of the water below as she continued to think through the possibilities. Maybe the other woman was in his thoughts? Maybe Wolfe wasn't ready to be a father? He liked stability, calm, normal. Children shattered that lifestyle like a hammer through glass. All his favorite pieces would have to go into storage or locked cabinets to be safe from sticky little exploring hands. Was Wolfe sweating his new predicament?

Never liked to think he would wait to panic in the moment. She could visualize him freaking out after a 3 a.m. feeding or diaper change. Maybe his new woman reviewed those realities with him before he decided to break the news to Never last night. Maybe that was the key to understanding his desperation.

There was so much she didn't know. Never thought she had everything figured out before his disclosure. She thought he planned to impress her with his choice of proposal sites when he asked her to meet him by the lake. Justine had let it slip that she saw him with a bag from the jeweler's two weeks ago and begged her not to tell. They both had reason to think he was going to propose. Last night, Never dressed up, expected cameras, and thought he would get down on one knee. She had been terribly wrong about his intentions.

A baby! She couldn't have been more shocked. He didn't even try to soften the blow, or offer her a nice bauble as a parting gift for her silence. His brush-off was crass and selfish. She in no way expected that kind of treatment from him. Why would he be so asinine?

Never stood up straight and looked at the beach with new eyes. Was Wolfe planning to admit his sins and go to his grave before anyone found out about his indiscretion? The information about the baby might have a ripple effect, she supposed. The college might fire him over the affair, but it wasn't likely. If he married this mystery woman, his colleagues might talk behind his back, but the administration would look the other way unless there was a political fuss.

None of the information she could come up with made sense, but it made less sense to think someone would murder Wolfe. What would be the angle? Mad student, angry faculty, was there more than one jilted lover? She shook the thoughts out of her head. Wolfe wasn't that exciting.

Never knew several things about him. The most stirring things she knew about him were that he liked to smoke cigars after sex, and that he hid a bottle of scotch in the filing cabinet in his study. She had no idea he liked to have sex in his office at the college. That could have livened things up during their lunch dates.

She wasn't averse to exploring alternative locations, but Wolfe always struck her as a traditionalist. How had she pegged him so wrong? Three years, they practically lived together and she had no clue he would ever consider the events of the last twenty-four hours.

Chasing Wolfe

Watching the slight waves dance across the surface of the water, she wondered if the kayakers would return next week. Would the images of Wolfe's lifeless body outweigh the need for outdoor gaiety? Even now, she could see boats anchored in the distance, reluctant to give up their weekend adrift. Brightly colored canoes crisscrossed paths and a trail of water marked the path of a jet ski as it sliced its way along the water's surface. Homeowners on the western shore gathered in clusters on the end of their elaborate wooden docks for afternoon get-togethers or pre-dinner drinks. They had seen it play out before. Potential drowning was a fact of life along the water. Every busy season produced another grouping of obituaries.

Just last weekend, birds gathered and kayakers carried their bright gear in and out of the shallow water near the shoreline. Small children splashed, ignoring the parent's stern voice that carried over the rumble of midgrade stereo products. Occasionally, an unusual accent, foreign and enthralling would cut through the din. Balloons marked birthday celebrations and volleyball nets were taking the brunt of attempts by out-of-shape participants. Picnic tables were occupied with towels and bodies content to stay on dry land as dedicated swimmers were drawn to the water's edge. Squirrels roamed about unconcerned by the multitude of humans invading their refuge. Unlike the rest of their cousins, they refused to twitch and run for cover. Teens shared their trees and curled around each other in hammocks mere feet from the prying eyes of strangers.

This afternoon, Never averted her eyes from an amorous pair of lovers as she walked down to the rocky shoreline. She studied a pale blue sky consisting of small puffs of clouds that would stretch and drift away as she watched them. Any other time she would enjoy these quiet moments sandwiched between the rushed hours that made up her workday. Today it put her on edge. Her eyes roamed without direction.

The shoreline was peaceful in its vibrancy. There were no smells of hot dogs or burgers in the gentle breeze ruffling her curls. Shade and sun existed in harmony. Dead trees fully exposed during the winter months drifted along the edges of the waterline. The faint smell of smoke from a cherry or specialty cigar drew her gaze back to the shore's human occupants as a group of walkers passed the spot where she had taken root.

The scent of cherry took her back to conversations on Wolfe's back porch during the summer when the warm breezes would blow his cigar smoke towards her as she listened to him describe the new landscaping project he had planned for next spring or when she would grab his hand and dare him to streak across the lawn with her in the moonlight. Those were the happier times she should hold on to. There was still so much promise in those late night conversations.

CHAPTER 7

Nashville Tennessee,
Two Months and 29 Days Earlier

The flights back and forth to Paris were long and cramped. The fact that Wolfe always had trouble sleeping near strangers made the trip feel even longer. He was rumpled and cranky with the guy in the seat next to him for hogging the armrest. By the time the people ahead of him cleared the aisle, he was miserable and ready to go. His shoulder bag threw off what little balance he had left. His strides were slow and unsteady as he cleared customs and weaved his way through the hive of Nashville airport workers and patrons to the parking garage level where his Jeep waited for him.

   Wolfe was eager to post on the treasure hunting group page. He pulled out his phone once he closed the door. His impulse was to take the box out and snap a picture of it to put with his message, but he didn't want to open it here in the parking garage and risk breaking the statue inside. He would have to settle for letting everyone know of his find. A weary smile creased his lips as he typed out a quick message that he had found the box and photos would be posted soon. Wolfe checked his statistics board and was proud to note that he was still among the top five finders in the group. The other four were retired with as many hours in the day to look for outstanding clues as they pleased. Wolfe was the most highly-ranked working member on the tally board, and that pleased him beyond reason. He hit "send" with satisfaction before putting the phone back in his pocket.

This trip had been longer than his usual trips around the adjoining counties, but the prize was beyond anything he had unearthed so far. His find reassured him that the trip was worth the expense and that an American traveler abroad would hide something worth his efforts. Even the sleeplessness could not pull down the tilt of his chin as he cranked his vehicle and shifted into gear.

A soft ding from his pocket stopped him short. He shifted back into park and pulled out his phone. Wolfe's post had elicited a quick reply from Pierce.

What box?

Didn't the man know what he buried?

Wolfe typed back, *I found a wooden box buried at Saint Acacius Chapel.*

I didn't hide a box at Saint Acacius. My clues were for St. Vincent's Chapel on the other end of the street.

But the clues match.

Wolfe slumped back against his seat and waited.

Nothing else appeared.

Care to explain? Wolfe poked harder on the keypad with every letter as his patience started to wane.

I mixed up the numbers. I tend to have a dyslexic streak from time to time.

Mixed up the numbers! What was Pierre talking about? He couldn't possibly be saying the box wasn't hidden by him. What did Wolfe bring home?

So the box I found isn't related to your clues at all?

No, I have never stepped foot in that courtyard. Maybe it's a real treasure.

Wolfe leaned back in his seat and read the words over and over again. What had he done? Something clenched inside him as he read the words. Could he have taken a real treasure from its resting place?

Maybe just another enthusiastic group like ours. Wolfe returned a few minutes later, hoping it was the truth.

Yes, that has to be it.

Wolfe tried to remain calm, but he couldn't shake the feeling he would regret his impromptu trip to Paris. The weariness from his spontaneous trip was sitting heavily on his shoulders as he eased out of the parking space and tossed his phone on the seat beside him. The novelty of his new find was wearing off. Exhaustion was creeping in. He didn't want to deal with the new questions swimming around in his head.

Had what he found been just another prize or was it something more? He knew it was fancier than anything his group would hide when he opened the box to inspect it. Now it could be a real treasure he lifted from the courtyard by mistake. Should he march back into the terminal and get a ticket back to Paris? How would he ever return it without drawing attention to himself?

"Maybe I need a night to think it through," he muttered through his fingers as he tried to rub the sleep from his face.

Wolfe took the first right out of the garage to find a nearby hotel. Driving back to Folman was out of the question at this point. He wouldn't go anywhere else before he had a few hours to sleep and time to think things through. His new find was more of a surprise than he ever expected. Now he had to figure out if he dared to keep it.

CHAPTER 8

Folman Tennessee, Present

Sunday and Monday came and went in a blur for Never. She finished her account of the night of Wolfe's death and it ran in the Monday edition. The *Folman Gazette* was back in the game, and so was Never. She went from having her job hang in the balance to being a unique source of information. The paper agreed to pay for any other legal fees accrued as long as they were handed exclusives about every encounter Never had with investigators. She was relieved to find that the end of her social life didn't translate to the end of her career as well.

Her boss, Jerry, had never been so happy to find her alive when the fan mail and sympathy cards started pouring in. The citizens of Folman were reading her work and they wanted to let Never know they believed and supported her. Telling everyone in the region about Wolfe's betrayal was mortifying, but she hoped her embarrassment would lead to moments of clarity in the future. Everything was still too raw for her to interact with others about her situation. She avoided and ignored the fan messages and letters, handing them over to Justine and others to sort. There was only one Never couldn't turn a blind eye to.

The envelope was made of quality paper with a large silver seal covering the v-shaped closure on the back. The faculty of Redmond College sent a personal invitation to a memorial for Wolfe Aaron Strickland on campus Tuesday afternoon at 2 p.m. She wanted to toss the invitation back into the basket on her desk. Her inability to cope was written on her pale skin, carried in the dark circles under her eyes, and measurable in the takeout containers of food she couldn't bring herself to eat. Reporters still haunted the shadows outside her building, but their numbers had dwindled. She did her best to hide behind umbrellas and her work bag when cameras came toward her.

Other than the public dash from Wolfe's house the morning after his death, she tried to keep herself visible only in her own by-lines. She wasn't sure she was ready to be seen in public for more than a few minutes at a time. The idea of going to a public event to cover Wolfe's death unnerved her, but she didn't have much choice. Never was doing double duty for the *Gazette* while she was there. Jerry promised her she could contribute her side of Wolfe's story. She and Landon had entered into an uneven partnership. Her readers wanted to know more about the man she lost and what he did before he died. If Landon wanted extra information other newspapers weren't able to obtain, he would have to share his by-line with her. Their joint venture orbited around the other stories Jerry expected her to cover.

"You want me to go with you for moral support?"

Justine edged closer to look over her shoulder at the information grabbing her attention.

"It should be a room full of boring academics." She shifted to block her friend's view. "I can handle it."

"You want to go out to Paisley's for dinner?"

Never didn't want to tell her everything tasted like pulp when she could manage to force something past her lips. Alcohol didn't even interest her anymore. The only things that seemed to pacify her were the searing hot showers she took late at night after her workday was finished, but she didn't want to upset Justine by confirming this new turn in her behavior.

"Maybe," she hedged with a smile she hoped was reassuring. "I'll call when I get back."

Justine was the closest thing she had to a sister, but it still didn't feel right adding another witness to her misery. At best, the event at the college would be a stuffy gathering of people that barely knew Wolfe. At worst, she would break down and bawl her eyes out after strolling through halls and buildings that reminded her of her loss. What would it be like to spend the afternoon talking to people about the man she thought loved her? Would she get there and come face to face with what they could have been? Never wasn't sure she was ready to face the blunt reality of being surrounded by Wolfe's mourning friends and coworkers.

She also knew she didn't have much of a choice. She had to go where the story led. This would be her assignment regardless of the personal invite. Her presence was required at anything pertaining to Wolfe

Strickland. She would have no choice in whether she was ready to be exposed at a public event like this one, just like she had no choice in the details surrounding Wolfe's last hours of life. Circumstance was pulling her strings and she had no way forward other than to comply, commit to do her best, hold her composure, and act like a professional in the distressing moments ahead of her.

Never decided she wasn't going to the memorial to be treated like the grieving ex-girlfriend. She would be all business. If there were questions left to ask, she wanted to be the one asking them. Never hoped it would be easier to hide behind her journalistic professionalism while she watched a parade of speakers describe a man she thought she knew.

To help her defense, Never still needed to prove Wolfe had mentioned another woman to her. No other newspaper had confirmed that aspect of her story. No witness or mystery woman had come forward to claim knowledge of Wolfe's office affair. A memorial was a good place to talk to people when their guard was down.

Looking for her rival made sense for her defense and for her readers. While Never was at Redmond College she could focus on looking for the woman Wolfe claimed was carrying his child. Attending his memorial service was the only way she was going to get any firsthand knowledge of the graduate students in the history program. If there wasn't a Chasity, there had to be someone, right? Never would make it her focus to find out how many there were and who talked to Wolfe last. Wolfe couldn't take his secret with him. She wouldn't let him.

So here she was, dressed in black, driving out of

town. Maybe after writing her article tonight she would be able to find closure and cry. She felt guilty for not doing it before. It was like everything in her dried up. Tears, joy, her taste buds, everything but the urge to find answers had gone away. Never was functioning as a husk of the person she had been. Everything seemed to be whirling past her like the scenes outside her car window and she couldn't process it all. It reminded her of every time she was sent to a new group home. She was in motion, gathering her things out of habit. There was no joy in the actions she was performing, and the car ride always ended with her facing a group of strangers overenthusiastic to make her feel better about the coming weeks of adjustment.

Contrary to the random moves throughout her youth, Redmond wasn't an unknown to her, but she was just as anxious about what she would find upon arriving there. Would other members of the press be there or would they be moving on to other stories? Would there be crowds of people or would it be a gathering of only faculty who were required to attend? Regardless of their numbers, they would all know who she was. There would be looks when she arrived and whispers when they thought she was out of earshot. She would have to steel herself to several possible realities before the true situation was forced upon her.

Alone on the highway, Never had plenty of time to fight with her demons. Her phone was already on silent. She didn't want to focus on anything other than the task ahead, and reception on the ridge was spotty at best.

Justine had already checked on her twice before she left Folman. Once to help with her outfit and once to make sure she hadn't changed her mind about needing a friend to come along for support. Never loved her, but today she had to view this trip as a professional trip. It was the only way she would get through it. If Justine was beside her, regarding her with those big sappy doe eyes, Never wasn't sure she would be able to hold it together. She needed to push away feelings until she could be alone tonight writing a final farewell of her own.

She had taken this highway several times throughout their relationship, sometimes with Wolfe and sometimes to meet him. Never was accustomed to its quirks and switchbacks. It was surrounded by an endless sea of green peaks and valleys. Never let her mind drift as she drove. Her thoughts landed on other trips as Aurora charged up the steepest section of the ridge. Focusing on the past was much safer than evaluating the present.

A southern boy at heart, Wolfe would tell her about the history of the area, point out landmarks, and tell her how he planned to pitch a summer class offering to the dean just on the local history that intersects here. The current town of Redmond wasn't much more than a stylized four-way stop in the shadow of the ridge, but the layout of the college was elegant for the sleepy little hamlet that surrounded it. Built on the grounds of an old fort from the civil war, Redmond had a strategic location not many colleges or universities could boast. The college president's house sat on a hill overlooking the Red River and the other halls clustered around it like a nest around a chick. A permanent bridge was erected for automobile traffic down the bank from the original Redmond train bridge that used to carry passengers all the way to Illinois. Every time they crossed the bridge, Wolfe would gesture to what was left of the train bridge's metal skeleton and remind her how the Red River and the Northern Stage Coach line turned the area into a boomtown in the early 1900s. The community had a long history as a commerce and travel hub between the towns of northern Tennessee and north beyond the looming southern border of Kentucky.

Looking at the family farms and mom-and-pop diners she passed, it was hard for Never to imagine the type of town it was then. Thriving with shops and travelers, teeming with soldiers and miners, a place that drew people in, historic Redmond seemed like an ambitious mayor's pipe dream. How could all that progress come screeching to the standstill exemplified by the main streets of Redmond today? That kind of drastic change was hard to fathom, but there was no denying it. By the middle of the 20th century, Redmond had become a shadow of the town it once was. Closed were the silk mills and the passenger train depot. Cars that used to hit the state routes connecting Chicago to Florida zoomed by on the new interstates farther to the west. Businessmen fled to Nashville or over the border into Kentucky and Illinois. Buildings were shuttered for good. Everything but Redmond College and the original Baptist Church closed to future generations, and the town morphed into the sleepy farming community it was today. How many times in the last three years had Wolfe scoffed at how the natives were forced out on the Trail of Tears, the southern soldiers were forced out by the northern forces, and the settlers were forced out by a changing economy. For so many years everyone who wanted to be here was forced out by someone who wanted it more, and now Redmond College struggled to interest spoiled kids from the suburbs of Nashville to come study here. How times had changed. Now, Redmond was a bump in the road. It didn't even warrant a stoplight.

Wolfe delighted in the history around the college that fueled his work, but he soon decided that living over the ridge in Folman was far more comfortable for a modern man. That's where Never met him three years ago while she was covering cycleball, the new sport he had created. When she was assigned the story, Never by no means thought it would be more than a strange evening she would have to report on.

When she heard about the new sport, Never had imagined men on unicycles bouncing balls on their heads, and she wasn't far off. Folman's newest sports enthusiasm was for a version of soccer that was far more difficult than remembering not to use your hands. Six players on each team battling it out on full-sized bicycles to get the ball into the other teams net. People were tossed over handlebars, two referees on Segway chariots flew up and down the field trying to stay ahead of the action. It wasn't until the postgame interview with Wolfe that she began to see the charm of the game. After his team's 6-4 victory over the Cross Blaze, Wolfe was charismatic for a man covered in sweat. Sitting with a bandage above his left eye and a wrap around his right ankle, he explained why he created the game and how happy he was to see the league taking off in the way it had. There were now enough teams to merit a playoff series at the end of the season. The league and its new teams were attracting sponsors and gaining community support. Wolfe thought it could become a new American pastime.

Never didn't know if she agreed with him, but he was well-spoken and his enthusiasm was refreshing. When the interview was over, she walked away wishing she had more questions to ask. When he called the next day to ask her out for coffee, Never was surprised but enthused by the turn of events. They were well on their way to being a solid couple when he announced he bought a house on the outskirts of Folman a few months later. Everything seemed to be lining up for the two of them. How had they strayed so far off-course?

As Never made a right turn onto the bridge over the Red River, she eased to a stop and watched the kayakers in their yellow boats gliding through the low levels of the fall water table. Southern tan lines and warm weather would hold for a few weeks longer, but autumn crept into yards and windows in every other way. Hay bales with pumpkins, posters advertising ghost walks, colorful wreaths, and flyers advertising harvest-themed dances littered every window she passed. Even the warmer-than-usual winds wouldn't slow the seasonal transitions for long. Dropping temperatures would be apparent to everyone in the coming weeks.

Looking out over the campus, she never thought anything would lead her to a day like today. The distress was sharp, unexpected, and felt wrong in so many ways, but still it stayed with her, pushing her to find the end of her musings. She couldn't accept the circumstances surrounding Wolfe's death, but she was sure of their accuracy. All the local media's accounts agreed with her, but she still could not reach a place of acceptance. How would she ever get over this anger and reach the place where she could mourn? She couldn't forgive him now that he was gone. She wasn't able to cry over her loss. Wolfe stripped her of that with his shocking admission and sudden departure. Never just hoped her formerly amiable outlooks would return, like the water table of the Red River in March.

Easing into a space at the end of the commons parking lot, Never remembered she could easily avail herself to a visitor's parking spot like she used to when she was rushing to meet Wolfe for a lunch or dinner. Today, they were all taken by cars with out-of-state tags. Places like Texas, Georgia, and North Carolina were among the variety of states represented here today. The unexpected collection of vehicles with out-of-town owners made her curious. Who would drive to the small town of Redmond to say goodbye to a colleague? Never could count former teachers and colleagues she would go out of her way for on one hand, three fingers tops. She had no idea Wolfe was so popular within the history community. She expected a small, but respectable group of academics and their spouses.

Looking around the parking lot, Never had to admit Wolfe's memorial had turned into quite the gathering. She hoped the mystery graduate student would be among the scattered groupings she saw before her. Never was determined to find Wolfe's admitted side-chick. She had questions for the other woman and couldn't wait to shove her knowledge in Sergeant Henderson's face when she proved Wolfe was seeing someone else.

As she entered the large hallway leading to the gym, Never weaved her way around the edges of the groups, listening to snatches of conversation and saying hello to familiar faces as she went. No one grabbed her attention during her initial sweep. Maybe the other woman was already in the gym waiting for the service to begin?

Never didn't want to rush. If she went in early she would have time to think and she didn't want to break down in front of people watching her for signs of vulnerability. She elected to hover by a far wall waiting and watching as the last of the attendees rushed in from the parking lot looking harried and strained by their efforts. Watching their discomfort distracted Never from her own.

The service attendance was what you would expect for one of those academic social affairs. People she had never met milled about in suits and utilitarian dresses. Most of the men wore gray or the dark blue suit colors that were popular this autumn. The females wore a range from office casual to new-age flowing skirts with layered sweaters in earth tones. Never felt overdressed in her black dress standing next to some of them as she waited to be steered toward the open doors in the last seconds before the service swung into motion.

She could make out ferns and potted lilies spaced out across the front of the small platform stage from her place in line. A dark, thin podium with the college seal stood vigil over the empty chairs lining the wall behind it. A projector broadcasted the faculty picture of Wolfe from the college promotional materials used for recruitment with a brief statement about his time at the college. There were faculty members handing out hastily printed orders of service to everyone entering the gymnasium. Suicide hotline information glared up at her from the bottom of the page.

Never spotted a couple she recognized from one of the college faculty appreciation dinners Wolfe had invited her to. The woman was petite and cropped her dark hair so that it hung along her jawline and frequently had to be untangled from her dark square-framed glasses. The man was average height, his scalp reflected the harsh florescent tubes suspended from the high ceilings, and he wore a black armband to hold his phone at all times. *Susan and Paul Gilbert*, Never recited to herself. Susan always said her name kind of nasally, like the wide black frames were cutting off her air supply. Then she would let out this little giggle after the fact as though having the name Susan struck her as funny. The habit made Never wonder if she had an online avatar that went by Demetria and was a secret falcon trainer. But it was the way she pronounced her spouse's name that sent creepy tingles up Never's spine. There was always this elongated, higher than usual pitched *ah* turning Paul into an oddly orgasmic sound that Never wanted to avoid hearing again. Jumping into conversation mode, she rounded on Susan before she could pioneer the awkward road to reintroductions.

"Susan, I'm so glad to see you and Paul."

"We're so sorry Never." Susan came in for an unsolicited hug. "We thought the next big thing for the two of you would be a wedding."

"Honey, maybe you shouldn't mention that," Paul reminded as he tugged on his wife's sleeve.

"It's okay Paul," Never assured him. She didn't share what a nice change it was not to be accused of Wolfe's murder everywhere she turned.

"Are you going to speak today?" Susan asked as she took in Never's black dress.

"I think I would rather listen to the thoughtful words of his colleagues."

"Sure you would," Paul tried to console. "I bet

everything is still a shock for you."

"I don't think anyone would have seen it coming."

"He seemed so focused on his work."

"True, I have seen few professors so fixated on their work."

"What do you mean?"

"He was in his office at odd hours, and he always seemed to be researching," Susan confirmed.

"Yes, we thought he was gearing up to write a book."

Was this her opening to find the mystery graduate?

"Anyone else with him on those late nights?"

"Not that I can recall," Susan replied as she readjusted her frames. "He liked his privacy."

I bet he did.

"He was a very private man," *and secretive,* Never added to herself.

"It is such a shame," Susan went on.

"I guess his grad students are pretty torn up about things."

"We all were," Paul agreed.

"The college has provided counseling support for everyone," Susan volunteered.

"I'm sure there are some students that need the extra support."

"And faculty...losing Wolfe was a terrible shock."

"Yes, it was," Never had to agree.

Paul and Susan encouraged her to come with them and sit in one of the front pews with the rest of the full-time faculty, but Never refused.

"I need to be able to take notes for my article," she begged off. "I wouldn't want to distract anyone."

"I guess we should get to our seats." Paul motioned his wife to come along.

"We truly are sorry Never," Susan repeated as she turned to follow him.

Never kept her distance from the other faculty congregating around the back of the auditorium. Several had read her retelling of the night before Wolfe's death, and she didn't want to rehash it. She wasn't the grieving fiancée. Wolfe made it clear she would never be his plus one again and she intended to maintain her dignity while she was in attendance. She watched the crowds in the main hallway, taking notes, and pretending to be interested in the workers setting up the refreshment tables for after the service. She resisted the urge to straighten her dress and run her fingers over her curls. It felt cowardly, but she made a show of checking her recorder and looking through the small printed handout she received as she breezed through the wide double doors of the auditorium. Never spotted some long looks in her direction, but their eyes skittered away when they meet her gaze. After all, it wasn't polite to gape in situations like this.

When she couldn't stall any longer, she ducked into one of the last seats in the back pews set up for their weekly church services. She nodded to the woman next to her for making room as she tucked away her purse. Never straightened her dress and lifted her gaze just as the speakers walked onto the small stage in the front of the room and settled themselves into black folding chairs that would crease their clothing as well as their spines.

She listened to snatches of speeches and jotted down a note here and there, but her main focus was scanning the room for anyone that could be a candidate for the elusive Chasity. She tried to distract herself from thinking about the speeches at the memorial by scanning the room looking for anyone that would fit the description of Wolfe's knocked-up grad student. She couldn't make out anyone under forty in the seats near the stage. There were a handful of people under thirty in the rows ahead of her. Most were male. Some, Never recognized from the cycleball matches. There were two or three young women about the right age range. One was a willowy brunette, with long hair and a black suit jacket. Another was a platinum blonde with thick make-up and wide shoulders. Both seemed somber, but neither woman had the emotional flare of a pregnant woman left to fend for herself.

If Chasity was here, she had to be a great actress. Never didn't see anyone that looked like they suffered a loss of composure. Maybe the other woman decided to cut her losses and didn't show?

Never couldn't blame the other woman for being angry. Wolfe had left her with a child on the way and no means of support. It had been a few days since she found out he was running out on her, and Never was still pissed at his betrayal. She bet she was nowhere near as enraged as she would be if she knew she was carrying a child that neither one of them wanted. Top that feeling off with Wolfe's death on the morning news. How was a hormonal girl supposed to process that? How was anyone supposed to process the events of the last week?

Never wished Wolfe was alive so she could shake him and demand he reveal the other woman to her. She was becoming obsessed with sniffing out a possible candidate for his affection. She used several excuses to justify her efforts: it would make a great story, it would give her closure, they could be supportive to one another. But it was all a lie. They were all excuses you give yourself when you don't have a justification for targeting someone. She wanted to know her competition, she wanted to expose her to the world the way her life had been exposed, and she wanted Wolfe's memory to pay for the things she couldn't forget. It was angry. It was pitiful. It was weak. And it still wasn't stopping her from pursuing it. It was eating at her in a way that no other lead ever had. Never had to figure out who Chasity was. It irritated her so much that there was no trail to follow. It was as if Wolfe created a ghost and then complicated matters by becoming one.

Probably the only way he thought he could keep me from beating it out of him.

The thought brought a brief smile to Never's lips before she reached up to cover it with her program.

CHAPTER 9

Redmond College, Redmond Tennessee,
Two Months and 27 Days Earlier

Rebecca Batson had stopped by his office again today with questions about her project. She was a promising young graduate student, but she needed constant reassurance she was on the right path. Other confused undergraduates wouldn't find their way to his door until he assigned paper topics next month, and he was prepared to conduct his regular classes later in the week. Rebecca's presence was an interesting way to break up the long blocks of time he found himself with during his first official week of office hours.

She usually didn't need much in the way of a push. Wolfe would give her a direction or ask a few questions about part of her work and she would be digging online for more information. He had mentioned wondering why black market crime had spiked in the art world and if it was more or less violent than regular crime-family activities. She was already clicking away on the laptop she used as a buffer between them. If her normal patterns held, she wouldn't need his input for thirty minutes or more.

Wolfe picked up the newspaper he had been working his way through when she arrived, and leaned back in his chair to catch up on the news in the southwestern region of Nevada. He was going over pictures from a recent earthquake when her voice caught him off-guard.

"That's funny," Rebecca said as she leaned over the screen.

"What's funny?" he asked as he lowered his paper to study her.

"The statue on your shelf looks like a stolen Peruvian art piece from the 1500s."

"What are you talking about?"

"Look at this article," she said as she turned the laptop and pushed it across the desk in front of him.

A grainy photo of the statue he had found in Paris glared up at him. The short article was from five years ago in a small Peruvian magazine. Rebecca had unwittingly stumbled across the origins of his statue while she was researching for her dissertation.

It couldn't be, but it was. The small statue he had placed on the shelf behind him after his return from Paris was glaring up at him from the article. "Priest Killed in Robbery," the headline screamed. Warning bells went off in his head. The tiny figure behind his desk was stolen, once by someone who killed a priest and once by Wolfe from its hiding place in Paris. What had he done? He couldn't let Rebecca keep believing his statue was stolen. He had to think of a plausible reason for the statue's similarity. Wolfe couldn't reveal what he had found in Paris.

"It is very good for a gift shop purchase," he deflected with a smile as he tried to remain calm.

"Copying is an epidemic now that 3D printers are available," she followed his train of thought without question.

"Exactly, everything from shoes to cars now-a-days," Wolfe agreed.

"It's still cool that you have a copy of something that someone would literally kill for."

"It definitely changes your perspective on things."

Rebecca gathered her laptop and notes to launch into another set of questions about her paper as Wolfe struggled not to expose the misgivings she had brought to light about his new acquisition. She was a sweet girl, talented and curious. Wolfe had the feeling it wouldn't take too much to deepen their relationship beyond the student and teacher guidelines. Rebecca Batson seemed eager for his approval and he caught her watching him from time to time when she was pretending to be working on her notes. She would chew on her pen or twist the ends of her long auburn locks while she gave him inviting looks with her dark chocolate eyes.

In a few years, when they were colleagues passing the weekend at an out-of-town conference, he might allow himself to follow her up to her room after a few drinks at the hotel bar. With his job on the line and a stolen artifact on the shelf behind his head, Wolfe wasn't reaching for low-hanging fruit. He had his heart set on spending the rest of his night alone trying to come up with a plan to get out of the mess his obsession had created.

His senses barely registered the musky scent of her perfume as he ushered her out an hour later and locked the door behind her. Wolfe pulled his laptop out of the bag leaning against the leg of his desk and cleared a space for it. He needed to find out if anyone had more news on the statue or the priest's killer. It wasn't long before he recognized the publication she showed him. He clicked on several articles and added them to twenty other tabs he had open.

The stolen art scene had gotten far hotter than when he was in college. Paintings were being ripped from the walls of museums all over the world and taken from private collections at an alarming rate. War-torn countries of the Middle East were decimated by the modern shadow market, but South America was increasing in popularity among thieves and smugglers. Adding to his current predicament, all roads in the black market pipeline seemed to lead to Europe, Paris in particular.

It will be okay. He tried to soothe himself. No one but Rebecca knew the connection and she thought he was telling the truth about it being a fake. As long as she never questioned his story, he would be alright. Wolfe only told Pierce about his find in Paris, and even then he only mentioned the box. He never uploaded pictures of the contents. The statue was still a secret. He hadn't even had a chance to brag about it to Never.

Marcy Christopher from the college newspaper, the *Redmond Recorder*, was in here yesterday he reminded himself. She was taking pictures of him to run with a piece in the paper about the summer local history class project he was trying to get the board to approve for next summer. Images of his latest find would soon be in more places than an obscure Peruvian website article.

Wolfe let out an expletive as he looked at the display shelf behind his desk. The photos for the article would scream his guilt. In print, the statue could be seen by anyone willing to look for it. Wolfe knew he should have listened to his gut. He had a bad feeling as soon as he opened that wooden box in Paris. He knew it couldn't be a treasure hunt prize. He should have returned it. Instead, in his arrogance, he brought it home and put it out for everyone to see.

"Why didn't you just buy a billboard?"

He lowered his head into his hands and let himself get caught up in his despair. The odd squeaks and groans of his office furniture were his only counsel on the matter. The statue sat behind him like a cartoon devil looking over his shoulder.

As he pulled himself up out of the funky mixture of his own emotions, Wolfe switched to defense.

"There has to be a way to stop this from getting out."

Whoever took the time to bury the statue wasn't someone Wolfe wanted to tangle with. The article said "no amnesty". If he was caught with it, Wolfe could be charged with the murder of the priest as if he had held the blade himself. If he did find a way to return it to the church where it belonged, what would he tell them?

Wolfe dug the statue up on private property in the dead of night and had only the flimsiest excuse to defend his actions. Who would believe he wasn't a trafficker with special instructions to retrieve it? Shit, he might as well walk himself into a life sentence. Looking at the details again, Wolfe wondered if he hadn't already.

Art thieves were notorious for being involved in drugs and organized crime. Five years was a long time to bury something. Maybe the thief was in custody for another crime and couldn't come back to retrieve it? There was a slim chance the thief was dead. Wolfe wanted to believe that was the case. But what if he was wrong? He couldn't ignore the possibility of things going sideways in a hurry. If the thief was in prison or waiting to reclaim his stolen property until the heat died down around the murder, Wolfe could be in very big trouble. Everyone he knew could be in danger before this was over. His career would be gone. He still owed years of payments on his house and new Jeep. Everything he had worked for could be in shambles if the statue's new owner and location ever came to light.

"You're an idiot," he muttered as he sagged back into his chair. "Why did you go to Paris?"

Wolfe turned and picked up the statue, tempted to bust it into a thousand tiny pieces and scatter it in the deepest woods he could find. In reality, he couldn't bring himself to do it. The article said it was early 1500s Catholic Church-influenced art. There were some lines he wouldn't cross.

What could he do? Rereading the information about the last person that met this art thief in a church yard, Wolfe felt his hands tremble. The priest was stabbed more than twenty times. That denoted someone who had no interest in mercy. Did this killer already know Wolfe took his prize from the courtyard? He needed to find a way out of this without attracting attention to the statue or to himself. The first thing he needed to do was get the statue out of sight. Wolfe wrapped it in his jacket, shoved it into his laptop bag, and said a short prayer that he wasn't already too late. He had to get this someplace safe where it would remain out of a killer's line of sight.

CHAPTER 10

Redmond College, Redmond Tennessee, Present

After the service, Never walked back out to the front hall to talk with some of the speakers and verify some additional information for her story while refreshments flowed. She turned at one point to find four men engrossed in her actions as she weaved her way between a group of staff members and teachers. There wasn't anything overly distinguishing about any of them as individuals, other than that the tallest one had the mustache of a young Howard Hughes. It was uncanny how similar they were. They all had comparable haircuts with salt and pepper creeping into the sideburns. The shortest one had applied his hair gel more liberally than the rest. They were a group of men in the same age range, three of the four were of average height, and they all had an interest in her movements. Overall, they looked respectable in their somber suits.

Never was struck by their familiarity, but she was sure she had never met any of them before. Is it possible they were security or off-duty police? Because of its size and close ties with national park lands, Redmond only had one park ranger. The college had their own security. If these men were on the campus security team, Never thought she would have recognized them. And why would they make their interest so obvious if they were watching her? Maybe they were just curious former students working up the courage to talk to her? Never continued to ask questions for her article and mingle with college staff she recognized. She was hoping they would either decide on a plan of action or leave.

She finished speaking with the dean's secretary, Paula Avery, who promised to send her updates on campus events scheduled for the next spring. The hallways had cleared out and Never was ready to call it a day. The sign above her head pointed to restrooms around the corner. Never closed her notebook and tucked her phone in her bag. She wanted to freshen up her lipstick and take care of a few necessities before driving home. She was almost to the corner when she noticed a gray wall of fabric shift in her direction.

Her group of gawkers was still following her every move. When she strayed too far out of their line of sight, the men moved as a fluid group to catch up to her. Were they going to follow her inside the restroom as well? Never had heard of dedicated wingmen, but this was ridiculous. They were tracking her. And they weren't being subtle about it. Other reporters maybe? Never couldn't tell which group to blame. She couldn't place them in any of the local groups. Why were their faces so familiar?

After returning from the restroom, she turned to find their eyes on her again. Never was ready to leave. Whoever they were they had missed their shot to talk to her unless they followed her out into the parking lot. Tired of the cat and mouse game, tired of holding a pleasant, but not too pleasant look, well...tired of pretty much everything, Never walked over and introduced herself.

"Hello, I'm Never Martinez reporter for the *Folman Gazette*. I don't believe I have seen the four of you around campus before."

"Wolfe said you were direct," the closest one said as he stepped forward to greet her. "He always admired that about you."

"And you are?" she pressed.

"James Branch, social studies teacher at Oak Hill High School and summer legal assistant at Taylor, Murphy, and Greer."

None of that rang any bells for Never as she glanced around for his shadows. She didn't search long. The others set aside their flimsy, clear plastic cups and came over to join them.

"This is Kevin Painter, Scott Cup, and Leonard O'Tool," he motioned to the line of males beside him. "We were classmates of Wolfe's."

"You all went to Oglethorpe?" the realization finally hit her.

"Yeah, we all met in Jacobs Hall."

"Was Jacob a friend?"

"No, Jacobs Hall was one of the residence halls on campus."

"And you all lived there?"

"All except Leonard, he had a boyfriend he came by to visit."

"He was my math tutor," the mustachioed member of the group corrected as he leveled a glare at his companion.

"So he had a full service math tutor and stopped by on a regular basis."

"Wolfe never said much to me about his time at Oglethorpe."

"Once he got his PhD from Emory, Wolfe was 'the history professor' and he ran full-force to embrace his new persona."

"Would you mind answering a question for me?"

Everyone gave her a solemn nod.

"Where did he pickup cycleball?"

She got a few chuckles.

"Who knows," Scott piped up. "Wolfe never could run, tennis and baseball were a struggle for him and chess wasn't exactly a magnet for girls."

Never felt the first real chuckle she had experienced in days well up in her throat.

"You think cycleball was his way of dealing with the handicap of being slow at running games?"

"Possibly," James shrugged. "He was never one

to give up easily."

But he had given up, Never wanted to shout as they all fell silent.

"So, you said he talked about me, you have kept in touch over the last few years?"

"We tried," Kevin spoke and the sharp tips of his ears moved as he elaborated. "We all sent him updates once a month, like a newsletter of our lives, he rarely ever responded."

"But he talked about me," Never prompted.

"He mostly mentioned your work in relation to his job at the college."

"The last time he emailed it sounded like he was thinking over something important."

"We all thought he was going to propose," James commented as Leonard elbowed him.

"Not to me," she confirmed. "I guess none of us saw this coming."

"We all thought it was a joke when we read the news."

"How did you read it?" Never wondered aloud as she thought about the local channels and regional papers that would carry Wolfe's story.

"Wolfe sent us subscriptions to your newspaper," Leonard explained. "We're all news junkies."

"It looks like things are breaking up here, would

you like to join us for a drink?" Kevin glanced around the emptying room to reinforce his point.

"I need to get my story turned in tonight."

Never was curious about Wolfe's friends, but she still had a drive ahead of her. If she started drinking and thinking about Wolfe's last few hours she might not be able to drive home tonight. She tried to be polite and stayed until they were the only group left clustered together in the hallway. They asked her again to join them for a drink or dinner, but Never shook her head and begged off.

"I wish it was under better circumstances, but I am glad to meet all of you."

She hoped she was giving them a warm smile as her eyes roved over their familiar faces. Her cheeks, shoulders, and back were beginning to throb from the rigid stance she had held throughout the afternoon. Her black dress was bunching around her waist and she itched to straighten her twisted bra strap. She imagined freeing her feet from her shoes and driving back to Folman with her toes against the wavy ridges of her accelerator.

A curious thought struck her as she walked out to the parking lot. If Wolfe was so tight with these guys in school, why had they never come up in conversation? It was true that Wolfe wasn't interested in reliving his glory days at college in Georgia, but wouldn't he mention an email now and then? Never was confused. It was just another layer of deception she hadn't been aware of.

Never paused by her car to regroup before the

long drive home. She listened to the murmur of voices, dead leaves crunching under heavy footfalls, and the sound of large, gas-powered engines charging to life around her. The world seemed to be signaling, whether anyone was ready or not, it was time to move on. As much as Never wanted to go hide in her apartment, she had no desire to get in her car and drive away.

She couldn't spend the rest of the afternoon standing by her car as other people went about their day. Never remembered a snug little café on the edge of campus that Wolfe had taken her to on some of their rushed lunch dates. Maybe she should take one more swing at finding her mystery girl before she headed home. If she hurried maybe she could get a table for dinner before the afternoon classes let out. Leaving Aurora in the parking lot, she set out on foot.

The Red Gator Café was a gem on this sleepy little campus. It was loud and Never loved the tacky Christmas lights strung across the windows and around the jukebox. It had a Cajun feel with a bluegrass clientele. There were beer cap collages on the walls and patron's initials were carved into the outdated wooden table tops beside the coolers full of ice to hold alcohol on a dry campus. Fiddle music was blaring from the jukebox in the corner, and a tall blond offered her a beer from his cooler as she sat down near the wide front window. Never suspected the offer was out of pity. By now, everyone within fifty miles of Redmond knew who she was and what she looked like, but Never accepted his offer with a thin smile.

She came here to look for her mystery woman. Maybe her new friend could help her? She sipped the strong IPA and took a menu from the metal rack on her table as she waited. Students drifted by the window as she peered through the outlines of happy shrimp and dancing alligators, conceivably painted by a student years ago in exchange for free food. If she tilted her head just right and squinted, Never could get a fleeting view of the deteriorating remains of the original Red River Bridge.

"You look familiar," floated over her shoulder as she heard the front door squeak closed.

Never stopped peeling the label on her free beer and turned to look at the newest arrival, intending to shoot him down. She came face to face with Wolfe's college friend Kevin instead.

"I guess I had a few extra minutes after all," she admitted as she invited them to join her by the window.

"Looks like you lost a drinking buddy," she pointed out as she watched them take their seats.

"Scott stopped outside to take a work call."

"I guess the four of you are hanging around for a while?"

"We can't get a flight out of Nashville until tomorrow afternoon. Might as well make the best of it," James told her as he reached for a menu.

"You would find better nightlife in Nashville," Never reminded them.

"I'm sure Scott and Leonard would love it, but the two of us old married men are holding them back."

Married or not, Never hadn't taken in the Nashville nightlife in a while herself. When co-workers joked about Justine's bachelorette party, they suggested weekend trips with pub crawls and outfits involving phallic-shaped accessories. It was hard to imagine Justine and the rest of the wedding party promenading on the cold streets of Nashville the week before Christmas in plastic crowns and short dresses. Never hoped a trip to the local bar after work with their co-workers and a weekend of massages and facials with her best friend would be an acceptable celebration before Justine's big day.

Never thought about what a wild weekend away in Nashville would entail. It had been close to ten years since she toured the bars of the strip on a weekend away. She didn't even know if those places were still in business, or if they were hip enough to impress a girl on the last night of her single life.

After she met Wolfe, they would travel to the city from time to time, but their last trip to the capital was for a quiet stroll through one of the galleries. He wasn't interested in touring the new wineries or trying the latest microbrewery. Despite her unrelenting efforts to persuade him to stay longer in the city, they were back in Folman snuggling on the couch by eight that night.

Never was glad she stayed. Wolfe's friends proved to be amiable dinner companions as they shared fried green tomatoes and fried alligator with her while they waited for Scott to show up. James dominated the conversation, but Leonard seemed to focus his charm offensive in her direction. Never got the feeling that Leonard imagined himself something of a throwback to the dapper southern gentlemen in history whose lives he worked so hard to archive. His slick black hair and mustache were curious. Paired with his sharp green eyes and tall build, he would rarely go unnoticed by either sex. She could imagine him in a white suit with a wide planter's hat standing on a sun-kissed veranda surveying his fields.

Their plates of shrimp and grits, crab po-boys, and red beans and rice were being delivered as Scott pushed through the crowd to join them.

"Sorry guys, hey Nev...good to see ya again!"

"That must have been some call."

"Several teams are going to the Gulf of Mexico next week."

"Company trip," Never asked as she licked sauce from her fingers.

"You could say that," Scott deflected as he bit into his crab po-boy.

"He works with scientists who study water pollution," Kevin explained.

"They want to test levels after the last hurricane cleanup in Texas."

"That sounds exciting."

"If you like being surrounded by smelly water and people who love talking about it," Leonard chimed in with one of his white-capped grins.

"Better than hanging out with people who reenact wars their ancestors lost."

"All of it is better than teaching snotty teenagers," Leonard fired back as though it had been rehearsed.

"You got me there."

In spite of their complaints and jabs Never got the feeling the four of them had stayed close over the years. When she got out of foster care, she moved around a lot and struggled to work her way through community college in Athens. There were several times throughout her twenties she wished she had a sisterhood of friends, but it never worked out. People drifted. Sometimes it would be a few days then weeks. Settling for one email or card a year was nothing like having long term friends.

"It's a shame we couldn't have gotten together while Wolfe was still around," she admitted as she sat her empty bottle back on the table and gathered her things.

"We tried, but short of showing up unannounced and refusing to leave his couch there wasn't much we could do over the years to attract his attention," Leonard admitted as he threw down his napkin. "His last email was the only one that gave us hope of seeing him in the future."

And now he had run out of future, Never thought as she watched the rain drizzle down the window in front of them. After tonight, Wolfe Strickland's legacy would be set. Never still had to go home and figure out what she thought about that legacy, and how to put today into the wording readers would expect from a final goodbye. She would need the lengthy silence of the drive back to think about how she would eulogize a man she wasn't sure she liked toward the end of his life.

"I hate to break this up, but I really need to get back to Folman."

She paused to gather business cards from everyone and receive a hug from Leonard. They offered to pay for her meal and walk her back to her car, but Never refused. She enjoyed their attention, but didn't want to be "taken care of" like a weeping girlfriend. She wanted everyone to understand she was on her own. She liked Wolfe's friends. If things had turned out as she had planned, she would have insisted he make them a bigger part of their life together. Now, Never didn't get a say in that version of the future either. She took a deep breath and fixed a smile on her lips before she turned to wave at the small group of men gathered behind her on the sidewalk. It would be her last glimpse of them before she crossed the street to the campus commons and disappeared beneath the shadows of the trees.

CHAPTER 11

Redmond College, Redmond Tennessee,
Two Months and 25 Days Earlier

Rebecca shifted in her chair and smoothed the navy pin-stripe skirt over her thighs. Wolfe couldn't remember a time when she was so withdrawn. Had something happened with her paper? Did another date get handsy? He didn't think he had done anything out of the ordinary to cause her reaction, but he had been so distracted of late, it was hard to tell. Wolfe figured he would come right out and ask. Taking his lump of coal with his lump of sugar wouldn't be any more than he deserved.

"Is something making you uneasy today?"

"Your statue is missing," she mentioned as she looked across the desk at him.

So, she was keeping tabs on it. Great. Think fast Wolfe.

"Yes, I loaned it to a colleague who is doing a

lecture tour. I mentioned our conversation and he asked if he could use it as a visual."

"That's a great idea!"

She relaxed and brightened into her usual self as she assessed his latest lie. *Keep going Wolfe.*

"He was pleased when I said yes."

"He should be, that statue is a brilliant fake," she agreed and slipped back in her chair to stretch out her legs.

He couldn't help but follow their silky, slow movement to the edge of her skirt line and wonder what it would be like to run his fingers under the thin fabric. Would Rebecca be as enthusiastic then? In a few years, he might revisit those thoughts. Talking his way into her bed might be fun.

"It is eye-catching," Wolfe agreed and turned back to his paperwork hoping that Rebecca would believe him in the coming months when the statue never resurfaced.

They moved on to go over a section of her paper she was having trouble with. She was making great progress. If she kept up her pace, Rebecca might graduate early. Wolfe wanted to aid that outcome in any way he could. The earlier she graduated, the less time she would have to worry him about the disappearing statue. He sent her away with a list of libraries to call and a few notes to help her search.

As office hours dwindled to a close, Wolfe paced the small room. The first hurdle was accomplished. The statue was safely out of sight, and one of the few witnesses to see it up close believed his lies. Few people would ask about the statue's disappearance. Wolfe could only hope that no one was looking for it, or had seen him exit the courtyard that night. If he wasn't connected with the statue, he would be safe. The picture in the school paper was a problem, but it had a small circulation, 250-300 people. He should be relieved that it hadn't appeared in Never's paper like many of the articles from the *Redmond Recorder*. If it had been an article confirming the new college offerings, or asking for regional involvement, Wolfe would be giving the tip to Never himself. If it wasn't for the bloody photograph, he wouldn't have to worry at all. Most of the locals were clueless about art and how that world existed outside of their elementary school fieldtrips to the local museum. There was a very tiny chance that any of them would recognize the statue for what it was, but Wolfe still felt uneasy to have pictures of the statue in print. The consequence wasn't just a ticket or a fine if he got caught.

By all accounts, Wolfe stole from a murderer, possibly a professional criminal. This person was smart enough to hide the statue in a place no one had looked in over five years. Would he be smart enough to track Wolfe down? Was he in jail for other crimes? Was he dead? Five years was a long time to wait. Wolfe didn't like that there were so many variables, so many unknowns. He could chance mailing it to someone, but it was possible that Rebecca would put the pieces together and out him as the sender. He didn't need to rouse suspicion. A statue showing up somewhere it shouldn't would cause questions. He didn't know if he should run or just keep the statue out of sight from now on. How long should he wait before deciding the coast

was clear? Weeks, months, years even? Was it worth it?
Not to go to prison, give up his career, maybe his life,
yeah...it was worth it. He just had to rent a locker for it.

No! That's traceable you imbecile.

"Okay, bury it," he offered aloud.

In the woods near his property line, there was an
old stone cottage with three of its four walls still
standing. It was all that remained of the Folman
Witch's home. Children told tales of the witch that used
to live there and still haunted the surrounding area.

There was no historical data to prove that one of
the former owners of the property, Ellen Ratner, was a
witch. Still, the urban legend persisted. Locals
memorized the stories surrounding the property. They
left bundles of herbs and trinkets as offerings near the
front steps of the cottage for her protection and
blessings.

The property welcomed heavy traffic near
Halloween when Widow Jenkins' donated the proceeds
from ghost walks and hay rides on her farm to support
the local festival, but most people fled when their
imaginations got the better of them. No one would
bother to dig on the overgrown property surrounding it.
He would be trespassing if he hid it there, but neither
Mrs. Jenkins nor her guests would be the wiser if he
added a fresh mound below the fallen leaves.

Hopefully things wouldn't go any farther. His
grad student had spooked him just in time. The statue
was safe, out of sight for now. Wolfe was sure things
would get back to normal once it was re-hidden.

CHAPTER 12

Redmond College, Redmond Tennessee, Present

Never had stayed too late in Redmond, but it was the first meal she had enjoyed since she met Wolfe by the lake. It was a shame that Wolfe's friends hadn't come for a visit sooner. The two unmarried men were huge flirts. Maybe that was the reason for her changing mood. Never argued with her inner critic that just getting the memorial behind her made her feel lighter, unburdened. She didn't need to review how she got dumped like a sack of rocks when Wolfe told her his news. She could put all the drama Wolfe created behind her.

The buildings of Redmond College faded into dark edges and angles as Never pulled out of her parking space and concentrated on the drive home. As she crossed the bridge, Never could tell that driving conditions had changed. The landscape around her was already taking on the frightening characteristics of a campfire tale. The long, skinny lampposts around campus gave off an eerie glow and did nothing to fight back the thick floating fog that covered the mountains after a rain shower. Her only path to Folman was a winding narrow two-lane state route through the national park. The drive would take longer than she expected.

Never pointed her car toward home and eased along the highway. Streetlights disappeared as she drove farther from the college. Redmond was, after all, a farming community first and foremost. There was no reason to light a sleeping downtown. There were no street lamps for bikers or walkers. No one worried about how anyone would find their way to third shift jobs or whether strangers would miss their exit. There was no nightlife on the other side of the campus bridge. Lighting was limited to an outbuilding here or there, a house in the distance, or the two pump gas station at the edge of town.

Before long, Never's headlights would be limited by the shadows of thick old-growth trees. She watched as the national forest closed in around her to obscure what the fog left in view of her headlights. Never slowed as the road snaked up and around the side of the mountain toward home.

When she accelerated up the steepest grade, the engine quieted and the gas pedal went to the floor without any change. The engine stalled and her breath caught as she watched Aurora slide back down the path she had just climbed. A shriek passed her lips, but she did not hear it. Never struggled to see headlights in the fog and guide the wheels. She asked the air in the seat beside her what to do, but all she heard was the crunch of something under the tires. A second felt like a pregnant pause and a twitch of her eyebrows all at once. She couldn't make the car stop. The brakes weren't responding. Silence descended over the interior as the back end swerved to the left and hit the shoulder. She heard the scratching of metal as Aurora made contact with the guardrail and a blast of mountain air sailed through her open window. The ground was coming up to greet her but she couldn't see it. Her shoes flew up to the ceiling as she swung from the stained tan fabric of her seat like a ragdoll. There were things moving, sounds of protesting machinery, and the light from one headlight bouncing off of random objects. Her gaze was joggled from one disjointed thing to the next. And Never had no power to stop any of it. She jammed her eyelids closed and waited of the motion to end.

There was a ringing, thumping, and pain as she opened her eyes. The side of her head ached and she couldn't tell if the liquid on her hand was from her leftover coffee or her own blood. The slight skirt of her dress was flipped over and climbing toward her trapped waist. Her remaining headlight cast a disconcerting glow out into the trees. Never strained to find sense in the strange collection of images. From her suspended position everything looked out of place. The engine choked and gargled one last time before it went silent. The only drone of noise left was the one playing on a loop inside her skull as the headlight faded to match the shadows outside.

Everything she needed was on the ceiling by now. She could make out one of her shoes and the small purse where she kept her phone. Her work bag worried her the most. It housed her laptop and all her recording equipment. If any of it was damaged by the roll, she didn't know how long it would take her to repair it. Like the situation she found herself in now, Never didn't have the time to spare. She needed to get right-side-up and figure out how to get help.

She didn't have the wherewithal to grab for the keys or shift the transmission into park. What would be the point anyway? Gravity and several large trees would be her partners in this collaboration if things went south. Was Aurora getting her back for all those missed oil changes and all the deferred maintenance paired with being her main source of transportation?

Maybe this was a warning from Chasity?

Never's addled brain came back to the mystery woman. She let out a sigh as she tried to scoop unruly curls from her line of sight. Not finding the woman today was maddening, but Never knew she shouldn't turn her rival into a phantom.

Wolfe is gone and she blames you, a little voice slurred back at her in the darkness.

The night looked like a Kaleidoscope. Never tried to focus on something, but the effort just increased the throbbing in her temples. When she used a hand to steady her swimming head, it came away with blood dotting her fingertips.

Was the ground outside slanted, or was it a by-product of her injury? Never couldn't tell. All the images took on a strange look from her overwrought, upside-down angle. She latched on to the one sense she thought she could still trust: smell.

The contents of her coffee cup dominated the scent of the car. Salt and stale fries trapped under the seats were dislodged and adding grit to the discomfort of her situation. There was a musky smell like oil or warm lubricant coming from the car. It interrupted the delicate tinges of pine drifting in from her lowered windows.

Fog caressed her cheeks like a damp sponge, keeping her awake. Never wasn't cognizant if the highway was above her or beside her. She couldn't take too long to figure it out. Passing out was a possibility. Maybe she already had. The situation had already made her a little fuzzy-headed. Coupled with the blood drying on her fingertips, Never didn't know how long she had before she would run out of time to act.

"I've been hanging here too long," she whispered as she tried to get her bearings.

She needed to find the release button and tried to decide how she would attempt to angle her body as she fell. The gearshift and the steering wheel were her main obstacles, but there were dozens of little shapes, plastic points littered throughout the controls on the dashboard that could reach out to snag her. Taking a chance of hitting the steering column when she released the seatbelt wouldn't be ideal, but she needed to get out before the car moved again.

Most people would say a prayer, but Never believed in always using her last moments to clear her conscience. Reaching her arms out from behind the shoulder harness first, feeling the lap belt tighten, Never counted to three like she was ready to rip off a bandage and closed her eyes. Whatever happened, this was her choice. She hoped it would prove to be a good one.

Announcing to the emptiness around her, "I'm not taking the easy way out!" Never punched hard at the release button with her thumb and forefinger. There was a brief weightlessness before she hurtled into the hindrances piled on the roof below. She tried to roll as she fell, but the pain coursing through her right arm told her she made contact with something unyielding. Another flare of pain traveled up her right leg as she focused on regaining her breath. Metal cried out in protest to her shifting weight. Aurora didn't throw Never out or renew her trip down the mountainside. The car simply echoed her final groan of protest before they both fell silent.

Never grabbed the heels she had discarded as she crawled slowly in the direction she thought was the road. Her hand struck gravel and was nicked by pieces of litter as she emerged through one of the open windows. Mud stains were added to the other liquid splattered across her dress and skin as her knee pressed into the damp earth for traction. Her right shoulder hurt and she had to use her other arm to pull herself up the slight incline like a lopsided dumbwaiter. Never gave a passing thought to the blood leaking from her head as she shuffled her body toward freedom.

Once she reached level ground, Never looked out into the foggy darkness surrounding her. The forest was dark and quiet. No lights approached from either direction. It would surprise her to find phone service this far from Folman. She might be here for a while.

Never reached up to brush her hair out of her face and felt the strands pull at the blood drying around her forehead wound. She detached the drifting curls with concern and hoped her injuries wouldn't require stitches or attract wild animals ready to finish her off. She needed to find help, but she needed to rally first.

Never sat on the shoulder of the road with her possessions clustered around her. She moved far enough away that she hoped she would be safe if the car had any more surprises in store for her. She waited, trying to collect her thoughts as her breathing returned to normal. Dirt decorated the surface of every object she managed to pull out with her. Her arm protested when she tried to raise it. Her leg was greening into a bruise on one thigh, but it was functioning. She didn't know if she could get to her feet and remain standing in her heels. She might need to crawl to the guardrail or a near-by tree to help her try out her balance with one working arm for support.

She was surprised to see that, from the outside, everything inside the car looked intact. The airbags hadn't deployed thanks to the slow creep back down the mountain and off the road. She was thankful a broken nose and extra bruises weren't added to her current uncomfortable situation.

Aurora looked like an old, tired beetle flipped on her back. She wasn't crushed or missing side mirrors. Aurora just looked exhausted from the struggle to right herself.

"You and me both girl," Never muttered as she pulled her phone out to check it.

The screen hadn't been cracked, but the light didn't come on when she pushed it. She shook it and pushed the button over and over again. The same black screen greeted her after every action. On the last frantic try, she held the button in and dropped her hands to her lap in defeat. In the next few seconds, the light from her screen glared up at her. She had forgotten about turning it off while she was at the memorial. After being distracted by Wolfe's friends, she hadn't turned it back on. She had a light but no signal. It seemed like a hike out of the woods was her only option. She had plenty of battery life for the flashlight feature. If she could get to her feet, Never could make it to the next house before the battery died. She just had to hope her bruised leg would hold up long enough to get her to safety.

CHAPTER 13

Folman Tennessee,
Two Months and Three Weeks Earlier

The article for Wolfe's new summer school offering
would run in the monthly edition of the *Redmond
Recorder*, accompanied by the picture displaying the
statue for anyone to see. He had removed the statue
from the shelf behind his desk and taken it home for
safekeeping, but he was running out of time to give it a
hiding place. Wolfe needed to distance himself from the
prize he brought back from Paris. If he wanted it out of
his hands, tonight was his last chance before the article
came out.

The box he extracted from the courtyard in Paris
sat in the bottom drawer of his kitchen island for the
better part of a week. He had agonized over a proper
hiding place for days. Tonight he would follow through
with his strongest solution.

The woodlands next door would hide his secret
without having an explicit connection to him. The

property connected to the Folman Witch was shrouded in urban legend and contained trails frequented by trespassers. Wolfe would have deniability if the statue was ever found.

It might be dangerous to keep the statue so close, but he would be one of the first people to know if it was ever unearthed. It gave him some comfort that he could look out his back door and know that his secret was guarded by the strong roots of the tallest tree on the ridge. The area around the old witch's cottage had grown into bushy undergrowth years before his next door neighbor's husband passed away. Plowing for spring crops was moved to the other side of the ridge in response to the damage done by trespassers enthusiastic to reach the local landmark.

Wolfe wasn't beyond hoping that the Folman Witch would protect his offering as well. He didn't believe in superstition and curses, but if he thought a misconception would keep others away, Wolfe would use the legend to his advantage. He hoped burying his secret near the famed cottage would prove safer than any bank deposit box.

Tonight, while the rest of the neighborhood slept, he would sneak up the hill with his secret treasure. He checked the statue in the box one more time before lowering it into a dark bag. Wolfe had singled out the Hanging Tree on the ridge as his hiding place. He just had to get the box containing the statue off of his property without attracting attention from any of his other neighbors.

He had rearranged his schedule to focus on getting into the woods without being followed by prying eyes. He begged off on seeing Never tonight under the ruse of prepping for his upcoming classes. He couldn't have her in the same room with him until his task was final. He couldn't trust himself not to give up his secret. In his current state, she would be able to see through his deflection and deceptions. It was one of the things he admired about her. Never always went straight to the point, and Wolfe didn't want her to get to the point of his current situation. She couldn't come back to his home for a visit until he had things under control. If he could get the statue box hidden before dawn, he might have time to take her out to Sunday dinner as a celebration.

Wolfe had paced his kitchen floor throughout the night waiting to make his trek into the nearby woods. He tried to keep his focus on the task at hand. It unnerved him to think of wandering through the dark timbers alone, but he would have to fix his little slip-up without help. The wooden box sat in the dark bag on the table, urging his coffee consumption. It was the only spectator to his sporadic mood changes. With each sip of hot liquid, there was a running chant in his head. *This will all be over by tomorrow.* Wolfe had to believe that. For the second time, he would be trespassing on private property.

Wolfe promised himself things would go back to normal. Once the statue was out of his life, he could get back to his normal routines. No one needed to find out about the lengths he went to tonight to hide his secret. The box and statue within it would be out of his hands and off his property. All he had to do was clamber up the slope and dig a final resting place for the statue. It was unlikely anyone would dig it up until everyone involved was out of the picture. Even if the old widow died tomorrow, the witch's cottage was an unofficial county landmark. He couldn't see any new owner of the farmland bulldozing the cottage or the woods surrounding it without heavy protests. Wolfe hoped the superstition surrounding the ruins would protect the statue longer than he would be alive. He wanted to finish out his time at the college, retire to the peaceful existence of contemplating the long chapters of his memoir, and be interned in his own special box before anyone unearthed the contents he buried beneath the shadows of his neighbor's tree.

"A few more hours and it will be out of my hands," he whispered as he walked by the box to scan the view beyond his kitchen window.

Wolfe wanted to time it just right so his neighbors would not notice his movements. He decided on a timespan between three and four in the morning. In his thinking, it was late enough for the night owls to be nodding off to sleep and too early for everyone getting up in preparation for Sunday morning church services. He hadn't slept well since he brought the statue back to his house. A few more sleepless hours wouldn't matter. He could nurse his coffee and remind himself to be patient.

When the clock on his phone boomed its alarm jingle, Wolfe jumped to his feet. In his haste, he spilled the remains of his cold coffee down the front of his shirt. He didn't waste a minute changing. Dabbing at the wet spots for a few seconds, Wolfe threw the towel on the counter and covered the damp stains with his jacket.

It was time to go. Wolfe grabbed the new hand shovel and gloves. The dark bag shifted as he picked it up and swung the straps over his shoulder. Wolfe did a final inventory as he zipped the front of his coat and headed out the back door to the line of trees that distinguished his property from his neighbor's.

Navigating beyond the tree line without a light, Wolfe could understand why the local teenagers thought this place was haunted. The old-growth trees, oaks and beech, were hung with kudzu and swayed even without a detectable breeze. Shadows were everywhere and an active imagination could summon figures weaving in and out of sight. Wolfe found the whole place unsettling. The fact that he was sneaking around outside in the woods like a teenager trying to hide his pot stash before his parents came back early from vacation didn't help matters. He felt ridiculous in his felt hat and oversized black coat. Every shadow gave him misgivings about his plan. Twiggs snapped, leaves crunched from years of autumns left undisturbed, and light filtered in at odd angles before disappearing altogether. Wolfe wished he could take the statue to a locker or a bank deposit box and have it safe and distant, but all those options left paper trails. So here he was, traipsing around in Widow Jenkins' woods like a pirate hoping to hide his loot.

Wolfe's actions only exuded stealth in his own imagination. When his steps threw him off balance, the sharp new hand shovel tucked in the inner lining of his coat would jab into his ribs. His feet found holes and roots over and over in the darkness. A few quick jabs with the hand shovel kept any ideas of swiftness in check. Branches scratched at his face and wild pockets of bush knocked against his shins after every misstep, but he didn't dare use a flashlight.

The simple hike felt like it had gone on for hours by the time he reached the rise where the cottage was located. Wolfe was comforted when he could make out the outline of the remains of the stone house's walls ahead of him. Holly bushes still guarded the front entrance with its missing door and broken windows. Part of the stone chimney had toppled when one of the support walls fell. A small tree grew up through the opening, casting an eerie shadow. It had pushed its way through a hole left when the shingled roof supports gave way, and acted as a makeshift support to the remaining walls.

In any other place and time, Wolfe would be curious to see if the current owner would let him partner with the archeology department and lead a local dig here to train students. When he first moved here, Wolfe imagined his name in connection with pieces added to the local history museum on Main Street housing artifacts dedicated to early settlers of the region. Now in his quest for secrecy, he never wanted anyone to fancy the idea of digging here or anywhere close by.

Wolfe proceeded up the incline behind the last remains of the house and looked for the base of the largest tree on the hill. The one he could see from his back porch. He figured it would make as good a marker as anything. The remains of the witch's cottage already drew too many curious interlopers this time of year and throughout the winter when it was easiest to spot through the naked trees. Wolfe didn't want his secret misrepresented to the press as an occult piece buried on the property. It might be more than he cared to explain away. Trespassing on his neighbor's land in the early hours of the morning was one thing. Explaining how a statue from South America, lost during a crime that killed a priest, came to be buried there was quite another.

Wolfe was almost to the tree he sought. The small box nudged him in the side with its hard angles as it swung with his uneven strides. Imagining the relief of walking home without its weight encouraged Wolfe's last few steps. The Hanging Tree loomed before him in the darkness. He leaned against the base of a small tree for a breather before a hand went up to the zipper on his coat. He was just about to whoosh it down and pull out his hand shovel when a twig snapped off to his left.

Wolfe's head pivoted, but the rest of him remained still. His instincts told him to call out, but he clamped his lips shut. If someone else had followed him here, the worst thing he could do was to give the game away. He rushed into a nearby stand of trees.

When he peaked out, Wolfe thought he saw movement beside the tree across from him. Someone could have poked their head around the side. He stayed still behind the stand of trees and waited.

It wasn't long before a set of shadows much bigger than squirrels came around a section of brush and proceeded in his direction.

"Shouldn't you watch out for trail cameras or something?" Wolfe could make out a faint female voice.

"Sydney, I told you there is nothing out here."

High school kids. They were ten feet from him and closing in fast.

"Keep your voice down!" a female whisper drifted by.

"You think the witch will get us for talking too

loud?"

Wolfe heard a scuffling sound and a shriek, but he tried to stay still.

"You're such an ass, Tyler."

Sydney's short protest was followed by giggling and thrashing around in the leaves. Wolfe thought they would get up and leave after their horseplay was exhausted. Then he heard a soft moan. *Great, he was stuck here at the mercy of horny teenagers who were trying to scare what little wit they had out of each other.*

Wolfe had no interest in seeing the sunrise from behind this tree, or signaling Sydney or her beau Tyler during his retreat. The only thing he could do was hold his position. Hopefully, Tyler would have a short fuse. Maybe his lover would be frightened by something else going bump in the night? Until they got moving in a vertical fashion again, all Wolfe could do was curb his annoyance, wait, and listen for signs of their departure.

He doubted by the way they were carrying on that it was the first time for either of them, maybe not even the first time tonight. Wolfe had to admit Tyler was outperforming all of his high school attempts. The sounds of "Oh Tyler" from his adventures tonight would be haunting Wolfe longer than any witch's curse.

After he was sure Sydney and Tyler had departed, Wolfe eased out from his hiding place and buried the box just before sunrise. The shadow of the large oak and the shallow impression carved into the soil near its trunk would protect his secret. Covering the scarred earth with dried leaves and twigs, Wolfe directed a tight grin toward his accomplishment. The enthusiastic melody of a goldfinch accompanied him as he zipped his jacket and turned to make his weary journey through the predawn light.

CHAPTER 14

Folman Tennessee, Present

After hours in the emergency room at Cedar Brook Regional Medical Center, Never wasn't excited about the new twists and turns her life was taking. There was still no sign of Wolfe's mystery woman, and now her car was in disrepair and her arm was confined to a sling. She couldn't even have a decent dinner away without falling off a mountain road, and having to explain to Justine why she needed a lift.

"We need to go by Elliot's and pick up your meds," Justine's words broke into her thoughts.

"It's just pain meds," Never argued. "I'll be okay until tomorrow."

"The doctor wanted you to sleep tonight."

"I will."

"Not without your pain pills."

"I have aspirin."

"Have you broken bones before?"

"It isn't broken."

"You should probably stay with me tonight."

"I'm going home Justine."

"Then I guess we're going to Elliot's first."

"Fine," Never bit out. "I want a lollipop too."

Justine was smug for the rest of the ride to the pharmacy, and Never knew she should have called her bluff. She wanted to be with the rest of her things, the ones that weren't broken or covered in road juices. Her black dress was ruined. They had to cut her right sleeve up to the shoulder to examine her. The fabric was already speckled with coffee, blood, and several other things from her crawl to safety. Years ago when she was struggling to afford work clothes she would have taken it home and tried to revive it, but tonight she was learning to let things go. Most of her outfit would go into the trash after she cut her way out of it. Her heels were scratched and needed a permanent marker to hide the evidence of the hike she took them through. Her car, Aurora, was sitting in a lot somewhere waiting for a guy with grease-stained hands to work her over and see if she could be coaxed back to life. Never was lucky the scratches on her forehead didn't need stitches, but she suspected the skin would need more than cocoa butter to return to the way it looked in her bathroom mirror this morning.

Her world was still tilting. She needed to force

everything back where it belonged. The trouble was she didn't even have the energy to make Justine obey her. How was she going to make everything else fall back in line? She needed to see her things. Her bed, her clothes, and her desk nook were her only concern tonight. If she had to go to Justine's, she wouldn't be able to reassure herself everything else was okay. Never needed everything else to be okay. She still had a deadline tonight. She might have to type it with her teeth if her arm refused to cooperate, but she would get there.

There was a strange static that charged up the thin hairs in the back of her neck as they exited the car and mounted the short set of steps outside her apartment building. Justine rambled on about the instructions on the bag from the pharmacy, but Never ignored her. She had learned through foster care to heed those physical warnings. Somehow her body always knew when things weren't right. The strange tingle ramped up when she stepped inside her apartment. There was no one waiting by her door. There was nothing in the shadows beyond her hallway, but the feeling continued to crawl up her spine.

Never couldn't put her finger on a certain spot, but things were different. Her front door was closed when she reached it, but she suspected it had been unlocked when she turned the key. Trying to manage the sling and the things she rescued from her car before it was driven away on a flatbed, Never hadn't noticed the difference in the key's resistance. She wished she had.

Something was off. Two drawers in the kitchen were slightly ajar. It was something she would notice, but not many others would. Never had to use extra force when she closed them to get them to budge the last quarter inch.

"You really should sit down and let me bring you some water," she could hear Justine behind her.

Never ignored her and moved into the living room, leaving Justine and her reclaimed items behind. The chair in her work nook was moved and the books on her desk were in a different order.

"Nev where are you going?"

She continued back to her bathroom without responding. She did not want to alarm Justine. She wouldn't tell her friend until she knew the full scope of the problem. Whoever entered her space had rifled through her bathroom closet. Toilet paper rolled along the floor at her feet when she opened it, and towels-once neatly folded-were scattered throughout the space. The words "it doesn't make sense" kept repeating in her head as she closed the closet door and made a beeline for the end of the hall.

The look of her bedroom made things more obvious. Whoever was here got impatient. The drawers in her dresser and nightstand were open and rearranged. All the shoeboxes in the bottom and top of her closet were dumped, and her large coat was falling off its hanger. She pulled it the rest of the way off and examined it. She thought it was fine and was about to try putting it back with her good arm when she saw a flash of color. The lining had been cut in a place she repaired last winter. Whoever was here cut through her crude stitchwork like it was offensive to them. Never didn't see a whisper of activity anywhere else.

"What were they looking for?" she whispered as

she held the coat.

It was silly to think it could tell her who wounded it. Whatever they were looking for had to be small. The cut was only five inches long.

"Did they think I hid my nest egg in there?"

The sleek, designer coat was as close to a nest egg as anything else she had. Whoever broke in didn't violate her by touching her physically, but it made her skin crawl all the same. Strange hands had mingled with her most intimate apparel. She could wash everything and reorganize, but she would always imagine a stranger touching them without her consent.

Whatever was going on, she wasn't safe here. She needed to get Justine moving before something else was set in motion. Never had a sneaking suspicion she wasn't having a run of bad luck. Maybe these latest events weren't random after all.

Justine was still fussing in the kitchen, making tea or something that required water. Never could hear the soft whine of the water heater kicking in. Should they both leave? Should she call the police? Nothing seemed to be missing. She really didn't want to deal with *Sergeant Tons-of-Fun* tonight, but what if someone was targeting her now? She tossed her ideas about changing clothes along with her damaged coat and headed for the kitchen.

"Justine, we need to leave."

"For where?"

It was a good question. It shouldn't have been a

hard one to answer, but it was.

"Where the hell should I go?" Never muttered as she clumsily retrieved the card from her purse and dialed the sergeant's number.

It went straight to voice mail.

"Someone broke into my apartment," was the only message she left before she hit the "end" button.

"We need to go to Cora's apartment," she decided as she motioned to Justine.

Justine was still standing by the stove with a tea pot in her hand trying to work out this latest change.

"Why?"

"The police will need to talk to us."

"About what?" she leaned back and crossed her arms. "Never... talk to me."

"Someone was here while I was gone."

"Is something missing?"

"No, they didn't take anything."

"Maybe it's the meds, Never?"

"I haven't taken any."

"I watched you."

"You saw me palm pills and pretend to take them."

"Where are they?"

"Check the cuff of my sweater."

Never's last comment got Justine moving. She walked away from the stove and to the coat tree by the front door to inspect the garment in question. Never watched her pull two long white pills from the shallow cuff.

"How?" Justine held them out to her in confusion.

"We need to go."

The apartment was small. The interlopers only checked a few places. What did they think she had? They weren't after drugs or electronics. All of her possessions were still within reach of where she left them. Maybe whoever was here just wanted to listen? The thought forced a smirk to her lips. She had never thought of herself as an interesting personality. She was sure her neighbor, Mrs. Basket, would have far more interesting conversations.

Maybe the sheriff's department was still trying to pin Wolfe's death on her. Whoever did this didn't care if she found it. But what was this slow-moving train of intimidation leading to? Did someone develop some fantasy that she took something more valuable than coffee and peanuts from Wolfe's house when she had her photograph taken by every newspaper and two-bit press in the region? Why target her jacket? She wasn't wearing her jacket that day. Why cut it open? With or without a blow to the head things weren't adding up. Whoever was after her wasn't being clear about their motives.

Never checked the hallway before she walked out and grabbed Justine with her good arm to keep her close. In all probability, someone would have grabbed them before they entered the building if they were interested in kidnaping, but nothing about tonight made sense. She took it slow and guided Justine out beside her. She watched in every direction for someone to emerge. No one seemed to be waiting in the shadows for them to resurface. Never didn't bother to lock her door. She felt Justine turn to pull it to and they both bolted across the hall to Mrs. Basket's door.

Trying to tap on the wood in a normal tempo, Never ignored the uncomfortable way Justine's fingers were clutching her arm. She focused on the sound of shuffling feet coming from behind the closed door. She never stopped to wonder if her neighbor would be home tonight. It seemed like the older woman was always dogging her footsteps. How many times had she shoved her head outside the door and called to Never as she returned home from work or a date? It felt like thousands.

"Just call me Cora," she would correct when Never tried to be off-putting.

Mrs. Basket wanted to talk about every article Never had ever published, and often offered tips on where to find her next scoop. Retired for the last ten years, Cora showed no signs of slowing down. She got up every morning and smoothed her snow white hair into a bun and readied herself for company in what most would call work casual. She was always in some shade of pastel to match the pink and purple frames supporting her thick lens.

Never manufactured a smile as one pink oval

peered around the creaking door.

"Hi, can we come in?"

"Have you brought a friend to see the kittens?" she brightened as she swung the door open. "They're going to be grown if you wait much longer."

"Kittens," Justine mouthed to her, but Never ignored it.

"Yes, I hope it's not a bad time." She tried to remain polite as she barged in. "This is my friend Justine from the paper."

"The *Folman Gazette* is my first read every morning," she chattered as she ushered them both into the living room. "Mel is here too."

"I guess we can make it a party."

Cora motioned for them to follow her down the hall. Their trek ended beside a small enclosure lined with towels where her cat Domino sprawled encompassed by offspring.

"This is Patches, beside him is Cookie, Boots is in the corner, Checkers is a mama's boy, Marble is the biggest, and Houdini is always getting out of their enclosure," Cora introduced as she pointed to each one like a proud grandmother peering through a nursery window. "I'm going to have to run an ad in the paper to find homes for them."

"I could take some pictures for the social media page, and caption it so people know the kittens are going to be up for adoption," Justine offered as she picked up Houdini. "I bet my message box will be full in minutes."

Looking over the active group, Never was glad for the sling. It kept her from being badgered into holding a squirming kitten of her own. The nerves jumping around under her skin would send the small fluffs of energy into a frenzy in her arms.

"Domino will be single in no time," Never agreed as she tried to sneak a look at her phone.

"Would you girls like to play poker with us?"

Mel seemed content in his chair, but he smiled up at them as the short parade of women reentered the living room.

"I didn't know you were a card shark Mrs. Basket."

"We play every weekend, Mel and I. Betting is limited to oyster crackers, and the loser has to bring dinner next time."

"Sounds good to me." Justine seemed excited as she cuddled Houdini in her arms.

The phone rang just as everyone was waiting for Never's response.

"I have to take this."

"Mrs. Basket would you mind if I took pictures first?" Never could hear Justine working her magic as she took the older woman's elbow and guided her away from the door. "Then I will help you set up the table for cards."

There was another gentle reminder, "call me Cora dear" before Never closed the door and checked the screen on her phone.

"Took you long enough," Never baited as she answered.

"Wasn't exactly waiting by the phone for your call," Sergeant Henderson's dry reply mirrored her own.

"It wasn't on my list either."

She heard a rustling in the background, and a door closing. The irritation in her voice must have registered as genuine because he flipped into professional mode from then on.

"Why not call Folman PD?"

"I thought it might be related to your case."

"Where are you now?"

"Justine and I are at Mrs. Basket's apartment across the hall."

"Is Justine your roommate?"

"Coworker," Never corrected without adding any explanation for Justine's presence.

She could hear an engine coming to life.

"I'll be there in a few minutes, crime scene is on the way," grumbled its way to her ear before the line went dead.

"Great," Never said to the empty hallway. Maybe

she should call her lawyer? Another round with Sergeant Henderson wasn't in her best interest. She really didn't want him in her home. Going back to Mrs. Basket's apartment too soon would cause more questions than just waiting out here.

"He will want to talk to all the neighbors anyway," she muttered as she shoved the phone into the end of her sling for easy access and shuffled back through her neighbor's unlocked door.

Their party of four was halfway through their second hand of poker when a firm knock on the door made them all look up.

"I'll get it," Mel offered, but Never was already out of her seat.

"You three enjoy the game," she tossed over her shoulder as she opened the door. "I'll be back in a few minutes."

Justine made a small protest, but stayed to play cards with Houdini dozing on her lap.

She heard Cora speculate, "I bet that's a source for her next big story."

It was all Never could do not to roll her eyes as she looked out at Sergeant Henderson.

"Romance interrupted?" she needled as she stepped into the hallway and took in his suit and tie.

"Folman Volunteer Firefighters Annual Fundraiser."

So...he was on a date or being auctioned off for

the evening to some desperate woman. Even with her sling, Never thought her evening was looking up compared to his. She wasn't that far down on her luck yet. Next year, who knows, she might be there with the catcalling masses hoping to find a little more than that good feeling one gets from donating to charity. Images of boiled burgers and runny mashed potatoes came to mind and Never quickly turned away. Some hometown amusements didn't have the flare or the flavor associated with southern cooking and hospitality. The volunteer firefighters' fundraiser was one of them. She had a hard time writing a fair and honest article about it her first year at the *Folman Gazette*. She was glad the assignment now fell to an eager junior reporter. The whole gathering seemed sad and a little creepy to her.

"Sorry I missed it."

"I thought you would be in Redmond today."

"I was," she gestured to her sling. "That's where I got this."

"So you found the other woman after all?" she heard a hint of a grin in his voice, but she didn't turn back to look at him.

"Not unless she's the one who tampered with Aurora."

"Who?"

"I don't know who she is."

"No, no, now slow down." He shook his head at her as though he was trying to clear an etch-a-sketch. "Who is Aurora?"

"My car. Something made me lose power."

He looked at her as though he was the one suffering from a head injury and not the other way around.

"This is your second issue today?"

"Yes, things are moved, but nothing was taken," Never explained as she opened the door.

"Are you sure?"

She nodded. "I don't have much of value."

"I guess we should have a look."

Never got the feeling he thought she was lying, but she didn't care. Something strange arose when Wolfe died, and it felt like it was ramping up. If *Sergeant Snotty* didn't believe her, he still had a duty to keep her safe. Never didn't like the idea of having him go through her underwear again with a group of his colleagues, but she would cope. As frequently as they were being put on display, she was entertaining the idea of going commando for a few weeks. At the very least, she was going to ask Justine to take her by the nearest mid-sized store on the way over to her apartment. She would grab her laptop bag from the table and her tennis shoes. The rest she could come up with along the way.

"You must be quite the neat freak," his voice snapped her back into the present.

"What?"

"Single guys never have things this organized, with or without a break in."

Her thoughts trailed to Wolfe's house. The stacks of books, papers on every surface, sports equipment piled by the front door. She missed that part of her week, that sense of connection that had been severed after his betrayal and finalized by his death. Never looked up to find curious eyes studying her. She jumped into a ramble of explanation to distract from the feelings she was on the verge of divulging.

"I found the drawers in the kitchen that are hard to close sticking out, the books on my work table and drawers in my bedroom were rearranged, but the bulk of the mess is in my closets."

"Closets?"

She nodded.

"Bathroom and bedroom," Never pointed to the hallway before leading the way.

She led him to her bedroom closet first and showed him the piles of shoes and boxes littering the floor before she gestured to her coat.

"They had an interest in the lining of a coat I repaired."

"They cut the seam back open." He looked curious, but masked it when he saw her look up.

"You said closets," he prompted as she struggled to hang her coat back on its hanger.

Judging from the way he was hovering by the bedroom door, he didn't want to spend any more time with her than he had to. Never was happy to get him out of her private world and back to his date.

"The bathroom is this way."

He took notes and walked her back to the living room before he spoke.

"Someone tossed a few shoes, cut your jacket, and unrolled your towels in the bathroom closet. Your jewelry, electronics, and prescriptions are all accounted for?"

"Yes, I checked those first."

"It could have been a lot worse if they decided to slice and dice the place."

"You make it sound like it was no big deal."

"Oh, on the contrary, small changes are worrying, but easier to clean up."

"I'm worried that my car and this break-in are connected to Wolfe's death."

"You think Wolfe is haunting you?"

"I think his death set someone off."

"And it wasn't you?"

Never wanted to strangle someone tonight, but a few biting words were all she had the strength to deliver.

"There is nothing I want badly enough to seek out your attention."

A knock on the door announced the techs had arrived.

"If you're right, Miss Martinez, we both may have some uncomfortable days ahead of us."

He dismissed her by turning to issue instructions to the crew lining her doorway. Maybe Justine was right. If she had taken the pain pills she wouldn't have let herself be enticed to snap back. Being accused of murder on a regular basis by this man had a funny way of setting her off.

By the time Never made it back across the hall to Mrs. Basket's apartment, Justine and Houdini were on their fourth hand of cards with Mel and Cora. Judging by the pile of oyster crackers by Mel's free hand, Cora was on the hook for dinner the next time they met.

"Does your handsome source have a name dear?" Cora asked without looking up.

"He's not a source and handsome isn't how I would describe him."

"Dashing, sharp...what is it you kids say now...sick?"

"Illness comes to mind," Never agreed as she seated herself. "I'm afraid Justine and I will have to be going after this hand."

"And Houdini," Justine added as she stroked the sleeping bundle in her lap.

"You're keeping him?" Never looked at her friend with confusion.

"Disappointed?" Justine looked up at her with mischief radiating from her face. "You could pick out one of your own."

"It might turn out to be the first decent male in my life, but no," Never declined. "I'm godmother or cool aunt material."

"Come on, Cool Aunt," Justine motioned for her to follow. "We need to stop by the store on the way home."

"Yes, someone needs some extra special toys for his first night," Never agreed as she dashed out the door.

"Next Saturday is game night!" they heard Mrs. Basket's voice echoing down the hallway as they made their escape.

"Can you hold him with your sling?" Justine asked as she followed Never to the passenger side of the car.

Never nodded as the kitten sniffed and pawed at her good shoulder. "I just hope he likes car rides."

If it wasn't for the adrenaline, Never would be ready to collapse. The kitten fed off her energy like a struck match and moved around in her arms in full adventure mode. He was like a slinky with fur as she tried to contain him with her good arm.

"I may need to add a cat carrier to my list." Justine eyed them both as she engaged the engine.

Everything was going fine until the force of the

air vents hit him. Tiny claws came out with a high-pitched growl that would have embarrassed a larger cat. Never struggled to pull him away from her, but he evaded her clumsy attempts. Houdini ran his claws up and around her neck, trying to burrow under her hair.

"Do you want me to pull him out?" Justine asked as she reached out to pull a still-struggling Houdini from his hiding place.

"No, turn off the vents," she pleaded. "He could take out an eye if he starts swinging again."

"I'm buying a carrier when we get to the store," Justine promised as she flipped off the air and shifted into drive. "You'll need antibiotic cream too."

"I'll be fine with a few clothes and a toothbrush for the night," Never waved her off. After all, what's one more injury to add to tonight's adventure.

"I just need a shower and a place to work."

"Rory is out of town and the office has a futon in it."

Never liked Rory Scott, but they came from different planets. Rory had a big, loving, catholic family, and was consumed by sports and the men who played them. He worked for a big ad agency on the outskirts of Nashville, and traveled for work. He and Justine were not officially moving in together until after the wedding this Christmas, but Rory was a fixture in her apartment. It made things awkward when Never dropped by. Not only was she a third wheel, but Justine was the one thing that they both had in common. With Wolfe gone, there wouldn't be a buffer between them, or a reason for double dates.

Never tried to focus on the positive as Houdini dug another razor-tipped claw into the back of her neck, "He is going to be surprised by your latest addition."

"We discussed having animals after the wedding, but I think he was leaning toward a dog."

"To play fetch with?"

"He wanted me to have protection when he's on his trips."

"You don't have to sift litter for a baseball bat."

"True," Justine laughed. "But a home should be full of life."

Never had been in many places throughout her childhood that were overflowing with life and bodies, but none of them felt like home. She knew if anyone could find happiness in the crazy up-and-down world of traditional marriage Justine could. It was evident Rory was head over heels in love with her, and Houdini would be chewing on his shoelaces in no time. They would both lose their hearts and scratch-free furniture to the cuddly little demon, but they would accept his addition to the family all the same.

"I'm sure Houdini will deliver on that."

"He is adorable isn't he?"

Never could see the thoughts churning through her mind. When she wasn't behind a camera or worrying over Never's social life, Justine was wedding-planning. As her maid of honor, Never could see the kitten wreaking havoc up and down the sanctuary of Our Mother Mary's Holy Catholic Church. Dresses would be pulled, flowers would be eaten, people would be scratched, and the ceremony would be delayed until they could control the little escape artist. After tonight, she wasn't volunteering for that duty.

"If you make him your ring bearer, we can't be friends anymore."

"But think of how cute he would be in a wagon pulled by the flower girl," Justine pleaded as she pulled into a parking space at one of the local department stores.

"And we both know how much he loves being in something that has wheels," Never told her as she motioned to the clump of fur she was trying to detangle from her curls.

CHAPTER 15

Redmond College, Redmond Tennessee,
Two and a Half Months Earlier

Wolfe's copy of the *Redmond Recorder* was waiting for him when he arrived this morning. His article hadn't made the front page, but the photo of him seated at his office desk glared up at him all the same. The statue was clear behind him on the shelf and larger than he would have liked. His brows knitted together as he scanned the *Features* section. His secret was there for everyone to see. Wolfe suspected the ink from the paper would leech into his skin and brand him as he carried it back to his office.

Despite the cool weather and his struggle to stay calm, Wolfe could feel the perspiration. He eased the paper into his bag and checked the trash for other copies before turning down the hall. Several people stopped him to chat about the new class or ask about his plans for the upcoming holiday break. He resisted the instinct to check his watch or grip his bag closer as he returned their friendly banter. He hoped the moisture collecting near his collar wasn't visible to the world around him. The statue was gone from his office, but proof of its existence was circulating around campus before he pulled into the faculty parking lot this morning. The campus newspaper would be in everyone's box and gracing tables in the library and common rooms at the dorms. Wolfe would not need to look far to see his mistake peering up at him.

A select few people in the world would be able to decipher where it came from, but everyone would see it connected to him in print. Wolfe hoped no one would ever come looking for the statue or the man in the photo. If they did, they would find a trail to follow.

CHAPTER 16

Folman Tennessee, Present

Never's phone rang early the next morning when she was waiting for coffee to finish brewing.

"Miss Martinez this is Gary Dunham from Ridgewood Towing and Bodywork."

"Do you have news on my car?"

"It looks like your alternator is shot," the gruff voice on the other end of the phone informed her. "It will be next week before I can get the parts to start on the body damage."

"Was anything out of the ordinary?"

There was a short pause.

"You think someone tampered with it?"

"I was in Redmond for a while that day and I had no trouble going over the ridge."

"I didn't see any obvious signs. In a car this old, it is hard to say."

"But it is a possibility?"

"I can't rule it out," he admitted without enthusiasm.

"What about the brakes?"

"What about them?"

"I wasn't able to stop when the engine died."

"I didn't see anything wrong with the brake lines, but I can go over them again."

"Could there be any other explanation for the sliding?"

"Your tires are worn, but still have tread. The only other factor would be weather."

"It did rain," Never admitted. "There was fog."

"So far, I can't say there is anything to be alarmed about, but I will recheck the brakes."

Was her accident a scary coincidence? Aurora was older than most of her contemporaries, but Never was always vigilant about new behavior and sounds. Could it be that the car part had failed without help and she was just in an unlucky spot? It all seemed pretty odd to her, but she needed proof.

"It would make me feel better if you went over them again Gary."

"No problem, I will check them while I wait on your part to come in. You should be back up and running by next Thursday."

Never thanked him and wrote notes in her notebook about picking up Aurora before ending the call. Grateful her insurance covered most of the cost, Never was still eager to get rid of the SUV as fast as she could. It wasn't ideal for her to be dependent on Justine or anyone else for transportation, but driving the rental still made her uncomfortable and nervous. She couldn't wait to return it.

She worried about cars parking too close to it, and she couldn't hide it when she was trying to sneak around. It was like driving a big, silver blimp. Add to the fact, everyone knew she had a rental car after the aggressive coverage of Wolfe's death and the memorial.

It was possible that her car crapped out on her, but Never found the timing convenient. It was the same night someone took a chance at breaking into her apartment. Why would someone do that if they weren't watching her movements? Maybe the whole situation was making her paranoid, but it wasn't unreasonable to think that someone tampered with her car. She was in Redmond for the afternoon. Anyone could identify her car in a parking lot. If they had enough skills, sabotaging her car would be easy.

"I guess there is no point getting dramatic," she muttered as she closed the notebook and thrust it deep in her bag. "I'll just have to wait and see what Gary finds."

She picked up her full mug of coffee from the machine, and sat down at the table with a sigh. She had hoped that Wolfe's memorial would be the last time she would have to think about him. She had written her good-bye. Readers had sent cards and flowers. It seemed like a fitting end to his tragic death.

She was healing from her accident, but Never couldn't find any relief. She never thought of herself as vulnerable. In her life, things were always happening around her. It just felt as though after Wolfe's death things were directed at her. It was a very different situation. Never hoped she could clear it up by hiring a therapist instead of a bodyguard. Her decision would be prompted by Gary's final report on her brake lines. She reserved no enthusiasm about the possibility of her winter fashion choices shifting between a slimming straight jacket and the ominous bulk of a bulletproof vest, but she couldn't rule them out either.

CHAPTER 17

Folman Tennessee, Present

Never opened the door with a groggy look of confusion for the person gazing back at her.

"Susan... I ...didn't expect to see you here," she stuttered out.

"Sorry to catch you so early Never," Susan replied as she strode past with a large cardboard box. "I have to get back for morning classes."

Never followed her and set her coffee cup aside.

"What is this?"

"These are some of the things that Wolfe left you."

"He left me a box of papers from his office?" Never asked in confusion.

"Not, just one," Susan explained. "Paul is helping

me with the rest."

As if on cue, Paul stumbled through the door with another box stacked high with books.

"Hi Nev, where you want these?" Paul's voice emanated from behind the tower advancing on her.

Where did she want them? She wasn't sure she wanted them at all. Should she say that? Why would she want Wolfe's old junk?

"The table or floor is fine."

"Good, we may need both," Paul huffed out as he set his load down next to Susan's.

"Is there that much?"

"Close to a dozen," Susan admitted as she grabbed Paul's arm and headed back outside.

"A dozen!"

Good thing she already set down her coffee mug. A dozen boxes of Wolfe's stuff. Where would she put it? What in the world was this about?

Never tried again to get answers from Susan and Paul when they returned carrying more overflowing boxes. "I don't understand why he sent them to me."

"It is a terrible thing all the way around," Susan agreed. "But Wolfe put you on his paperwork as the person to contact if something happened to him."

"But...that can't be binding."

"As far as the college is concerned it is," Paul said as he came huffing through again.

"Otherwise, it would go straight into the trash." Susan looked forlorn at the thought.

Never wondered if that would be her next step. The idea of being saddled with Wolfe's old papers and forgotten junk wasn't sitting well. She couldn't blame the strong coffee for the irritation brewing in her stomach. He could have left her his house or the contents of his bank account, but instead boxes and boxes of stuff from his cluttered office were invading her small space. Why didn't he just donate it to the college library and be done with it?

"Why wouldn't they keep it for use at the library?" she voiced as Susan and Paul headed for the door to bring in another round.

"It has to be donated directly or they can't keep it," Paul paused to answer and shrug. "It's just one of the strange rules of institutions."

So here she was in her pajamas being forced to play the part of Wolfe's donation bin. Never might chuck the entirety of her allotment after Susan and Paul went on their way. She didn't owe Wolfe another hour of her time. It would take hours to sort through the boxes and take inventory of what was there. She had other things to keep her distracted, like figuring out what Archie Gordon and Mayor Ball were up to at night. She had been out late watching both of them, but still couldn't come to any conclusions. They were beginning to be as irritating as her former lover. She had no ring and no story. She shook her head, but the images of stacks and stacks of boxes covering her floor and table wouldn't go away. On top of Wolfe's strange behavior and death, she would now have several boxes of his research to crowd her space until she decided to get rid of them. What a gift. Was there no length the man wouldn't go to in a quest to anger and humiliate her?

Never stood by and watched as Susan and Paul made trip after trip into her apartment with overflowing boxes to stack on and around her small table. She felt like she was watching a time-lapse video. People were moving and boxes were multiplying, but it all seemed too fast.

"I think that's the last one honey," crashed through the silence before Paul lowered the box in his hands to the floor. "We should get back to Redmond and let Nev get back to her morning."

"Yes, Never we're so sorry to intrude." Susan gave her a delicate hug and moved to stand beside her husband. "Forgive us for being such a whirlwind this morning."

"I suppose it couldn't be helped." Never sighed as she eyed the takeover of her kitchen. "I just don't know what to do with all this stuff."

"Think of it as a treasure hunt," Paul offered as he steered his wife out the door. "Think of the possibilities."

Treasure hunt indeed! If she worked hard enough, she might find her kitchen again.

She mumbled a thin, "thank you" as they disappeared down the hallway. The door swung shut behind them and she was left in the wake of their departure. Never glanced down at the chipped red paint on her toenails. The last time she painted them was after her last call with Wolfe. He had been adamant about their plans to meet at the lake the next night. She had been letting herself go for weeks now. Had it really been that long ago?

Instead of taking a seat at the table, Never looked at all the boxes and thought what a shame the thieves hadn't come after Wolfe's office supplies showed up. Maybe they would have taken some of them off her hands by mistake. She would have happily parted with all of it.

The sounds of an engine retreating caused her to raise her head and peer around the room. Paul and Susan were headed back to Redmond. She was alone with all this stuff.

Boxes and papers accosted her everywhere she looked. Never had heard of baggage from past relationships, but this was ridiculous. Why should she have to sort through a dead man's things after he dumped her?

"Please let this be the end of it."

Never hoped there weren't any more boxes, treasure or otherwise, coming her way from Redmond College. The memorial should have been her final obligation. Everything since then added another layer of confusion. Her car, her apartment, nowhere was off-limits to Wolfe's incessant interference in her life after his death.

Maybe the sergeant was right. Maybe Wolfe really was haunting her. For her sake, Never hoped he was. At some points it felt like she was losing her mind. She had readied herself for a long-overdue proposal that night by the shore. Her hopes were so high she could have forgiven Wolfe for almost anything. Anything but the secret he wanted to tell her.

"You really were a sick bastard."

She couldn't let him continue to torment her from beyond the grave. She may not have a choice in the way things turned out, but she didn't have to archive his papers like an assistant professor hoping to uncover a path to tenure. His boxes could crowd her all they wanted. Crouching in her floor and covering her table, it didn't matter. It was all trash to her. She didn't have to acknowledge it until she was ready.

Never knew the coffee in her cup was cold before she reached for it. Navigating her way to the sink with more willpower than grace, she dumped the contents. She should be in the shower by now, but she headed for her closet instead. Stripping off her pajamas, Never replaced them with workout leggings and a hoodie she could carry her phone and keys in. She needed to get fresh air into her lungs, and that meant getting far away from here.

CHAPTER 18

Redmond College, Two Months and 13 Days Earlier

When Wolfe opened his campus mailbox there were several envelopes, flyers for campus events, and a large manila envelope with December graduation instructions. He thumbed through and read some of the announcements. The cheerleaders were having a car wash, the English and drama departments were joining forces to collaborate on a spring production of *Hamlet*, and the new outdoor club was selling t-shirts to pay for their kayaking trip on the French Broad River. Several professors from his graduate days still kept in touch and often mailed him listings for job openings in their programs. There was a small white envelope obscured by the rest when he gathered them up to tuck them under his arm. It had no return address typed in the corner. When he broke the seal, a folded piece of newsprint fell out and fluttered to the ground. He could see a message written on the back of it that read, "I know."

Wolfe picked it up and evened out the creases.

The clipping was the photograph of him from the *Redmond Recorder*. Someone had cut the photograph of him with the statue out of the article and written a message on the back.

His first thoughts were of Rebecca. Had she seen through his attempt to slide the statue's disappearance by her? What about Marcy Christopher at the *Redmond Recorder*? Could she have figured out his secret after looking at the photo? What would be the point of sending him a creepy message? It was someone with knowledge of his work address and access to the post office on campus. It had to be someone within close proximity of the college. His thoughts made him leery until he turned the clipping over and realized there was more to the message.

"I know" was followed by "what you're doing next summer!"

That seemed like a strange way to make a threat. Summer was months away. Wolfe dug around in the envelope and found a cheap, hand-printed card with balloons on the front of it. He opened it to find. "Best Wishes for your new proposal! We're beating our drums and sounding our whistles in support of your achievement." It was signed by Susan Gilbert and a few other teachers in the English department.

Wolfe breathed a sigh of relief and chuckled. It was just an oddball encouragement card from Susan. He needed to pull himself together. The statue was making him paranoid.

Lights and ghosts were going up in dorm windows across campus, and more than one tree had toilet paper sweeping across its lower limbs. Students were gearing up for Halloween. Parties were being planned. In his nervous state, students wouldn't have to work hard to make him look foolish.

Wolfe smiled and tried to be rational. He couldn't react to everything like killers from Paris had found him. It was silly to worry about someone finding him here. The town of Redmond wasn't a hotbed of tourism like Nashville or the bigger college towns near the Kentucky border. If anyone did seek him out, they wouldn't go unnoticed in Redmond like they would in a bigger city. Locals would notice them as soon as they reached the town limits, and Redmond College campus was even smaller. There wasn't much room for a stranger to hide.

With a grunt, he tossed the newspaper clipping on top of a stack of fall carnival flyers in a nearby trash can. Wolfe needn't put so much energy into worrying about the hidden statue. He was safe from scrutiny. Thinking otherwise would only succeed in making him jumpy.

Wolfe pushed away his unease and returned the strange card to its envelope. Maybe after Halloween and the fall break, his students would calm down and focus their enthusiasm on their studies. Term paper assignments were due next week. Wolfe wouldn't put it past some of his weaker students to try to spook him into distraction as a way of extending their due date. If he continued to react to everything like a boogeyman was chasing him, his students might get the upper hand. Wolfe was determined not to let the "statue mishap" affect his work. Tucking the white envelope under his arm with the rest of his mail, Wolfe headed for the sanctuary of his office.

CHAPTER 19

Folman Tennessee, Present

It was funny how the new rental car made her nervous.
Her doctor gave her the go-ahead, but Never still felt
hesitant. Driving had always been a time of reflection, a
calming freedom. This new car, this unknown quantity
injected into her life was a different matter altogether.
It was bulky in places she was used to having a clear
view, and lights beyond the dashboard came on
whenever another car got close or when she decided to
pass. The bulk of it reminded her of a large silver potato
bug. It felt silly to miss Aurora, but she did. Never's old
Nissan had, in fact, seen better days. Most people would
be horrified to get behind the wheel of her old clunker.
It was almost twenty years old with enough parking lot
rashes to give a person reasons to scratch. It was
unprofessional, unattractive, and over the hill. Pushing
200,000 miles, it led most people to believe she would
be pushing it one day. All of that should have bothered
her, but it never made her as nervous as all the lights,
sounds, and smells of this fully functional SUV.

Jessica P. Morgan

Never longed for the worn leather seats, dusty dashboard, and the ever-present lights echoing all of her transportation's infirmities. She supposed it looked like she had a full house spread, but she was holding out for the final collection to announce her royal flush of automotive breakdowns. To a sane person, this probably wasn't calming, but for some strange reason it soothed her. She knew what to expect. She enjoyed surprising people when the car projected a much different kind of person. If nothing else, it gave her room to exceed their expectations. Aurora was likely to become a fireball the way Never maintained her, but she couldn't deny the love she felt for the big hunk of junk. Aurora wasn't plush. Whatever Aurora lacked, she made up for it in determination. Never admired that bewildering quality in people as well as machines. Somehow, the car kept spluttering to life when most cars in her condition would give in and resign themselves to the idea of one final, slow trip on a flatbed to the scrapyard in the valley.

The steering wheel on the rental car felt firm and unfriendly. Not like Aurora's constant, yielding companionship. Never had been through so many changes and almost-changes in the past few weeks. Somehow Wolfe set all this in motion. Him and his obsession with Chasity and whatever she represented to him.

Because of Wolfe, Aurora had been fished from the side of the mountain by a tow truck and checked-over by a mechanic. Never was left with this flashy, silver stranger to navigate her assignments and hunt for clues. The cleaner they used to refresh the fabric seats made her stomach turn. She didn't like sitting in the strange new pod, couldn't imagine eating a meal in it, and didn't remember the last time she had driven a car that had been recently vacuumed. *When was the last time she had done that for Aurora? Was the great birdseed debacle in 2009 or was it 2010?* She couldn't remember, but the image of birds swarming her parking spot after the incident was firmly planted in her memory.

Speaking of birds...Gordon was on the move.

In his three-piece black suit and tight Windsor-knotted tie, she would know him anywhere. His eyes were close-set to the bridge of his long flat nose. His brown hair was receding on top and turning gray around the temples. His short, buzzed haircut made his average ears look larger and his wide, thin lips look even thinner. In all other respects, he projected respectability with sensible loafers for a day at the office. The interesting thing was, he wasn't heading the direction of the third floor office he occupied in his father's prosperous packaging and shipping company. That business was on the east side of town. Something didn't add up about Archie Gordon's trips to the south side of town, and Never was determined to prove it.

So far she had come up with zilch. No drug ties to the businesses he frequented like a shadow and nothing illicit at the pier or park. He wasn't trading in anything, but he returned again and again. He would just walk and gape in his slow unusual strides. Most people would shame her for picking on a disabled man, but Never couldn't let it go. He was up to something and she wasn't going to stop until she had proof. If he wanted to play cat and mouse she would give him room to get comfortable before she moved in to corner him.

It was possible he already knew of her interest two weeks ago on Becker Street when he saw her pretending to window shop outside a business selling geriatric dog beds. It wouldn't be hard to find out she didn't have a dog or a need for such equipment for her relationship with Wolfe or otherwise. That mistake might have cost her.

In all likelihood, Archie Gordon was a suspect in sabotaging Aurora. But just like the inkling she had about him for the last few weeks, she had no way of proving it. Never had followed him to different businesses around town, down to the pier on the banks of the Cumberland River, and to Bash Park. Nothing stood out except his odd canter and the slow methodical way he checked out every direction before he left his car. Maybe he was paranoid or eccentric, but Never's gut told her if she followed him long enough she would figure out either who he was hiding from or what he was attempting to hide.

It was harder to hide in the rental car. Never became a local celebrity for the second time this month when the story of her accident graced the pages of her paper. Speculation raced like wildfire through the gossip chains woven into the fabric of Folman like the thin strips of material in a rag rug. She might as well have a news station logo on the side of her car and flash the lights in Gordon's direction for good measure. Her only saving graces were the plethora of other "mommy-mobiles" in the area of the park sporting the same color and the businesses on the south side of town were flanked with delivery vans and dumpsters she could shield her new burden behind.

Gordon was a strange one, but she would never mistake him for a fool. Her phone buzzed. She gave it a quick glance to see Justine's name before lifting it to her ear.

"Something wrong," Never answered without taking her eyes off Gordon.

"I have to get a few more pictures of the middle school production. I need you to check on Houdini for me."

"I am following Gordon, but he's as exciting as dishwater," Never admitted. "I can run over and make sure Houdini isn't throwing a wild party."

"He would look so cute in oversized sunglasses!"

Never couldn't help but smile, "I can see the New Year's posts already."

Houdini was an instant star on the newspaper's social media page. Everyone loved the furry little terror and Justine was a proud momma with all her updates. When an event allowed, she would take him with her for pictures on location. Houdini was becoming a celebrity and all his siblings received homes within a week of Justine's pictures and pleas. The little guy was wiggling his way into hearts across the region, and he had attitude for miles. Never hated to admit she was becoming fond of the kitten despite his claws.

"Wouldn't he look cute in a hat, with beads...," Never could hear Justine's voice pickup as she changed ears.

"Get your photos for tonight first."

"Yes, thank you so much for going by," was followed by a click.

"I guess he has to be more entertaining than

Gordon," Never grumbled as she took one last look at the man before shifting into gear.

She left Gordon walking the playground in the park and headed east to Justine's apartment. Never didn't plan to stay long at Justine's. Houdini was still in full kitten mode and was shredding anything his little paws came in contact with. She didn't want to give him a shot at one of her best sweaters. She gave herself a mental reminder to wear the worst clothes she had the week of Justine's honeymoon.

Never had agreed to be their cat sitter while the happy couple enjoyed a cruise to Jamaica. It would be a Christmas wedding. She had no family to celebrate with now that Wolfe was gone. She would watch movies or read to Houdini while they both ate leftover takeout and wedding cake. She could wrap him in thin, shiny garland and see how long it would take him to untangle himself. Maybe she should buy a couple of catnip balls to serve as distractions? Either way, it would be the most magical first Christmas Justine's adventurous kitten has ever seen.

Never was just passing the mailboxes when footsteps sounded behind her. She turned to see a stranger with dark, flyaway curls like her own. He stopped and watched her as she took in his black dress pants and dusty steel-toed work boots. A smile curved his lips as he pulled mail from his box.

Never was getting ready to head to Justine's door when she heard him call out, "You're Justine's friend?"

"Yes, I don't remember meeting you before."

"Forgive me, I am Marcel Weaver." He extended

a hand. "I moved in a few weeks ago."

"Never Martinez." His hand was firm but not harsh as it encased hers. "Are you new to the area?"

He chuckled. "What gave me away?"

"Weaver isn't a common name in Folman."

"I am working on a hotel project in town for the next several months."

"Is that what's going in on Jackson Avenue?"

"You don't miss much around town do you?"

"I would love to interview you about it for the *Folman Gazette* when you get close to opening."

"With the current delays it looks like I will be sticking around until late spring."

"I'm sure I will be seeing more of you then."

"I hope so," was backed up with a smile that could audition for toothpaste commercials.

If conditions were different, she would be tempted to get to know him better. Never couldn't tell if Marcel's mocha skin extended well below his waistline, but she was surprised by her thoughts on the subject. Physical attraction was natural. It shouldn't make her feel uncomfortable, but the thoughts were unwanted all the same. She felt herself stiffen. As her eyes raced back up to meet his, the motion of his angular jaw caught her attention. It twitched. Did he recognize her discomfort? Had she imagined it along with the smooth contours being hidden under his wine polo shirt? The clean-shaven skin along his jawline was smooth and she felt an overwhelming urge to trace it with her fingertips.

"If you're looking for Justine, I think she went out earlier with her camera bag."

Stop ogling him and talk.

Never held up the key in her hand. "I need to feed Justine's cat, but it was nice meeting you."

Maybe Justine's new neighbor wasn't long-term material, but Never still wasn't ruling out short-term plans in the near future. It wasn't often that she ran into attractive, eligible men in Folman. If watching him walk away was as enjoyable as imagining what was under his shirt, Never should keep her options open for the next few months.

CHAPTER 20

Redmond College, Redmond Tennessee,
Two Months and 10 Days Earlier

Other towns could boast many advantages over Redmond, but they couldn't beat the way the sun lit up the river as it meandered down from the ridge and wound through town. Wolfe enjoyed the warm pre-autumn glow as he made his way back to his Jeep in the faculty parking lot. It reminded him of the photographs in one of those inspirational quotes calendars his mother used to love. He waved to another professor hurrying in for an early meeting. Everything pointed toward being a pleasant day on campus.

On any other morning, he would be halfway down the hallway to his office, but this morning he had forgotten his coffee. It only took him a few minutes to get to the main door and turn around again. When he approached his Jeep, he suspected the piece of paper under his windshield wiper was a flyer from one of the fall activities committees.

"They don't waste any time," Wolfe muttered as he pulled it out.

The Harvest Ball was a great moneymaker for the college and the faculty was encouraged to sell as many tickets as possible. Wolfe looked around the lot, but didn't see anything on the cars nearby. Glancing down at the paper in his hand, he stopped. He clutched it in his palm and headed straight back inside, the second trip to collect his coffee aborted.

Whoever was interested in this particular prank wasn't letting up. It had been nearly a month since his trip to Paris. His confidence that this note was an early Halloween joke was waning. Yesterday he received a picture of his office window accompanied by a picture of his home with a message to expect a call at 10 p.m.

His office hours and contact number were listed in the fall catalog. Many of his colleagues knew he lived beside the witch's cottage in Folman. It was an urban legend landmark and a favorite of local kids as far away as Orlinda. Wolfe knew that information wouldn't be hard for someone on campus to come by, but the ring of the phone last night at 10 p.m. unnerved him.

This morning was a jolt he couldn't ignore. The note was paired with a picture of Rebecca Batson sitting in the commons. She was wearing the blue striped shirt she had on when she left class yesterday. Flipping it over, he stood clutching it as he read the short message.

It was time to see Larry at the security office.

Wolfe was still trying to put his nerves to rest when he found himself standing in the office doorway looking for the head of Redmond College Security. He didn't know if he could form the words to explain his story. It wasn't that Larry Harden was an imposing man. It was that Wolfe didn't want to reveal as much of his problem as he might be forced to tell. He had met Larry the first day he arrived on campus to move into faculty housing. Larry wasn't a white-collar type. He didn't blend in well with the spoiled suburban types that sent their children to Redmond College, but Wolfe liked that he didn't have to worry about pretenses with Larry. You couldn't razzle-dazzle him. He wasn't that kind of guy.

Larry Harden always looked like he lost interest in his graying hair and scraggly beard a decade ago. Wolfe doubted he gave a comb any thought before shoving an old Redmond ball cap on his fading red curls in the morning. His polo shirts and black dress pants sported worn Redmond Security logos and his boots had no visible name brand at all. Regardless of his looks, Wolfe trusted the man and, over his years on campus, came to call him a friend.

"Larry I have a sensitive issue I need to talk to you about," Wolfe commenced as he eased himself into a chair in the small office the Redmond College security team was allotted.

"What can I do for ya Wolfe?"

"I received a strange note in my mail yesterday. I thought it was a prank." He took the photo out of his pocket and slid it across the desk. "Today I got this."

Larry looked at the photo without much concern.

"Flip it over," Wolfe instructed.

He watched as Larry's eyes widened and he tried to hide his shock with a hand and a lackluster cough.

"Where did you find this?"

"On the windshield of my Jeep."

"Just now?"

Wolfe nodded. "I just went back out to grab my coffee."

"Is the photo of a student?"

"Yes." Wolfe nodded and gathered his hands together in his lap. "That's why I came to you. Rebecca Batson is one of my grad students."

"You think someone is jealous?"

"I don't know what to think, but I couldn't chance her getting hurt."

Larry nodded and tried to lean back in his chair, which hit the office wall with a smack.

"We can step up patrols in the faculty parking lot and near your office, but the post office is out of our hands."

"I can speak to Sarah about my box, I just want Rebecca protected without her knowledge."

"We will do our best, but it would help to have a list of her activities and classes."

"I can get those from her adviser without much trouble."

"Good, good." Larry nodded and sat for a second rubbing the collection of scraggly hair patches he called a beard.

"And you have no idea who this could be? No mad students, girlfriends, ex-girlfriends?"

"I haven't sent anyone away in the last few weeks." Wolfe tried to think of something to direct attention to. *Nothing, I got nothing.* "You know Never and I have been together for nearly three years now."

Larry nodded as he continued to rub the small round point of his scruff-covered chin and peered at the photograph.

"So, we are looking at a possible stalker."

"It seems to have passed the realm of enthusiastic prankster," Wolfe agreed.

"Talk to Sarah, we'll step up patrols, and if there are any more threats bring them to me."

"Thanks Larry." Wolfe reached out to shake his hand.

"It goes without saying that we need to keep this quiet," Larry instructed as he gave Wolfe the strong pump of a well-practiced handshake.

"You'll have no arguments from me." Wolfe nodded as he turned to leave. "I'm going to check in with Sarah."

It was a short walk to the campus post office. Until lately, Wolfe enjoyed going by to pick up his mail and talk to the postmaster. Sarah Wilkerson was a petite, black woman in her fifties, but she had the energy of a woman in her twenties. She always offered Wolfe a wide smile as her curls bobbed around the sides of her face like springs set into action. She had been in charge of the Redmond campus post office for the last ten years. She had seen hundreds of her "kids" grow up and move on to better things. Sarah showed up to graduations as regularly as the faculty and since Wolfe's installment here as a full-time history professor, she never failed to greet him with a smile and a few kind words.

"Hey Sarah, how is your morning going?" he asked as he leaned against the counter.

"I can't complain." Sarah smiled and tilted her head in his direction. "Harvest ball and fall flyers are keeping me busy."

"It is that time of year."

"What brings you by?" she asked as she studied his empty hands.

"I had a disturbing note in my mailbox yesterday," he leaned in and whispered. "Larry said I should talk to you about it."

"What kinda note honey?"

"Strange scrap of paper without an envelope." He left out the photos for now.

"I wouldn't put nothing in your box like that." Her stance changed as she watched him.

"I know that Sarah, but I wanted you to be on the

lookout for someone who would."

"Are you sure it's not a prank?"

"I thought that at first, but a new one showed up somewhere else today including photos of students Sarah."

"Oh, sweet Jesus!"

"I know." He reached out to pat her hand. "I went straight to Larry."

"How can I help?"

"Check your cameras, keep an eye out for someone acting strange, and report it to Larry."

"I can do that sugar," she told him with a fire in her caramel eyes that told him she accepted her mission. "No one better hurt my babies."

Wolfe talked with her for another few minutes until a student approached with a letter to mail. He felt a weight shift off his shoulders as he turned to leave. Maybe he should have gone to Larry yesterday? At that point, Wolfe still thought it was a prank.

Larry and Sarah would have thought the same thing he did. Kids were being kids, but targeting Rebecca changed everything. Like Sarah, he couldn't stand by and let harm come to any of his students. He needed to find a way to distance himself from Rebecca. And he thought he knew just the person that could help.

CHAPTER 21

Folman Tennessee, Present

Never had no idea how to approach the papers and books from Wolfe's office. Avoiding the boxes for the last few days hadn't given her any answers. She had purposefully driven to the furthest track in town this morning to do her daily run. She needed time to think. There had to be a better way to approach this new development.

Despite her anger, she was curious. Never couldn't help wanting to know what was in them. After work, she found herself sitting on the couch peering at the contents brimming over the top of some of the boxes. She watched the new occupants of her kitchen from a safe distance or walked around the new clumps of material, straining to make out as much detail as she could from the things she could identify.

Showered and changed on a Sunday afternoon, she was running out of ways to stall her inspection. Grabbing a cold beer from the fridge, a bag of chocolate-covered peanuts, and a notebook and pen from the kitchen table, Never flopped down on her tan sofa and glared at the closest box. She took a deep swig of the cold, bitter-tasting liquid and set it aside.

"I guess we should get this over with," she muttered before pulling the box closer.

Noting that she might need more than a six pack when this trip through Wolfe's files was over, Never held the notebook to her chest like a shield and reached for the first paper.

Categories made themselves known as she worked through lunch and another bottle. There were books on every mystery jewel theft imaginable. Antique catalogs with firm dots beside items that caught someone's attention, but it frustrated her to note that there were no circles or notes about his objectives. Confusion turned to exasperation as she pored over page after page of catalogs that might as well been selling seeds for all she knew about the subject.

Wolfe never mentioned any of this stuff. He talked in broad terms about his upcoming classes and the prep work that went into them. She had to admit that they never had a traditional relationship. She never thought they needed a traditional one. Wolfe never opposed her assumption.

Never liked to think of their relationship as "spacious" instead of long distance. They spent several nights a week together when he was on break for the summer, and they both had keys to each other's homes. But, apparently, their relationship left a lot of room for gaps. She had plenty of blanks to fill in as she studied the piles of paper and books at her feet. She didn't have any ideas what the contents of this first box were about and was having her doubts that the other four nearby would yield better results.

Wolfe told her about paper topics and funny questions his students would come up with in class. There were fundraiser events at the local history museum and traveling exhibits in Nashville he wanted to take her to see. He talked of other faculty members and the likelihood of grants in the spring. He never mentioned any of the nuts and bolts of his profession that filled the boxes in front of her.

Obsessed with news, Wolfe was a faithful subscriber to several papers. The strangest thing about his habit was that the papers he subscribed to weren't national papers. Six were from small towns in various regions of the country. When she asked about them, he said he liked to have "regional perspectives before they were regurgitated into national news headlines." Never couldn't argue with anyone willing to help the little guys keep the presses moving. He always gave her the scoop on any upcoming news on campus and wanted her to provide interesting tidbits on her stories that the public wouldn't otherwise get to hear. It was a beneficial arrangement. She needed stories of interest, and he kept buying subscriptions. Her livelihood depended on people like Wolfe opening their mouths and their wallets.

The strangest part of this puzzle was the fact that he never wanted her to have anything to do with his work on a day to day basis. It didn't make sense for him to leave her the collection of work he had piled up in his office. She could have spiced up his afternoons with a little naughty professor action of her own, but he never asked her to come by. Why would he want her to have all his papers and books now?

Did he not want this Chasity person to have his research? Was he afraid she would co-opt it for herself? And what exactly was all this anyway? How would anyone fit all of these pieces together? Looking at the disconnected piles of information around her, Never decided Chasity must be one formidable woman if she could do all that.

The alcohol was establishing a calm within her when a thought hit. What if it wasn't an actual baby? What if it was a metaphorical baby? What if it was a book, a paper, or a presentation for a grant that he created with this woman? Would that be easier to stomach? Naw, she had to be grasping. Why would he seem so unhappy and pained if it was just a work coupling? As much as she wanted to believe it, she couldn't think of a logical reason. She didn't have any other explanation for his strange behavior at the side of the lake that night. Never lifted the beer to her lips and swallowed the last sip. She wasn't sure she could find that answer after two beers so she headed for the kitchen. There was a very slim chance that on the way back she would find an on-ramp to enlightenment, but she could always keep drinking until it didn't matter anymore.

Never spent the better part of her Sunday afternoon hunched over this box or another. Stacks of pages littered the sofa and coffee table. She carried the books over to her office nook after the tall stack she had built on the living room rug threatened to collapse and crush her.

Looking around the room, it was easy to see why Wolfe's housekeeping was as lackluster as it was. Her only achievement this afternoon was moving the bulk of the mess occupying her kitchen and spreading it around her living room. How would anyone begin to get a handle on a project this size? How would she? And what would she do with it all if she managed to wrangle it into acceptable groupings? Should she donate it to the historic society or was there anything in these boxes worth saving? She really couldn't tell. There were several pages on historical finds, but nothing that would lend new information to the hunt for more sites like it.

The information seemed like a patchwork of random curiosities Wolfe had been briefly interested in. She couldn't think of any connection between a gold mine, a local potter, antique magazines, and the lost art of an Aguaruna tribe of Peru. None of his office bequests traced back to any common thread she could find. The reporter in her wished there was a story here, but she couldn't find a thread to follow. Nothing lined up.

Had Wolfe made the arrangements at the college before he became aware of the baby issue? Nothing else would make sense based on what he was trying to tell her that night by the lake. After they started dating, she was the closest contact he had.

That brought other uncomfortable questions: Should Never go to the trouble to seek out the other woman? Would Wolfe want his son or daughter to have his things?

"That might make an interesting story angle."

The contents of the boxes were hers now, after all. Never could use them as she saw fit. As angry and hurt as she was, Never's interest in exploiting her rival was abating. She wanted her pound of flesh from Wolfe's hide. Now that he was gone, she was forced to consider other options. Never plopped down hard on the sofa and upset the beer she left leaning against one of her southwestern throw pillows.

Never wished she could make some sense out of all these loose ends. It seemed strange not to be able to call Wolfe and ask him about all of this stuff. He was always a great sounding board when she was stuck on something for work or looking for a different angle to come at the same old information. Wolfe had the patience of a nerdy teenager with a new rubix cube. He made a natural teacher.

Now that her anger at him was subsiding, Never could feel the regret and pain seeping into her system. After Wolfe's big announcement, she would have only wished him dead for a week or two. There was a satisfaction that comforted her after visualizing several painful, lingering ends to his existence, but thinking about how trapped he must have felt to drown himself in the lake left her downhearted. The calm, even emotions that usually guided her were having trouble overriding the bewilderment that assailed her after the memorial and ratcheted up with every new surprise.

When something finally happened to her, only the legacy of her work would be left behind. No parents, no children, no husband. She would continue to the next world as she began in this one—on her own. She couldn't bring herself to throw everything in his boxes away. Never understood the meaning behind Susan's sickened expression when she mentioned that option. Now that Wolfe was gone, she couldn't throw away his legacy, no matter how burdensome and confusing it was to her. Looking around the room at the stacks blocking her in every direction, she just hoped that at some point the dots would begin to connect instead of looking like the world's strangest stacks of hording materials. Whatever Wolfe had planned, it hadn't worked out well for him or anyone else involved.

CHAPTER 22

Folman Tennessee, Present

Never was surprised when Carrie wanted to meet her with things from Wolfe's home.

"Just photos and stuff we won't be able to sell with the contents of the house," Carrie had said on the phone. "His mother didn't want them."

Never thought about the boxes of photos and old newspapers Carrie didn't want to deal with. She already had plenty of Wolfe's crap lounging around her apartment. She didn't want or need anything more, but Never said "yes" and settled on the local strip center near the newspaper.

She recited her mantra, "Give a little, get a little," before she drove off to meet Carrie and gather a new collection of Wolfe's homeless possessions.

Carrie Henson-Black was on the pep squad when she was in high school. She was sickeningly cheerful and Never swore she had the lungs of a horse the way she could outscream, outshout, and outcheer anyone within a mile of a sporting event. No one was surprised when she married the recently widowed football coach, Ken Black, before the ink on her realty certification dried. The two settled down together on Poplar Street in Ken's spacious craftsman home and wasted no time creating three little sports fanatics of their own. It wasn't the most comfortable friendship Never had cultivated over the years, but it was one of her more long-standing professional relationships. The straws that held their tentative friendship together were unlikely to change.

If Never was looking for a lead, Carrie either had one that hooked her in or knew how to get in touch with someone who would spill all the juicy details. In turn, Never would pass Carrie's card to anyone she ran into on her work beat that even hinted they might be interested in moving. Because of their joint effort, both were enjoying the sweet fruit of living and working in a town like Folman when others fled to larger cities right after high school.

"This one has kept me hopping," Carrie greeted her with a smile as she popped the trunk of her red BMW.

"I would have thought you had a cleaning company do most of the work," Never commented.

"Not physical work, I did find a great cleaning company, but there were several people bidding on it right down to the wire."

"A lot of broken hearts to go around?"

"My yes! Especially a motivated buyer from out

of town." She sighed as she lifted the last of the boxes into the back of the SUV. "He called several times to re-up his offer and still lost in the final minutes."

"Did he give a reason for his fervor?"

"Said he was tired of the pace of life in Chicago and this place looked like the perfect place for retirement."

"You can't get much more tranquil than Folman," Never agreed as she closed the trunk of the SUV.

"I'm sorry about how things turned out for you, I really am." Carrie surprised her by leaning in for a quick hug. "We all expected you to be living there with Wolfe by now."

"Thank you, Carrie, and thank you for meeting me with this stuff."

"You're welcome honey, I would have dropped it by your apartment, but you know how that rat your neighbor calls a dog makes my allergies act up."

"I remember." Never tried not to cringe. "It is hard to keep Pepper from meeting new people."

"She needs a trip to Paws and Tails for a flea dip and a shave."

"How is Ken coping? I guess he has the kids all to himself?" Never tried to steer the conversation away from her neighbor's very enthusiastic pet.

"Ken is a doll as always. George is trying out for the high school team next fall and Sam and Kirk are running drills from the sidelines with him when the team has afternoon practices."

"You must both be so excited!"

"Ken was hoping to coach all three kids before he retired. He is over the moon that they all love it as much as they do."

"Is Ken thinking of retiring soon?"

"Lord no, I don't think that man will ever turn in his head coach jacket. But sometimes when we get back from vacation or the team is having a tough year, Ken starts talkin' about it."

"I'm sure Ernie would like a shot at the big leagues."

"Ernie couldn't hold his own with those fundraising moms." Carrie chuckled as she leaned against her car. "He has made a career of hiding from Val."

Valkyrie Whitman, Val, was the scourge of the high school fundraising committees. Her husband ran Whitman Industries and left Val to bestow his monetary gifts on the town in any way she saw fit. She always reminded Never of an ostrich with her long neck, thinning gray hair, and ever-moving eyes. There was also no debate that she could chase you down before you comprehended you were in her presence. Val Whitman was a challenge no one wanted to face.

"How has Ken done it for so long?" Never wondered aloud.

"He and Levi Whitman are golfing buddies which makes him off limits to Val." Carrie smirked as she folded her arms across her chest. "Ken found that loophole years ago and swears our country club membership is worth every penny."

Never couldn't keep the laugh from escaping her lips.

"I've never heard a better reason to learn the difference between a wood and an iron."

"Sometimes it's all it takes."

Never had to admit it was an elegant solution to the Val problem.

"Give my best to Ken and the boys."

"Thank you for Justine and Rory's referral," Carrie shouted as she hustled back to her car. "Talk to you soon!"

Never watched her little red car speed out of sight before she put her key in the ignition.

Now the trunk of her rental car was full of boxes and her stomach was growling at her sense of priorities.

"I guess it is time to go get nachos and figure out what to do with this stuff." She agreed with her stomach as she turned to run by her favorite Mexican restaurant on her way back to work.

After her unexpected meeting with Carrie, Never returned to work to find requests for rewrites from Jerry and a message on her desk about dress fittings after work with Justine. She had another full afternoon in front of her. When she delivered her final assignment to Jerry, Never returned to her desk to find Justine waiting.

After another round of dress alterations at *Toss the Bouquet Formalwear*, Never didn't know if she had the energy to force herself out of the car when she pulled into the parking space in front of her building. She picked up a salad at the grocery store near work and hoped it was still edible. She wasn't going to worry about cooking if it wasn't. She couldn't fight her way up another unnecessary hill tonight.

She grabbed her work bag and reached for a few things scattered across her front floorboard before she eased from the driver's seat. Thank goodness the final dress Justine settled on for her to wear as maid of honor still needed some beadwork or Never would be dragging the plastic dress cover up the steps behind her. She had ignored the boxes in her trunk since her lunch meeting with Carrie. She opened the hatch and gave her cargo a look, but she wasn't up to lugging boxes tonight. She pulled a planner from the top of one box and a plastic bag containing a stack of photos from another before slamming the lid closed and lurching up the front steps with her burden.

After she demolished her wilting salad, Never pulled out Wolfe's planner and started to thumb through the contents. She was always amazed at the pride he took in making legible, consistent entries. It was more like a binder than simple calendar pages. He made schedules for classes and kept track of emails and phone calls. There were events at the college and birthdays for everyone he had ever met. Business cards were tucked in the back behind clear, plastic pages. There was a small yellow legal pad in the front for notes. It looked nothing like the environment he preferred to maintain. It was meticulous. There were no slash marks or rewrites within these pages. She wondered if he wrote everything out before he attempted a daily page. Her lips curved as she thought of him, his head bent over his desk in concentration, painstakingly writing each word one letter at a time to make sure he was forming them in just the right way.

Looking back at how Wolfe liked to keep his home and his office would lead most people to peg him as a disorganized slob. A person never had to walk too far in Wolfe's space to spy a pair of shoes or discarded socks sticking out from under a desk or chair. Papers were left where they were no longer of interest. Books were left open and waiting for someone to notice them and return them to one of the built-in bookcases. Never could usually track where his thoughts were by looking at what he had jettisoned along the way.

Several pages were missing from his yellow legal pad. Curiosity made her grab a pencil and rub it over the page. She expected to find a list of things from his last entry. The indentions made clear by the dark pencil markings were random letters and numbers. Never couldn't find any connection between them and Wolfe's final entry the day before his death. Class times maybe, or he was making appointments for something. Never couldn't connect the assortment of letters to anything she had ever written using shorthand. She typed the letters into her search engine and waited. It returned several links for a Chaste family tree page and one online treasure hunting website that required a login to view its content. She rifled through the family tree sites trying to find any link to Wolfe or any of the research he was concentrating on before his death. After hours on the floor, with her neck and back screaming at her to shift positions, Never plugged her phone in to charge and pulled herself up from the floor using the arm of the sofa. The sun would be up in a few hours and she had accomplished nothing more than making a bigger mess chasing after unproven clues in Wolfe's office clutter. She let out a tired sigh. She was turning into one of those people who see Jesus in toast and swears their dead grandmother is trying to contact them through their alphabet soup.

Looking around her, Never traced the trail of clutter she had made from the kitchen table to the living room sofa. She couldn't walk or even tiptoe through the room without disturbing one clump or another. In a week, she had made little-to-no progress in organizing and understanding it. Maybe she should give her efforts a rest for tonight.

The nagging voice in her head was still encouraging her to find the large leaf bags Justine insisted she buy for sledding last winter and fill every one to the brim for garbage collection day on Tuesday. Her shoulder was complaining and her headache was back. The only thing she seemed to be accomplishing was finding new ways to get to dead ends.

"Leave it to you to waste my time from the grave," she grumbled.

Even if she figured out the letters, there were still several numbers on the page. It could take her weeks to figure out what they pertained to. If Never had learned anything from following Mayor Ball and Archie Gordon around at night, it was that she didn't have the patience for long, involved research projects that didn't pan out. If Wolfe's papers didn't produce solid information she could follow up on in two weeks, Never would donate them to the library at Redmond College the way they were. Future generations would have access to his books and papers. She would take Justine with her to photograph a full layout for a donation story. It would be a fitting end to the saga of Wolfe Strickland's final days. She didn't owe Wolfe that, but she would do it. *Folman Gazette* readers would like the idea that his work would be helpful to future generations, and Never could go back to being a reporter instead of cataloging Wolfe's leftover missives. Everyone would be happier once she got all this mess out of her reach.

She still had to sort the things that Carrie brought her from Wolfe's house. She hadn't even brought the boxes in from her rented SUV yet. Never was willing to bet there were a few interesting items thrown in. Wolfe's home office papers could be added to the collection multiplying in the living room floor.

Meetings required Never's attention this morning, and Justine would be a nightmare disguised as a nursemaid if she reinjured herself carrying in books and whatnots. She would have to leave it for another time. Summoning all her energy, Never stumbled down the hallway to the bathroom to brush her teeth and take a shower.

There was nothing like lack of sleep to make her feel her age. Never let the warm water flow over her skin and hoped it would dull the aches and pains. She had a pitch meeting in four hours and a town council meeting to cover at ten. She wanted nothing to do with either one, but she would be in worse shape if she was left home to obsess over the riddle of Wolfe's notes and papers. As she stepped out of the shower to grab her towel, Never vowed she wouldn't think about Wolfe Strickland for the next eight hours. If he were still alive, he wouldn't be bothered by memories of her. There was no reason she should either.

CHAPTER 23

Folman Tennessee, Present

Never wasn't expecting to find a connection between any of the paperwork in Wolfe's office at Redmond College and his home, but one popped up while she was reading through his planner. The pottery article from Wolfe's office was about a man named Alvin Lucas who owned Lucas Pottery in Folman. By itself, it didn't mean much. After reviewing Wolfe's planner notes, however, Never noticed a notation about Lucas Pottery, a present, and a delivery time. Never was displeased to notice that there was nothing about a delivery location or recipient. It seemed out of character for Wolfe to start commissioning pottery pieces. She needed Alvin Lucas to connect the dots.

The white brick building on Porter Avenue wasn't as artsy as Never imagined. A weathered chocolate sign identified it as Lucas Pottery. Fliers hung in the main windows advertising gallery events and festivals. Two large urns filled with purple mums graced the sides of the propped-open front door she walked through.

Once inside, she was flanked by glass cases filled with pottery in every shape and color. Impressive combinations of track lighting and small pendant lights illuminated every corner of the room.

A small sign on the counter said, "Welcome! Pottery in progress. Ring bell for service."

Never hit the small hotel-style bell and waited. A man in dirty jeans, a t-shirt, and a blue Titans cap who looked like he had been putting up freight or doing construction ambled through the door from the back room.

"Excuse me, I'm looking for Alvin Lucas."

"That would be me." He extended a hand.

"I'm Never Martinez."

"From the *Folman Gazette*?"

Never nodded hoping her answer would give her some leverage to probe for the information she was seeking. "I was hoping you could clear up some questions I have about Wolfe Strickland's interest in your pottery."

"I don't know if I should be talking to you about that."

"I'm not here to research an article," she tried again. "I just need answers."

"About my customers," he summed up shifting his feet.

"About a customer who passed away," she reminded him hoping it would make a difference.

"You can ask, I may not answer."

"I can respect that Mr. Lucas."

"What has you curious enough to show up at my door?"

"Papers from Mr. Strickland's office included an article about your business and his planner was marked with an appointment time and date."

"He came to see me about a custom piece he wanted delivered."

"Have you delivered it?"

"No, it was paid for in full with a specific date and time."

"Next Wednesday at 10 a.m.," Never supplied.

He didn't respond, but he didn't protest her conclusion either.

"Will you tell me where the delivery will go on Wednesday, or do I have to show up and follow your van?"

He chuckled. "You shoot straight from the hip don't you."

"I just need a name." Never tried to keep her tone even.

"There is a celebration at Redmond College you

might be interested in." He grinned back at her for the first time.

"On Wednesday at 10 a.m.?"

"It's been nice meeting you Miss Martinez." He touched the brim of his hat before heading deeper into the recesses of his shop.

All trails lead back to Redmond College. A custom pottery piece was outside of Wolfe's normal gift-giving wheelhouse. He had always been willing to spoil her by spending money on little extras, but custom pottery with a delivery date wasn't something she would expect. Never could feel her excitement rising. Was the present for his new lover? Did it mean she was one step closer to meeting the mystery woman Wolfe dumped her for? She just had to wait until Wednesday morning and drive over the ridge to Redmond.

Alvin Lucas mentioned a celebration. There had to be some chatter about it among the staff. If she called Paul or Susan maybe they would feel compelled to invite her. But did she want the other woman to have notice of her presence in advance? Without a name, she seemed impossible to find, but Never had one new trail emerging in her search. She knew what Alvin Lucas looked like. He would lead her straight to her prize if she couldn't find her way alone. Wolfe's mystery woman couldn't lurk in the shadows forever.

As she passed through the door of the small storefront, Never's cellphone music jingled.

"Hello?"

"Miss Martinez this is Gary Dunham again about

your car."

"Did you get a chance to check the brakes lines again Gary?"

"There are small cracked spots in your lines that could be natural like an impact from something."

"You don't sound sure."

"I'm not," he admitted. "I have never seen a car with this type of cracks in the brake lines."

"And how long have you been working on cars?"

"Going on thirty years now."

"So you can't say they are unnatural, but in thirty years you have never seen this particular cracking on cars in your care?"

"That pretty well sums it up."

"Can you replace them and save the old ones in a sealed bag for me?"

"It will be tomorrow afternoon before I can get the new lines installed."

Never agreed to call him back after she made arrangements with Justine to schedule a pickup time for her car. As she pocketed her phone and crossed the street to her rental, she realized she had another argument coming with Sergeant Henderson. Never wanted to share her news in person. Her lawyer wouldn't like her rashness in the matter, but some things couldn't wait.

CHAPTER 24

Folman Tennessee, Present

In a few minutes, Never would take the highway across the ridge to Redmond College for the first time since Wolfe's memorial. Having Aurora back made her feel better about the idea. They could face a return trip together. She would take extra precautions this time, and an extra pair of boots.

"I wish you would let me go with you," Justine said as she leaned against the counter. "You might need a wingman if things get awkward."

"How much more awkward could it be?"

"Hair pulling, scratching, video of your face on the internet awkward," Justine insisted.

"I'm not going to attack a pregnant woman."

"What if she lied?"

"Would I attack a liar who exposed the fact that

my cheating boyfriend couldn't be trusted?"

"You don't know how much I want to say no."

"But you have doubts?"

Justine didn't answer. She didn't have to. Never could read the doubt in her brown eyes.

"If I go alone there will only be one of us on the internet."

"If I go too, I can help."

"But you won't stop me," Never warned as she gathered her things. "Best if you stay here."

She didn't pass a single car on her trip across the ridge. Never slowed down as she got to the place where Aurora came to a rest. There were still orange cones marking the spot where they had gone over the shoulder. In the afternoon sunshine, Never could see the full extent of her luck that night. Through the bare trees, it was a hundred foot drop beyond the shoulder. One good push or a jolt of speed would have sent her over. It could have been months or even years before someone found her.

"Let's not go for a repeat," she told Aurora as she pushed her foot down on the accelerator, not letting up until she saw the Red River Bridge.

Never pulled into a visitor's space at Redmond College and killed the engine.

"Now we wait."

Alvin Lucas would be here soon. Never still

didn't see his delivery van anywhere. He said ten. She still had time. She was a half an hour early so she would be sure to see him when he pulled up to unload Wolfe's special order.

Never was in her car for fifteen minutes before the delivery van rattled across the river bridge and onto campus. She watched as Alvin Lucas backed the van up to a door by the rear of the gym and hopped down from the driver's seat. The box he pulled from the back was simple and white. There was nothing distinctive about its look except the long, skinny dimensions of it. Whatever it was, it was tall enough to be an umbrella stand. Why would Wolfe buy something like that for a pregnant woman? Never got out, slammed the door, and raced to follow him inside the gym.

"Miss Martinez, you managed to follow me." Alvin smiled back at her as she entered the room.

"Someone told me where to find you," she joked as she walked up beside him. "What's in the box?"

"I can't tell you that, but if you stay for the presentation I am sure you will have the answers you need."

"And if I have more questions?"

He shrugged. "You don't seem to have trouble locating me."

"I guess I should scout out a good vantage point."

"I should be done blocking your view in a few seconds," he promised as he slid the box close to the podium and covered it with a dark tablecloth.

Alvin flipped her a wave and was off the way he had come. Never listened to the back doors of his van close and the sound of a motor drive off into the distance. She knew he would be back in Folman at his shop before this event got underway. If she had any follow up questions, she intended to find him there afterward. Never got the feeling he would cooperate for a little free advertising. If she had to promise a series of stories on local businesses like Lucas Pottery, she would be happy to do so. Anything that led her closer to ascertaining the identity of Wolfe's mystery woman was worth the price.

"I didn't expect to see you here today," Susan said as she walked up to stand beside her.

"I heard about the event and I came over to cover it," Never explained without elaboration. "Why are you here so early?"

"I volunteered to do setup and hand out programs."

"Is Paul not here to help you?"

"No, it is end of the month processing at the business office," Susan admitted with a tired smile. "He can't be dragged away until it is finished."

"Tell him I said hello," Never requested as she eased away. "I'm going to run to the ladies room before everything gets underway."

Never didn't need to visit the facilities, but she needed a way out of this conversation. Once the convocation began, the gym walls would be vibrating sound in every direction. Whatever was going on during today's events, Never didn't need Susan's nasally alto giving running commentary beside her. She would find a quiet spot near the aisle and get up to follow the box if she needed to. No one would block her from finding out who Wolfe was buying presents for, and how it connected to his mystery woman. Never was determined to chase her across the campus green if she had to.

When the program started, Never had a great view of the stage. Susan had given her the first program off her stack before disappearing to stand outside the double doors. The theme of today's program was service awards. They would begin with graduate studies students and work up to a presentation of teacher anniversaries.

Never sat tapping her foot as the program got underway. She listened to the usual opening prayer, a speech about the college and its interest in well-rounded individuals to carry the torch of academia into the future, and watched a slide show about how students and faculty had accomplished those goals in the past. Never heard the woman beside her clear her throat and looked over in time to see her glare targeting Never's bouncing leg. Never tried to smile and shift her leg to another position, but she heard a heavy sigh as her leg moved to twitch and tap again. How could people stay so patient and quiet during these boring things? The whole point was to hand out awards and let people clap. There was always thirty to forty-five minutes of filler before the announcement leading to the announcement that the awards part of the presentation would begin. By the time the first student rose to accept his award, the audience ranged from inattentive to impatient.

Never watched the first student walk across the stage to accept his award and return to his seat. She dutifully jotted down his name and the title of the award while she waited for the next. There were four graduate students in all. The first three were men. The last was a brunette with a name Never recognized.

"Rebecca Batson, please come up to claim your award."

Never's head came up and she watched Wolfe's graduate student cross the stage. He had mentioned her work on black market art and how proud he was of her progress. Was she the other woman? Had he waved her in front of Never's nose all this time?

The graduate student was attractive. Never couldn't dispute that. In her navy skirt and plum sweater, it was hard to hide her willowy figure. In a pinch, Never could see the similarities in their body-types. They both had long brown hair and pleasing figures despite the fact that Rebecca was fifteen years her junior. Was that what influenced Wolfe's decision? Was he looking for a young woman to make him feel alive again? It was hard to say, but Never didn't see any sign of a baby bump. Perhaps it was too early or Rebecca was a borderline twig creature before the baby weight. Never realized she was rubbernecking so hard she forgot to write down the name of the service award. She was already planning to have a conversation with Rebecca after the awards portion of the event came to a close. Never was determined to catch Wolfe's graduate student before she left the stage area.

It was surprising how far her focus had shifted since this morning. When the last award was announced, Never had no interest. She was already tracking Rebecca's movements like a woman possessed. She didn't even realize she was distracted from today's objective until someone came forward to pull the black tablecloth from the box by the podium. Like a child, she had already forgotten about the hidden object and moved on to another amusement.

"Professor Camille Bartlett had been a fixture in the Geography department for the last thirty years," the dean started his speech.

Never looked over at the woman in question standing by the box in her brown suit and tweed loafers. She had no problem imagining Camille Bartlett in a classroom. She could visualize her graying hair pulled back in a bun and a pencil stuck behind one ear as she held up samples and scrawled questions on a dry erase board with a dying black marker. The professor's back was hunched from grading papers and years spent doing research to appease the tenure gods that held her career in their hands. Her soft middle was the product of too many rushed cafeteria lunches.

If Professor Bartlett happened to be Wolfe's mystery woman, the revelation blew Never's younger woman theory out of the water. It didn't do much to salve her ego that the professor was not the beautiful cougar she would hope to lose to. None of this seemed right.

It was hard to take notes with her mind churning the way it was. Never set her notebook in her lap and continued to watch the strange production on stage. The dean was as awkward as a guy on his first date when he left the podium and began helping the professor pull out a long, thin urn from the box Alvin left this morning.

The urn was beautiful work. Greens, browns, and yellows swirled and danced around the outside. It almost looked like topography. Alvin Lucas deserved a local artist of the week article for producing something so stunning, and the professor seemed thrilled by Wolfe's choice. She picked it up and studied every side of it while the dean continued to praise her work at the college.

Never kept questioning why Wolfe was put in charge of a gift for this event. They weren't even in the same department. Was there something between him and the other professor or just a simple obligation to a co-worker? Never needed to talk to Susan about it later, but she was going straight for Rebecca Batson when the final speech ended.

Never cornered Rebecca as she was leaving the stage.

"Miss Batson, I'm Never Martinez from the *Folman Gazette*," Never introduced herself. "I was hoping to talk to you about your award."

"You were Professor Strickland's girlfriend?"

"Right, and you were his graduate student."

"Not for the last few weeks."

"What do you mean?"

"He transferred me to Professor Millhorn in the Law Department to broaden my dissertation work."

Wolfe had bragged about her work.

"Has it helped?"

"Surprisingly, yes, I have a new perspective on how art crimes are solved and what these thieves are charged with compared to other theft cases."

"That does sound interesting," Never agreed. "Were you ever seeing Professor Strickland on a personal level?"

"Wow! You really are as direct as everyone says."

"Then you're not surprised by the question?"

"No, and no I wasn't the other woman in his life," Rebecca assured her. "I never ran into anyone when I went to his office."

"No one was ever with him?"

"No, he was always working."

"That matches what some of the faculty observed." Never nodded. "Your award will be a great credit to you when you apply for jobs next year."

"Yes, I am so excited to teach full-time."

Never could see Rebecca light up at the idea and kept her talking about where she hoped her career would lead. After a page of notes, Never released Rebecca to go on her way while she looked for Susan. The crowd was thinning. Never hoped she wouldn't have to track Susan back to her office in the English and literature wing of Lethem Hall.

Never wasn't looking forward to a one-on-one with Susan. She was hard to deal with without Paul as a buffer. They didn't have enough in common to have a natural conversation. Paul would be able to tell her what she needed to know without all the chit-chat, because he would be forced to get back to work. Maybe Never should go by the business office and ask him first?

Never was finalizing her backup plan when she saw Susan come through the hallway leading to the back door.

"Susan!"

"Never, you're still here." She slowed to a stop.

"I have a few questions for you."

"For me?" Susan looked confused.

"You said something about a committee that rotates duties for events like these. That was why you were on duty today."

"Yes." Susan brightened. "The Service Committee is a sub-committee of the Faculty Engagement Committee."

"How does it work?"

"The Faculty Engagement Committee sets up events throughout the year to promote campus culture. The Service sub-committee is the committee that does all the legwork."

"Does the entire faculty participate?"

"Just full-time professors," Susan explained. "It wouldn't be fair to ask adjuncts and traveling professors to help at events when they are off for the semester."

"No, that doesn't seem reasonable," Never agreed. "Was Wolfe in charge of anything for this event? It would have been hard to pick up his extra work."

"Thankfully, he was in charge of ordering the urn weeks in advance."

"He was tasked with that small part?"

"He was supposed to handout programs with me, but I managed alone."

"It was a beautiful event," Never reassured her as she patted her shoulder. "Thank you for all of your hard work."

"It was good to see you again." Susan smiled as she drifted toward the empty stage to begin clearing chairs and refolding the black tablecloth left in a heap after the reveal.

Never read over her notes and tucked her notebook into her bag before pausing to watch the activity around her. She still had questions about the weeks before Wolfe's death. Rebecca Batson seemed to be telling the truth and Wolfe had an innocent reason to order a gift for Professor Bartlett. Nothing revealed here today connected the dots of her suspicion. It looked as though she would have to keep digging.

CHAPTER 25

Folman Tennessee, Two Months Earlier

Wolfe didn't know where to turn. The members of his online treasure hunting group had no experience in stolen art trafficking. He couldn't risk going to them for help. The same held true of every other body he belonged to. If anyone at the college knew about his trip or his accidental find, he could kiss his job in academia goodbye along with all hopes of future employment in his field. He thought he had selected the best option by concealing the statue and reburying the box in a place where no one would look for it, but he was wrong. The newest note was written on the back of the picture from the *Folman Gazette* article. The back of the photo had a clear message:

You have something that belongs to me. Call tonight (615) 555-7583 at 9 p.m.

If he tried to go to the police with it, they would want to know more than he wanted to tell. He filed a complaint on campus making it look like a stalking issue about Rebecca, but Wolfe couldn't tell the police the same stalker was after him too. They would never believe him if he claimed confusion about the stalker's motives. He had put himself in a dangerous situation, and he couldn't ask for help this time. Why couldn't this be a simple matter of returning the art, no questions asked? Peru didn't offer immunity. Other countries were happy to have art returned. Why did he find the one thing, from one of the few countries in the world that didn't?

How did this person know so much about him? Wolfe had been so careful after the photo was taken, but whoever was terrorizing him at the college had found their way to his house. There wasn't much hope they would back off now. They had devoted effort to following his routine, determined to get him to panic. Wolfe didn't have any optimism this person would quit even after he turned over the statue. There weren't any guarantees with someone like this.

Wolfe shoved the photo away. Now there was a new complication. Autumn was not ready to shift into winter, but Wolfe could feel his discontent. Every note created another punch to his gut. His proactive chats with Larry and Sarah had stopped the notes at the college, but now they were showing up in his personal mailbox. Should he tell Never to steer clear of his house? Should he tell her the story he was hoping to keep to himself the rest of his life?

He didn't like the idea of meeting with these people alone. Was there any better way to handle it? If he included someone else, would they be vulnerable as well? The ice in his whiskey glass wasn't telling him the answers he needed to hear. Wolfe picked up the cut-glass vessel he saved for exceptional occasions and poured again. He had two hours to come to a conclusion.

The second glass of whiskey made his hands seem steadier than his emotions as he punched in the new phone number and tapped the phone-shaped icon.

"Glad to see I finally got your attention. You made a mistake by thinking you can ignore me like one of the yokels. You're out of your depth with this one Professor. I want you to drive to Elkins Honeycomb and Custard, get something through the drive-thru, take everything out of the bag, put the statue box inside, go to one of their outside garbage bins and lean the bag against the side away from the street. My guys will collect it. Got that Professor?"

"Yes, yes...I can do that," Wolfe's dry lips stuttered.

"See that you do. I am running out of patience. You have twenty minutes."

The line went dead in Wolfe's ear.

Elkins was a favorite comfort food and ice cream joint for the locals. After 9 p.m. the traffic would be winding down. It was five minutes from his house. He had plenty of time to dig up the statue and make it to the parking lot on time.

"Hope you can figure it out Professor," Wolfe mimicked as he paced his study.

The snarky tone and patronizing comments irritated him. Wolfe was in the top five percent of his class at Emory. Why should he let this guy get away with humiliating him?

"I don't think he realizes who he is really dealing with. I'm going to call him back and tell him I already mailed it off."

He picked up his cell and hit redial, but the number had already been disconnected. Wolfe grunted as he slipped the phone back into his pocket.

"I guess he'll be surprised."

Wolfe rushed down the hallway to the linen closet. His sister, Angela, sent him a gift basket as a housewarming present. It had milled soaps, kitchen towels with lace at the bottom, and several other household things he had never found a need for. Tonight he could put one of the items to use. He remembered a tiny garden gnome that was tucked into the center of the arrangement.

It was bright red and blue with rosy cheeks, elfin slippers, and a bouquet of tulips. Wolfe pulled it out of a handful of kitchen gadgets and studied it. The gnome was plump where the statue was elongated, but the size was equivalent. In the bag, it would look like he had done what he was told if he left it by the trash can. He grabbed a pillowcase in a color similar to the cloth in the statue box and tore it into shreds. Wrapping the gnome, he walked to the bedroom and retrieved an old cellphone box from his nightstand. Nestling the new replacement statue into the lime green patterned lid, Wolfe covered his creation with the black bottom of the box.

"I guess it's showtime!"

Tucking the box into his work bag, Wolfe headed for the front door. If anyone was waiting, it would look like he was following orders. He locked the door, walked without haste, and acted as if he was meeting a friend. His neighbors would think nothing of his departure. Inside the Jeep, he shifted the bag to the passenger seat floorboard and checked behind him before locking the doors. As the engine roared to life, he checked his watch. Ten minutes left on the timer.

Wolfe hadn't made many trips to Elkins since he moved to Folman. It was always crowded on his way home. Families went for dinner and lingered to enjoy frozen custard. Every teenager in Folman had either worked at or been on a date to the establishment.

Although he didn't enjoy being forced to patronize this particular business tonight, Wolfe did admire it for its history. It started as a dry goods store in the early 1900s. When the economic boom in the region went bust, so did the store. The building sat empty and looked like it would turn into a shell of its original design until the structure was revived as a gas station and café in the 1950s. The café became popular with the locals for its honey-glazed pork sandwiches and the business was soon rebranded Elkins Honeycomb and Custard when construction of a new dessert counter was completed on the south side of the original building in the summer of 1976. With the expanded business came a drive-thru window, a spacious parking lot, and outdoor tables for warm summer nights.

Sitting in the parking space with the neon sign flickering in his side mirror and a foil-wrapped ham sandwich occupying the seat beside him, Wolfe scrawled out a note indicating he had already mailed the statue back to authorities in Peru. *That should make that little twit on the phone uncertain.* Wolfe tucked it into the side of the box before he closed the bag. They would have to wait for news from South America before they came looking for the real statue again. Wolfe hoped their communication was unreliable as he studied the cars parked in the parking lot. Two were SUVs by the front door. One was a ratty-looking Honda by the back fence. He watched the occupants of one get out and go inside while he was waiting at the window for his order. The other two looked empty.

Wolfe got out of his Jeep, walked over to the trash can he had parked beside, looked around, and bent down pretending to tie his shoe. When he rose, the bag had left his grasp. He returned to the Jeep without noticing any change in the parking lot. He locked the doors and switched on the radio as he backed up and drove away. The ham sandwich lay forgotten in the seat beside him as he headed for the interstate ramp and a hotel room on the outskirts of Nashville.

CHAPTER 26

Folman Tennessee, Present

Never was hoping to get a quick quote from Carrie about an upcoming chamber of commerce event when she called early on Monday morning. She didn't even get the chance to speak before Carrie's frantic voice came across the line.

"It's all destroyed!"

"Carrie, where are you?"

"I'm at Wolfe's old house. I had to do a final walkthrough to see what the movers needed to take to Benson's Auction Company."

Someone must have folded the curtains the wrong way or dropped one of the decorative pillows in the dirt. Never assumed she was blowing everything out of proportion before asking, "What happened?"

"Someone shredded the place!"

The passion and the direction of the answer almost made Never choke on her coffee.

"What...how?"

"The walls are cut open, all the cabinets were rifled through, and there are holes in the yard!"

It didn't sound like one of Carrie's overreactions. Never said the only thing she could think of.

"That's enthusiastic vandalism."

"Someone's a poor loser."

"Someone who bid?"

"Umhum," Carrie sounded so sure.

"Would they go to all that trouble?"

"The 'if I can't have it no one can' crowd would."

"Has it happened before?"

"Once or twice, but never this bad. I stay away from divorce cases now."

"How soon can I see it?"

"I don't want pictures of this all over the newspaper Never!"

"I won't bring Justine," she promised. "Can I please see it?"

"It will break your heart."

The fissures in Carrie's armor were starting to give.

"I'll be there with coffee in 15 minutes."

Never heard a sigh from the other end of the line.

"Make it 10, and no pictures."

"Yes, Ma'am."

Never was easing her way up the long driveway when she spotted the first series of holes. It looked like a major landscaping overhaul was underway. If the new owners wanted to add some bushes or trees to their landscaping, they were halfway there. There was a new hole every five feet. It must have taken a small army to make this kind of mess. The yard looked like a community of prairie dogs had colonized the space around Wolfe's front porch.

No wonder Carrie was freaking out. This was a mess and Never still hadn't been inside. She shifted into park behind Carrie's red BMW and flung herself out of the car. Grabbing the two cups of coffee she brought with her, she hurried up the steps.

"Oh, Nev, it is just a disaster!" Carrie greeted her as if they were still in the same conversation.

Never handed over one of the coffee cups and followed her inside. "I'm glad they didn't destroy the stained-glass inlay in the door." She tried to remain positive.

"They did do me that one small nicety," Carrie muttered then swept her arms wide to indicate the large living room. "But look at the rest of it."

Looking around the room, Never realized she owed Sergeant Henderson an apology he was never going to hear pass her lips. Her tossed closets and cut jacket were nothing compared to the chaos on display here. He was right when he said her apartment break-in could have been much worse. The room around her shared no resemblance to the house she snooped through the day she found out Wolfe was dead.

The sofa was overturned and the back was cut open. Seams in the drywall contained gaping holes. The built-in bookcases were reduced to firewood and splinters. Every picture frame was discarded on the floor, and several loose bricks around the fireplace had been removed. The beautiful oak flooring was pried up in spots.

"Is this the worst of it?"

"Not hardly," Carrie informed her before moving back down the hallway.

"The study was a few steps short of having a new entryway."

As she looked into the room, Never could see all the drawers in the wooden desk were dumped in the floor and the desk was thrown on its side to match the sofa. They didn't dice up the wood paneling, but the tan loop pile carpet was ripped to shreds in one corner of the room. Paintings were torn down as in the other rooms. She was confused about Carrie's complaints until she stepped inside and looked around. A thick, green leather office chair was covered in knife marks and embedded in the wall by the doorframe. It was clear that someone lost their temper.

Room after room displayed acts of destruction. The mattresses in all the bedrooms were torn open. The master bedroom's sturdy, pine headboard was missing from its usual spot. Instead it was leaning against a far wall. Every drawer in every room, including the one he had designated as hers, was taken out and dumped on the floor. There wasn't anything left in them at this point, but the sight was bothersome all the same.

The last stop was the kitchen. The room looked like a toddler, who refused to take a nap, had been released into the cabinets while its mom nodded on the couch. It was a disaster that would lead most people to wonder if they could burn it down for the insurance money and move rather than handle the cleanup. Anything larger than a macaroni and cheese box in the kitchen was sliced and poured out. Decorative jars of jams and sauces were smashed along with their dry goods companions. In one place syrup oozed, in another tomato sauce made a thickened blob on a mound of gritty cornmeal remains. It looked like an elementary school science project on a budget instead of the contents of an artisanal gift basket collection staged to tempt buyers.

"How did they have time for all this plus the front yard?"

Carrie didn't seem to hear her.

"I don't know how I'm going to deal with this mess before the buyer arrives this weekend."

"The cleaning crew will probably come back if you throw in some tears and a few extra bucks."

211

"Yeah, Mary is on the way over now to deal with the house," Carrie admitted as she scrolled through the messages on her phone.

"What could they be looking for?"

"I don't know, but I take it you didn't see the backyard?"

Never could have taken the long way round through the front and back the side of the house, but her tennis shoes had seen worse. She marched through the mess and out the back door depositing powdery footprints as she went. She expected to see holes in the yard like the front, but Carrie's shout when she took her first step had her clutching the doorframe. She heard Carrie's running feet and complaints about how the mess was going to ruin her new shoes. All Never could do was stare out at where the porch had been. What greeted her was the exact shape of the wooden structure in rich, black dirt. The remains of the porch were hunched in the far corner of the yard. It looked like a giant became angry and flung it.

"This would have taken an army."

"Or a very skilled construction crew," Carrie agreed from behind her.

"How did the neighbors not hear it?"

"One left for Florida for the winter, and the other thought it was someone working on the house for the buyer."

"They didn't see anything?"

"Just a white panel work truck and a few lights on in the house." Carrie shrugged.

They both looked out over the yard imagining men running and working with vigor to make this kind of mess using as little time as possible.

"At least six, without drugs," Never mumbled as she turned.

"You think they were looking for drugs?"

"No, I was just looking at the damage. It had to take at least six strong men, drugs would make it easier."

"Oh...I wouldn't know," Carrie gave a tilt of her head to register her disdain.

"You remember that thief last spring, skinny little guy, body slammed three cops twice his size."

"He couldn't keep his pants up, but he blew through them like a machine."

"Exactly." Never nodded.

They both fell quiet while they looked out at the yard.

"Well something blew through here," Carrie muttered as she turned away.

"Have you called Sergeant Henderson?"

She nodded and studied the lipstick ring on the side of her cup.

"He was inclined to think it was a crime of opportunity."

"Opportunity for what? Chaos? Did they take anything?"

"Most of my commission, but, wrecked as it is, it's all accounted for."

Never rarely felt a kinship with the woman, but today she thought she could relate to Carrie a little better. They weren't going to hug and sing camp songs together on the weekends, but she did feel a common bond forming. Carrie's frustration mirrored her own when the authorities dismissed her theory that all of the strange activity around Folman was connected. All she could do was wait and see where the unexplained would happen next. It was so exasperating.

"You need anything else before I go?"

Carrie just shook her head and glanced down at her white-powder-blotted leopard print shoes.

"It is, what it is, I guess."

Never couldn't argue with that. Saying sorry for her loss seemed inadequate, but she murmured it anyway. The state of the house was hard to compute as she followed Carrie back to the front door. The difference was stark. Wolfe was never a neat housekeeper. She had teased him several times during their relationship, but he never altered his pattern of leaving stacks of things littered throughout his private space. This was a different mindset. Someone slashed and smashed Wolfe's house like they wanted to murder it. It was purposeful and calculated. People must go insane when they lose their dream home.

Never couldn't relate to an obsession that compelling. She didn't know where to begin. As she drove back to her apartment, she tried to analyze a reaction like she witnessed back at Wolfe's house, but she couldn't figure it out. Never supposed she couldn't relate because she had never looked that hard at putting down deep roots.

The town of Folman was home to her. Where she slept within its boundaries wasn't of much concern. She wasn't what you would call a "nester" when it came to domestic matters. Foster care taught her to take care of her things, but not to complain about the details of the space around her. Paint colors, mismatched furniture, and decorating schemes outdated before she was born were of little interest or worry to her. She liked her things organized and accessible, but she deferred to Justine or someone else when it came to the world of fashion and design. She didn't feel the urge to let things like window dressing take up much of her time. She had plenty of other things to keep her occupied.

For one thing, Archie's strange behavior at night was still driving her crazy. What could the man possibly be doing? It had been weeks of skulking in alleys and watching him with binoculars at the park, and still she didn't have a clue why she felt compelled to do so. It had been weeks without a hint of what he was up to. Maybe it was time to be straightforward and ask him? If he was as shady as she thought he was, that approach might leave Never floating in the lake like Wolfe. She was still tempted to try it the next time she ran into him.

CHAPTER 27

Folman Tennessee, One Month and 29 Days Earlier

There was another email in Wolfe's in-box. It had a familiar, "Egret Society News" in the subject line.

Opening it, he couldn't help but ask himself, "Has it been a month already?"

Wolfe hadn't replied to one of the Egret Society group emails in months. He met James, Kevin, Scott, and Leonard at Oglethorpe University in the early two-thousands when he was finishing up his bachelor's degree. They were all southern boys from rural communities outside of Atlanta with an interest in the history of worlds their fathers and grandfathers had never seen. There wasn't a fraternity for history majors at the time so Leonard came up with the idea for their own secret social group. He called it, "a twist on a southern gentleman's club." They had a list of rules about preservation and a code for history majors to abide by. Kevin was into symbolism at the time, and the Egret Society was born. All members had gold signet rings made with the swooping egret design gracing the top. They all got a good laugh when others mistook it for the Oglethorpe mascot, the stormy petrel.

"We're hiding in plain sight," Scott would always joke after another student complimented them on their rings.

All five men wanted to be a combination of several popular adventure stars. They all had leather jackets and dreamt of motorcycles while they walked to the city transit stop. They ate takeout from some of the worst dives and tipped the homeliest strippers in the whole of Atlanta with five dollar bills when their birthday money came in the mail from home.

After graduation from Oglethorpe, the men in the group went their separate ways to careers throughout the southern region. Wolfe hadn't seen the other members after they packed up their dorm rooms. He stayed in Atlanta and entered Emory University for grad school. Wolfe never bought the motorcycle he was fantasizing about. He could have, but by then he was already interested in fitting in with another peer group.

When he drove out of Atlanta for the last time, Wolfe wanted to be seen as a professional among his co-workers in academia. He traded his college dreams for an expensive suit and a new four-wheel drive truck to head north from Atlanta to his future life in Tennessee. He had a new degree tucked in his luggage along with a full-time job offer from Redmond College. Oglethorpe and the Egret Society were far behind him.

The emails perched in his inbox every month were the only reminders that linked him to his former classmates. He was guilty of reading without responding to the bulk of their attempts, but he still wore his ring out of habit. He ran his fingers over the design as he sat reminiscing.

James and Leonard did their best to send out an email once a month with updates, photos, and interesting articles they thought the rest of the group would enjoy. He received invites for meetups throughout the year, but he rarely took time to consider participating or tapping out a response of his own on the keyboard. Maybe it was the picture of Never left in his mailbox, or the second empty glass of scotch, but Wolfe found himself clicking the latest email open to read.

Tonight, looking at the photos of his old friends and their families, Wolfe opened a new window on his laptop and began typing. He didn't want to bring them into the inner circle of his current problem, but tonight more than ever he needed to feel connected to something good. He mentioned his local history class proposal and how proud he was of Rebecca's work on the black market art trade. He couldn't mention the statue or the notes, but he told them about his lengthening relationship with Never. He ended the short correspondence with a glowing account of his expanding cycleball league and their ability to attract corporate sponsors for the end of the season tournament. Wolfe hoped his attempt to write out everything as he wanted it to be remembered would influence the outcome of the next few weeks in some small way.

CHAPTER 28

Folman Tennessee, Present

Never had been flipping through pages for most of the afternoon trying to find any connection or clues that would explain some of the events of the past week. Most of Wolfe's planner entries were pretty straightforward. There was only one entry that seemed unusual and repetitive. Wolfe had written in his planner that he received an email from the Egret Society. The entry still puzzled her. It was written in notes from every month of the planner. Did he give to charity every month? Wolfe had never mentioned to her that he donated any large amounts or that he had a love of birds. Even so, why would he write notes about an email from them in his planner? They would send him tax information at the end of the year if he gave that much money to an organization, or he could just check his bank statements. She didn't keep meticulous notes on all her emails from local charities or of the numerous requests from her college alumni association. Why would Wolfe find this one important enough to keep track of? Never looked up the name and found a handful of charities dedicated to the large, swan-like birds. She scrolled through several websites, reading through their offerings and mission statements. All were geared toward conservation in some way. One focused on the bird's environmental challenges, another took up the cause of fortifying their natural food chain, and the simplest plea asked for help caring for birds already in crisis. They were all noble causes, but why would Wolfe feel the need to keep track of their emails?

"It wasn't a mistake," she muttered to herself.

Never hadn't found as much as an un-dotted "i" since she started reading entries. If it was here, Wolfe had a reason to keep up with it.

"What was he up to?"

He listed it among his daily entries like one would a letter from a dear friend. Why mention emails from a non-profit at all in your daily notes of importance? Did he know someone who worked for the organization? If he did, why wouldn't they just use their normal email addresses? None of it felt right to Never. It was as if Wolfe was tracking his spam in a meaningful way. It had to be a cover for something else he was up to. Was it code for emails or meet-ups with his mysterious grad student? Never had a hard time imagining he would be able to push her off to one meeting every month. The excitement of their unintended hook-up would make it all the more tempting to increase the frequency of their interludes until someone either caught them in the act, or until the excitement of the situation played out. One wouldn't schedule an affair once a month like a dry cleaning appointment. What would be the excitement in that?

Never needed to get into his email account and have a look, but she would need to find the password first. She still had all the boxes from his house to search through, and it would be more likely for Wolfe to keep passwords and information in his study at home than his office at work. Her weariness couldn't outweigh her curiosity this time. If there was anything in those boxes that would shed light on what Wolfe was doing, Never was going to look for it tonight.

She moved the full boxes from Wolfe's house close to the sofa and dove into the contents. Lots of it was research and class prep information. There were several large stacks of newspaper clippings and promotional materials from several art museums. She found letters from former professors requesting names they might consider for upcoming positions in their programs. It was a hodge-podge of personal and professional papers that Wolfe had saved for one reason or another in the last few months. It was almost as confusing as the boxes she sorted from his office at the college.

It was late when Never came across an answer to one of her questions. Sorting through a random assortment of photographs, a framed photo caught her attention. She pulled it out and held it close to examine it.

The man grinning up at her in the center of the photo was in his early twenties and handsome in his leather jacket. It was a much younger version of Wolfe, but she could pick him out without any hesitation. Scanning the background, she decided it had to be Wolfe in college. He was standing on a campus green at Oglethorpe University with the four men she had seen at his memorial service at Redmond College. Some of them were already losing their hair when the photo was taken, but no one seems cognizant of it. They all looked ready to take on the world with their leather jackets and aviator sunglasses. Never would guess they were fraternity pledges the way they were all holding up their hands to display gold signet rings. All five men seemed ecstatic to have the wide black medallion overlaid with the golden outline of a bird grace their ring fingers.

She flipped the frame over and opened up the back. Written on the reverse of the photo in Wolfe's careful hand was: Egret Society January 2007. Never leaned back against the sofa and grinned at her stupidity. The notes Wolfe made in his planner were about an old friend, several in fact, and Never thought he was donating to charity. He was making notes that he received their emails, even if he didn't write his friends back.

Never fished the forgotten business cards out of her purse and sorted through them. She knew how to contact the other men in this photograph. It was one more place to look for answers. If she made the request, perhaps, they would share Wolfe's last email with her.

CHAPTER 29

Folman Tennessee, Present

Never was surprised when Marcel called her early the next morning to make dinner plans. She had thought about him several times since their meeting in Justine's apartment building. He admitted that Justine handed over her number when he mentioned his interest in asking her out. A smirk creased her lips as she imagined Justine playing matchmaker, no doubt, trying to find her a steady beau before the wedding this December.

Never had been so covered up with work and the mess created by Wolfe's possessions dumped in her apartment that she only found time to fantasize about Justine's handsome, new neighbor when she was too tired to enjoy it. Maybe tonight she would get a chance to see the real thing. She was pleased to accept when he suggested Bernardo's, an upscale Italian restaurant downtown, instead of the plethora of steakhouses throughout the city.

Never set up a lunch date with Justine to help

her find something to wear. Because of Wolfe, she was never wearing her red dress again. Because of her sliding trip backward down the mountain in Aurora, she didn't have a little black dress to fall back on either. The last few weeks had taken a terrible toll on her wardrobe budget, but Never was happy for the shopping diversion.

With Justine's help, she had picked out a little blue, off-the-shoulder sheath dress at a cute new boutique named Pando. Never liked the way it hugged her curves as she turned in front of the wall of mirrors. If Marcel had as much trouble keeping his eyes off of her as the male sales clerk she passed to get to Justine, Never thought it would be a stimulating night.

When her friend turned to look at her, Justine put back the handful of dresses she was weeding from the racks.

"That is perfect!"

"It really feels right," Never admitted as she turned from side to side.

"If he isn't turned-on enough to want to peel that off of you, there's nothing we can buy in here."

"You really think it looks that good?"

"I like it better than your red one."

Never got catcalls and traffic stopped at green lights when she wore her little red dress. That is why she picked it for her meeting with Wolfe by the lake. She thought it would be perfect for their engagement photos. Now it sat in the back of her closet shrouded in a dress bag that would probably never be unzipped again. Never smiled at the thought the blue dress could be its superior.

"I guess I should take it off and pay."

"You should, and while you're at it you should think about dropping hints that I should change the color of my bridesmaids' dresses."

"You've changed them three times already."

"But imagine how that color would look if we had snow," Justine rambled on as Never changed and headed for the register.

"Didn't the lady at the rental place threaten to charge you a fee if you canceled your order again?"

"She was pretty cranky when I changed from forest green to lavender."

"And from baby's breathe to forest green," Never reminded as she scooped up her dress bag and headed out onto the street.

"I know, I know, but there are so many catalogs and styles to choose from."

"You're doing an amazing job."

"But I shouldn't change the dresses again."

"No, the alterations are almost finished."

Justine looked as if she was about to protest, but she sighed and strolled along.

"Tell me if you're getting bored."

"This is your big date." Justine reached over to squeeze her arm. "Let's find lunch and stop by Sammy's for shoes afterwards."

They had a whirlwind of a lunch date together before Justine begged off to go home and check on Houdini. Never didn't find any new shoes, but Justine bought three pairs. After carrying her friend's bags to her car, Never returned to work in better spirits than she had in weeks. She had some tan pumps in her closet that would make her calves look amazing if his gaze wandered all the way down to her feet.

It was hard to stay focused at work. Every time her eyes strayed to the garment bag hanging on the wall of her cubical, Never couldn't stop a goofy grin from forming. Others would stop by to drop off copy or ask questions and she would have to explain the bag's presence. She got a variety of looks, but Never didn't see any reason to let it dampen her spirits. She turned in her latest column to Jerry at six and headed out the door with her dress bag.

It seemed so strange to be going on a first date after all these years. Never had only a few scattered group-style dates when she first moved to Folman. Meeting Wolfe had ended her habitual search for companionship.

In her mind, tonight was different. She wasn't looking for forever. Marcel was in town temporarily, but he had the potential to be an entertaining distraction. For now, an entertaining distraction was what she needed. Marcel was an enticing available male and she was interested. There was no need to complicate things before they started. Never smoothed her curls and tucked them behind her ear before putting on a final application of her sparkling red lipstick. Tonight was about having fun and feeling sexy. Looking back at her in the mirror was a woman ready to be the center of attention.

Marcel had offered to pick her up, but she opted to meet him at Bernardo's at eight. She didn't want to stumble out of the bundles and boxes of paperwork in her apartment when he knocked (or have to explain the origins).

Besides, this beautiful new dress deserved an entrance. Meeting in front of the carved wooden doors of Bernardo's would give her just the advantage she was looking for. Other couples in casual wear would be passing by on the street in their jeans and shabby work uniforms. Their appearance would amplify the difference in her curvaceous figure and the rich color of the fabric she was encased in. If Marcel was interested, she could give him plenty to consider. Never just hoped she wasn't overdoing it on their first date.

She was fidgeting with the clasp on the small evening purse Justine had insisted she buy at Sammy's, when Marcel strolled up to greet her. Gone were the thick work boots and casual work clothes. His dark dress boots were shined to a high gloss, and the open-neck red dress shirt and black suit made Never's mouth water. His hair was slicked back into shiny waves of curls and she would swear he was wearing lip gloss to draw attention to his lips.

"You look lovelier than I could have ever imagined," Marcel greeted her as he leaned in to place a kiss on her check.

"Thank you. You clean up well yourself," Never managed to get out as she continued to assess the changes.

"Should we go check on our table?"

Never nodded and followed his lead while he ushered her through the heavy wooden door. Marcel had an easy smile and the hostess wasted no time trying out her flirting skills on him as he inquired about their reservation. Never couldn't blame the woman for her efforts. He was a feast from front to back. Never couldn't kid herself into thinking he hadn't had plenty of options over the years.

Marcel reached out for her hand as he turned from the front counter. "Julia is going to take us to our table as soon as she has run one final check that it is set up as I requested."

"That is very thoughtful of her."

"I told her how nervous I was about disappointing you on our first outing together."

"I'm sure you have plenty of experience pleasing women," Never teased. "You're making a great impression on most of the females here tonight."

"I am humbly keeping up with the numerous men trying to catch your eye."

Never had to admit she liked the directness of his tone. Marcel was gorgeous without being overpowering, and he knew the right thing to say. Never could find no flaws in the way either of them were dressed for the evening. This date had a long way to fall before she would consider it a flop. At this rate, if she wasn't sneaking past Justine's door in the morning, she would be the one to blame.

"Never seems like an odd name for parents to give their child," he commented as he led her to a table.

"That's because they didn't."

"Did they have a contest?" he smiled across the table at her.

Never waited until the hostess had given them menus and turned to retreat before she answered him.

"No, I never knew them," she told him as though she were reading it off her menu. "They dropped me off at a church donation drive with a bag of clothes. The bag said Martinez Farms on it. I became known as Jane Martinez."

"I really can't see you as a Jane," he agreed as he studied her face.

"I guess it could have been worse."

"Yeah, like Cookie or Pebbles."

She made a face to counter his teasing grin.

"Come on, where did Never come from?"

"When I turned eighteen, I was free to search for any information regarding my parents. I didn't have much. I talked to the farmer about the bag I showed up with. He said he gave them out to everyone who stopped by his vegetable stand."

"So you were sure you weren't a Martinez?"

"Right."

"Why didn't you just change your last name?"

"To what?"

"Anything your heart desired."

"Everyone would still call me the Martinez girl."

"So you decided to make a statement instead."

She nodded. "I was looking for truth about my family. The only thing I could prove was that I wasn't a Martinez."

"You're sure?"

"Yes."

They ordered and sat in silence for a little while after the waitress disappeared with their menus.

"So what about your family?" Never asked as she turned the question back to her companion.

"My mother was a Hispanic woman who traveled from town to town with her family doing odd jobs. My father was an Irishman from Philly who worked construction like me. Thankfully, I got my mom's sexy Latin looks and my father's charm."

It was the first soul-deep laughter Never had unleashed in weeks. It bubbled up as though she had swallowed detergent. She couldn't seem to stop its steady flow. She might have to hand it to Justine. The dress made her feel like a temptress, and the man across from her was proving himself worthy of temptation. It had been a long time since she had a carefree fling with any man, but Marcel was making Never fixate on the possibilities as she picked at her dinner. Her fingers itched to undo another button on his shirt. She was imagining the mess she could make by running her hands through his hair when the waitress tipped over the water glass by her plate and sent a cold splash of water dripping down the front of her dress.

"Excuse me," Never muttered as she skirted the upset waitress and hurried to the ladies room.

The splotch encroaching on the front of her new dress was unappealing, but it wouldn't ruin the dress. Never tried to dry herself with the hand dryer as best she could, but her skin was chafed from the effort.

"Honey, you still look better than 90% of the women in this place," a tall blond evaluated as she eased up to the mirror beside Never to reapply her lipstick.

"Thank you."

"Oh, I was talking to me, but you good too girl." The blond gave her thick lips a smack. "Go out there and get you some."

Not knowing whether she was talking to her or not, Never closed her tiny purse and headed for the door.

When she reached the table, Never was surprised to see all their plates had been removed and large carryout bags were sitting on Marcel's side. He hadn't noticed her approach yet. A muscular man in a blue suit was leaning over the back of the booth and talking in hushed tones to Marcel. As the other man withdrew toward the front of the restaurant, Marcel looked up and smiled.

"Has something come up?"

"I hope you don't mind, but I wanted to take you somewhere special for dessert."

"Where might that be?"

Please say your bed. Please say your bed.

"Since I've had a chance to read your work, I thought it would be fair to show you mine?"

"Won't we need construction gear for that?"

"There is a suite model set up to impress investors," he explained as he reached for her hand. "I thought you might like to explore it with me."

"Over dessert?"

He nodded as he led her from the restaurant.

"I believe there is a pair of fluffy white robes in the model, if you need to let your dress dry," he whispered in her ear as they both settled into the back of a waiting cab.

"It would be a shame to spill anything else on it."

"Maybe a nice quiet night away from the crowds would do us both some good."

Never couldn't keep the stupid grin from her face as he reached to drape an arm around her bare shoulders. She wished the short ride from the restaurant to Jackson Avenue lasted longer, but her insides were jumping with the expectations of being alone with Marcel.

Never looked at the landscaped brick building they had pulled to a stop in front of. She didn't remember seeing it the last time she drove by. It had very clean lines with pops of color around the door and windows. Marcel's voice and the sound of a door being opened beside her redirected her focus.

He was standing outside with their bags holding out his hand to her. Never grabbed her purse and hopped out to follow him. When he opened the door to a luxury suite with a sleek kitchen and large sectional sofa, Never hoped she wasn't dreaming.

"What do you think?"

"Your work is impressive," Never admitted. "I don't remember seeing this building before."

"It's only been finished a couple of weeks."

"Did it encourage the investors?"

"We have several offers on the table."

"Did any of them stay for dessert?"

"I don't know. I left early." He grinned down at her as his hands circled her waist. "I was trying to get home in time to bump into my neighbor's hot friend."

CHAPTER 30

Redmond College, Redmond Tennessee,
A Month and a Half Earlier

Wolfe didn't want to have this conversation. When Rebecca walked in, he still wasn't ready. He wanted to make everything better without displacing her, but he couldn't figure out how.

"Rebecca, I am thinking of transferring you to Professor Millhorn for your dissertation advisement," Wolfe launched the words at her from across the room.

"Have I done something wrong?" she fretted with her purse strap as she walked over to the seat across from him and sat down with a thump. "Am I working too slowly?"

Smooth, real smooth. He really was screwing this up. Wolfe switched to a "it's not you it's me" approach in a soothing tone.

"No, no, nothing like that, I have come to realize that with my focus split between my current classes and preparation for a possible new course, I'm not giving you the attention you deserve."

"You think Professor Millhorn would be a better fit?" Rebecca looked skeptical.

"He has contacts in the legal world that might give you a perspective you won't get from art and history professionals." Wolfe tried not to think about how off-putting his colleague's loud booming voice or his hawkish eyes could be.

"You want me to widen my understanding of the legal side of black market art?"

"Yes, I think it would add to your discussion and impress the review board if you study it from different perspectives."

Rebecca looked like she was ready to argue, but Wolfe didn't give her the chance.

"I have spoken to him and he seems interested and informed on the subject matter." Wolfe wanted to assure her of the clarity of his decision. "But, of course, it is ultimately up to you."

"Will I still be able to come to you for advice if I need to?"

"Of course," *but I hope you don't* his inner monologue continued. "I just want you to have a fully focused guide through this process, and I don't feel like I can give it my all amid the new developments and the existing schedule."

"I understand Professor Strickland." She seemed

like she had just been sideswiped, but went willingly as she clutched her binder to her chest.

Wolfe stood by his office door and waited for her uncertain look back. *There it is.* He waved and smiled before closing his door. He did what he had to do. Right now he felt like he could use a drink. He went back to slide into his office chair with a sigh. He wished he had the nerve to store a bottle of scotch in his bottom drawer like the fictional professors he idolized as a teen. Instead, that drawer was full of old newspaper clippings he intended to use as topics of exploration in his spring classes.

Wolfe also wouldn't mind a ground floor window. He could crawl out of it when his office meetings dragged on too long. He had a great view of the commons, but using a window as an escape from his adult problems was only possible in fantasy.

Wolfe worried Rebecca would see through his words as he watched sunlight create shadows around a tree outside. He handled the situation without finesse. His reasoning sounded flimsy, but he wanted Rebecca to be as far away from him as she could be if any actual harm was involved with his stalker's notes. He felt like he had taken a sucker punch to the gut when she leveled disbelieving eyes at him. He could taste the betrayal lingering on his lips. He needed a drink to wash it away. On a dry campus, he would have to live with his actions in the glaring light of sobriety. Wolfe hoped his efforts were worth it.

His talk with Rebecca wasn't a decision he wanted to make, and it wasn't a decision he made alone during a game of mental chess. Wolfe had several talks with Larry over the last few days about their best course of action. They both wanted Rebecca protected without her knowledge. Getting her far away from a stalker's focus would reduce her risk of being injured by anyone coming after him. They both agreed on a scenario. They would fill Professor Millhorn in on the briefest of details and switch her over to him during office hours. Since much of Rebecca's research had to do with crime in art, switching her to the care of a professor of Millhorn's talents would look more believable, and change her habit of haunting the history hallways after class when they were abandoned.

Wolfe didn't know much about the colleague he was sending Rebecca to. He had only seen and spoken to him at campus events and heard details about him through the campus grapevine. Wolfe knew he hadn't lied when he told Rebecca her new advisor was a talented law professor, but he failed to mention two important points of interest.

Professor Millhorn had an office on the opposite side of campus from where Wolfe sat brooding in Guthrie Hall, and he, unbeknownst to most people at Redmond College, was an ex-marine. Wolfe had no idea if the crazy person sending him notes would ever appear in person, but spiriting Rebecca away to the other side of campus would be their best shot at keeping her from being an unsuspecting victim.

CHAPTER 31

Folman Tennessee, Present

Never's date with Marcel continued until the early hours of the morning, and she didn't want to close her eyes for any of it. When she hung up her soft bathrobe and slipped back into her clothes, Never was running on empty. It was the type of situation where six cups of coffee and an extra jolt of vitamin C were struggling to keep her upright.

She made it through her meetings and managed to stay awake through the town council debate over changing the paint color of the entryway in city hall from eggshell to alabaster. She ate a sandwich from Mambo's on the way home and walked around the clutter in her floor to go straight to bed. She was settling into a comfortable position with her body pillow when the realization hit her. *Wolfe wasn't saying Chasity.* He was taking about the website CHASETE she ran across earlier. His clue was leading her to the online group. She bolted to a sitting position and scrambled out from under her covers.

Never grabbed her phone off the nightstand and typed in the random letters again. The website she had ignored earlier popped up. College Historians Aggressively Searching Everywhere Treasure Exists, or CHASETE for short, was some sort of treasure-hunting club that consisted mostly of bored college professors and history majors. One might consider his obsession a possible mistress of sorts, but not a physical woman as Never had been lead to believe.

She pulled his planner out and checked his entries. CHASETE was listed several times throughout the pages. Wolfe was active in the group, and posted daily on the site until August. According to his notes, he found several of the prizes. He must have invested copious amounts of effort and income in this strange hobby. But why keep it a secret from her? It seemed normal compared to cycleball.

Many people enjoyed treasure hunting or geocaching as a fun excuse to explore the outdoors. Why keep it a secret? Never would have gladly gone with him on one of his hunts if he had ever mentioned it. Why was he talking about a baby? None of it made sense. Something changed in August. Wolfe said as much in his notes. If it wasn't a woman or a real baby, what was it? How does one conceive a figurative baby?

Never wished she knew his password. If she could look through his conversations from August maybe there would be a trail to the answers she needed. She could message the group members individually. It would take longer and she wasn't certain anyone would respond to her inquiries, but it was worth a try.

Never picked up Wolfe's planner and began compiling a list of names and clues related to the group entries over the summer and into August. It was the first real connection to Wolfe's strange behavior that had merit. Never couldn't go back to sleep until she had a plan to chase it.

Never's laptop slid from her grasp as a banging on the door jolted her awake. She maneuvered it back into a safe position and set it aside as she rose to her feet. Stumbling over some papers, she rushed from the sofa to her small entryway. Flinging open the door with a grunt, she found herself staring out at Justine.

"What are you doing here so early?"

"It isn't early Never," Justine insisted as she marched through the doorway and into the kitchen. "It's noon and we have a flower appointment at one."

"How did you know I was here?"

"Jerry already came by my desk twice to ask why he hasn't fired you yet."

Never gave her a sad grin. "It's always good to be missed."

She watched Justine shuffle around her kitchen making coffee and looking for mugs. Just the sight of the activity made her slump down into a chair. It was as if investigating Wolfe's death was sucking the life out of her. Every long night led to another. Never wondered if she would ever regain her energy again.

"You have to tell me about your date!" Justine demanded as she handed her a cup of coffee.

"It was good."

"It was good," she mocked her. "Dish, or I'm cutting you out of my wedding."

"He took me to the fancy Italian place downtown. He looked gorgeous in his red shirt and dark suit. The waitress spilled water on my dress, and he had the rest of our dinners and desserts bagged and ready to go when I came back from the bathroom."

"Go where?"

"He took me to see an upscale investor's model of his work."

"I thought he was working on a hotel remodel."

"He is, but there is a suite model built nearby to encourage investors."

"So he took you to bed in a fancy suite?"

"Well...we ended up in the bed eventually."

"How was it?"

"I didn't leave until the early hours of the morning."

"Anything interesting under his clothes?"

"No tattoos or scars."

"That is surprising for a man in construction." Justine considered the new information. "Even Rory has a few scars from his football days."

"This guy could be a model and there weren't any tan lines anywhere."

"You sound like you were thorough."

"We did take a long shower together while we explored the rest of the place."

"You two work fast for a first date."

"Yes, it may be the only one."

"You don't think he will call?"

"I didn't expect him to call the first time."

"Do you think there is anything beyond the physical?"

"He's a really good listener and he speaks more than one language."

"So he is classier than you expected?" Never could hear Justine's toothy grin without seeing it. "What did you talk about?"

"Oh, you know the normal things."

"Never..." Justine growled as she reached out to pinch her.

"Okay! He asked about my name, if I had family, about my relationship with Wolfe, and a few other things."

"Wow! Sounds like he is interested."

"Down girl." She sent Justine a warning gaze. "We both know what he was interested in."

"So no chance you're in love?"

"There can't be, remember, he is leaving in six months."

"You say that now, but I hope you don't decide to run after his truck when the time comes."

"I'll be too busy planning your baby shower by then."

"That is a nice thought."

Never downed the rest of her cup and walked over to pop another pod in her machine.

"So how is the house-hunting going?"

Justine giggled as she watched her over the rim of her coffee cup.

"Okay, Nev, I'll drop it for now."

"I need to get in the shower if we are going to make it to the florist on time."

"What about your coffee?"

"Put it in a travel mug," Never tossed over her shoulder as she disappeared back the hallway.

She would need every ounce of it to stay alert while looking at the entire flower selection of Robertson County.

CHAPTER 32

Wolfe whistled as he walked the hallway to his office. He had mail from one of his colleagues in Georgia. The most worrisome thing in his mailbox this week was a letter from the dean about his local summer history offering. Wolfe tucked that one away in the side pouch of his case to read later. He planned to open it tonight when he was alone in his study at home.

Since his last chat with Larry and Sarah, the creepy notes in the mail and on his car had stopped. His bluff of mailing the statue to Peru must have done the trick. Things were getting back to normal. He felt guilty for sending Rebecca away, but she was safe with Professor Millhorn in the Phillip Edgars Law Annex. He didn't want to spoil a beautiful day with ifs and maybes.

By all accounts, Rebecca seemed to be adapting well to the new turn of events. She acclimated to his ruse and added several sections to her work about the legal standpoints associated with the black market art trade. They all seemed to be better off from his unexpected changes. Everything was getting back to the way it was before his trip to Paris. An interesting and enjoyable week was swinging into gear.

Ellen Chase, the adjunct philosophy professor, came powering down the hallway past Wolfe in her gray suit and black wedges. The only pops of color in her outfit were the crimson earrings dangling through the layers of her chin-length brown hair and the red pocket square in her double-breasted jacket.

"Beautiful day isn't it?" he flashed her a smile and watched her green eyes slide up to meet his.

"How's it going Wolfe?"

"The sunshine has put me in good spirits this morning."

"You should enjoy it now," she instructed as her footsteps continued down the hallway. "The next few months will be nothing but thick clouds and endless rain."

Winter in Redmond was a slight concern when it came to weather, but not in the way most people would think. There was more snow here than his hometown in Georgia and it liked to make a guessing game of his attempts to traverse the ridge in the late afternoons. The patches of snow and ice weren't any more than his Jeep could handle, but snow wasn't the most effective use of the weather here.

The constant and common problem for the small town in the shadow of the ridge had always been the heavy and unrelenting rains. Water washed down from the hillsides and altered traffic routes while flooding basements. The college was usually safe from its frequent mudslides and the mess the heavy rains made when flood water overpowered the drainage systems. Once the heavy rains made it all the way to the banks of the Red River, it melted into the current like a long lost relative at a family reunion.

Today, Wolfe was going to follow his co-worker's advice and focus on what was right in front of him. Things were looking up for the first time in weeks. It was time to celebrate. Wolfe finished up "Yankee Doodle" and commenced whistling snatches of other songs from his childhood as tunes came to him.

The whistling slowed to a stop as Wolfe neared his office door. Something wasn't right. The heavy door wasn't locked. It wasn't even closed, and darkness greeted him from behind it. Wolfe knew he had locked it the night before. He was sure of it. He would never be so distracted that he would leave it open all night, and he wasn't in any particular hurry last night.

"What the hell," he murmured as he came to a halt.

Pulling out his phone he punched in the number for campus security.

"Hello, Larry speaking," greeted him after a couple of rings.

"Larry, this is Wolfe." *Was his voice shaking?* "My office door is open."

"Hang tight, I'm on my way," he instructed and

the line went dead.

The tiny flashlight on Wolfe's key ring stopped working around the first of the year and he hadn't bothered to replace the small watch batteries that would bring it back to life. He wanted to shine a light inside and see if anyone was peering out, but all he could do was hover in the hallway squinting into the darkness. He couldn't see much through the slit beside the wooden door with his brass nameplate on it. Other than the small section of laminate flooring illuminated by the iridescent tubes in the hallway, everything was cloaked in shadows.

Had someone figured out the statue wasn't on its way to Peru? Wolfe tried to ignore the thought. They knew where he lived. It didn't make sense for them to break into his office. Maybe it was just a group of opportunistic students. It was early in the year to be stealing answer keys, but some of his students might already be worried. Wolfe let out a weak chuckle at the thought. They would be disappointed to find out he kept testing materials at home this time of year, reviewing and revising questions.

"See anyone leave?" Larry asked as he hurried up behind him.

"No, and I was whistling when I walked up."

"Likely empty," Larry muttered as he switched on his flashlight and headed for the door. "It could just be a slipup from the cleaning crew."

Wolfe lowered his bag from his shoulder and placed his coffee on the window ledge across from his office. He wanted to be ready if Larry spooked someone.

The light switched on as he waited. Larry's shuffling feet and occasional swishes of paper were the only sounds of occupancy Wolfe could detect. It tried his patience to follow Larry's shadow around the room without being able to look himself.

Wolfe stood outside waiting for any sound of a scuffle or shout of all-clear. He kept track of the time by watching the steam from his hot coffee slow to a thin, wispy trick of the light as it leaked from the small slit in his travel mug. *What was taking so long?*

The longer it took Larry the more agitated Wolfe became. Stiffness transferred through his back and surged upwards spreading across shoulders that minutes before were well-rested and relaxed. He was going to need the number to a good chiropractor if Larry stayed in there much longer.

"I don't think it was the cleaning crew," came from inside his office before Larry reappeared.

"Any idea who?" Wolfe asked as he gathered his things.

Larry shook his head. "I think they have been here and gone."

"Did they take anything?"

"Hard to be sure." Larry shrugged as he moved aside and motioned for Wolfe to see for himself.

The first thing Wolfe noticed was that his desk drawers were all open. The small closet he used to hold supplies and his formal cap and gown for the college assemblies was open and boxes were shifted out onto the floor. Someone was being thorough in their search. There wasn't an inch they hadn't examined.

"I've had proctologists who weren't as methodical as this."

He could only nod at Larry's colorful assessment. Wolfe could imagine an individual creeping around his office in the dark groping in crevices and pushing past things that didn't live up to his standards. Then he imagined the intruder in a doctor's scrubs. He didn't want either of those images swimming around in his head tonight as he tried to sleep.

"Someone think you're hiding rubies in here or something?"

"If I had rubies, would I be teaching college classes?"

"Fair point." Larry reached up to scratch the collection of hair clinging to his chin. "They were looking for something."

He couldn't disagree looking at the mess around them.

"Maybe they were hoping to steal answer keys," Wolfe suggested without much conviction.

"Are you still getting notes?"

Wolfe shook his head. "Not since I talked to you."

"I'll go back and write it up." Larry looked over the room without moving to leave. "Call if you find anything missing."

Both men hovered, restricted by the things they weren't saying. Someone with knowledge of Wolfe's whereabouts was getting access to the campus. How long would it be before they escalated their efforts? How long would it be before they tracked down Rebecca?

"Can maintenance install a stronger lock?"

"I can get Rob up here to take a look."

"Thanks," Wolfe murmured as Larry disappeared out into the hallway.

The beautiful day outside was forgotten as Wolfe sifted through papers and straightened boxes. None of it made any sense. As much as he wanted to believe it was just kids looking to score higher on the midterm, Wolfe had a nagging suspicion Larry wasn't far from the mark when he asked about the notes. But the notes had stopped. Raking his hand through his hair, Wolfe tried to think. Was this mess the next step in an endless procession? Was his life going to be invaded from every angle until the person toying with him found what they were looking for?

Wolfe closed the last box and shifted it back up on the shelf in the closet above his robes. Everything was in order now, but he couldn't find anything missing from his desk or anywhere else in the room. Whoever ripped through his office left unhappy. The thought made Wolfe feel better about using his morning to clean up the mess.

Wolfe's phone rang with a calamity that made him stop and pull at his trouser leg trying to remove the jingling device from his pocket. For a split second he wondered if the would-be thief was calling to make demands, but the number on the screen was recognizable.

"Nev, honey, how are you?" he breathed into the phone as he picked up.

"I'm ahead of schedule for once. How about lunch?"

"That sounds great." He listened to the sounds in the background. "You're already on your way, aren't you?"

"I should be there in fifteen."

Wolfe looked around him checking to see if there was anything out of place.

"Why don't I meet you at the Gator?"

She voiced an agreement and the line went dead.

"I guess that's enough work for one morning." He looked around the room at his reorganized desk and closed closet door.

It would take him less than five minutes to walk over to the Red Gator Café, but he headed for the door. His office held no appeal at the moment. Fresh sunshine was still playing over the crisp lawns of the campus commons. He wanted to give himself time to enjoy the day. If he hesitated or retained a look of melancholy, Wolfe was sure to lead Never straight to the problem he was covering up. She would sniff his deceit out like a bloodhound. He needed to put some distance between himself and the problem at hand before meeting her.

Wolfe walked the commons and the garden spot behind the college president's house. He sat and watched the chrysanthemums sway in the breeze. He was so engrossed in their movements he didn't realize he had wasted ten minutes in the garden when he should have headed toward the Gator.

Wolfe raced across campus hoping that his late arrival wouldn't prompt Never to come searching for him. He couldn't have her near his office. Wolfe didn't even want her in the hallways of Guthrie Hall. The farther away from his problems the better off she would be. He spotted Never's car in the parking lot behind the Red Gator and came jogging up to greet her.

"Sorry to keep you waiting."

"I could've waited on you if you had paperwork to finish up," Never offered as he held the door for her to get out of her car.

He shrugged off her offer. "It's a beautiful day, and you sounded like you were in a hurry."

"I do have a meeting at two," Never admitted as she reached up to pull him in for a kiss.

She had on that red off-the-shoulder sweater that showed off her collarbone in a way that made his fingers itch to reach up and trace the exposed skin. There was nothing revealing about it. It paired well with the black slacks and black flats she wore.

He assumed she wanted to look professional for her meeting later in the afternoon, but Wolfe could feel himself harden as he watched her reach up to brush stray curls off her shoulder.

"I'm glad you could fit me into your schedule," he teased as he gathered her into his arms.

It had been over a week since he had seen her in the flesh. Wolfe enjoyed their daily chats, but being able to hold her in his arms was reassuring after the turmoil of his morning. He recited the "Gettysburg Address" from memory to squelch his physical enthusiasm for the woman he held in his arms. It was a trick he learned in high school and continued when he found it to be a competent way to stave off embarrassing physical displays in public. Once the union was saved, Wolfe gave her arm an extra squeeze as he released her. It was time to guide her around to the front of the building where students would be milling and watching them as they passed by the front windows.

He agreed with Never that they needed to maintain a certain level of professionalism on campus. They were both likely to work with numerous members of the staff and community throughout their careers. Neither wanted to set a bad example that would cause useful contacts to avoid them. Their public displays of affection on Redmond's campus were limited to short hugs and pecks on the cheek and lips that would not inspire yeast to rise.

Wolfe was tempted to throw out their rule and find a dark corner where they could act like hormonal college students between classes. It had been too long since he had taken Never to bed and seeing her here heightened his awareness. He was going to be reciting Lincoln's speech several times this afternoon.

The only seats left at the Red Grator were in the center of the room. He guided Never through the front door and eased into a seat beside her. Wolfe didn't need to look at the menu. When Sandy stopped by to take their order, he rattled off what he wanted. He overheard Never discussing the differences in the chicken and shrimp seasonings before she ordered chicken on top of her salad.

Wolfe made observations about students walking by outside the window, hoping to find a way to distract Never with other topics while she was here. He didn't want her straying to the topic of how his morning went or what he had been working to clean up all morning. He was compiling a list of topics to keep her talking when she snaked her hand through his arm and leaned so close to his ear that he could feel her warm breath.

"Would you rather be somewhere else today?" Never asked him as she leaned back into the seat beside him.

In bed with you, he wanted to tell her, but couldn't risk being overheard while they were the center ring at a campus hot spot. "Oh...sorry honey, I guess I was thinking about work."

Sandy interrupted to drop off their orders. If ever he needed a buffer, today was the day. He asked for extra napkins and hot sauce to guarantee Sandy would make a return trip to their table. Plastic silverware bags hissed as Wolfe and Never freed their utensils and rearranged them on the table beside their plates. Drinks were refilled with a flick of a wrist and salad dressing appeared from an apron pocket like a magic trick.

"I'll be right back with the rest of it, sugar,"

Sandy promised as she walked over to the newest arrivals with her ticket pad.

They sat in silence as Never cut up her chicken and Wolfe sipped his iced tea. After Sandy reappeared with hot sauce, Wolfe dug into his meal.

Wolfe was a few forkfuls into his bowl when he heard, "Jerry was really pleased with the reprint's response."

"What?" Wolfe paused the forkful of shrimp and grits he was about to devour and turned to look at her with surprise.

"Marcy approached Henry about using her story in the local interest section."

He tried to rein in his panic. "They reprinted my story about the class offering?"

"Yes, right after it ran in the campus paper."

Wolfe stayed silent thinking about the timeline. The reprint would have been around a month to a month and a half ago.

"I'm surprised she didn't mention it to me," was all he could muster in response as he dropped the fork back in the bowl.

"She thought Folman was close enough to Redmond to make it of interest and Henry thought it would tie in nicely with the fall lore and legends festival he was covering."

"I wish you had mentioned it to me sooner."

"Why?"

Why indeed.

"I would have given Justine some time to take a new photo," he improvised.

"The photo was fine." She waved him off with her fork.

"We could've done a location shot."

"You at the witch's cottage?" she turned to grin at him.

He shrugged. "Folman readers would be more interested in that."

That seemed to satisfy her because she went back to stabbing at her salad before she changed the subject.

"Have they accepted your proposal?"

"I got a letter today, but I haven't opened it."

She turned to study him again.

"Why not?"

"It's been a good morning and now you're here." He reached out to squeeze her hand. "I didn't want to spoil the day."

"You think there's a chance they'll say no." She summed up as she stabbed another clump of lettuce through the prongs of her fork.

"There's always a chance, but the campus

newspaper and several of the faculty and donors think it is a good way to give back to the local community."

"I can run another local piece on it if it is accepted."

He gave her what he hoped was an encouraging smile. He had lost all interest in his shrimp and grits. How had he missed the reprinted article? He read the local papers and several others. He looked up to see her studying him again.

"I will need local support and access to different properties around town."

"We could mention that, give people a number to call."

"I'll let you know after I open it," he agreed with a punch of a smile that didn't linger long.

A buzz from his phone interrupted them.

"Who's that?"

"Rob, letting me know he can change the locks on my office this afternoon," was out of his mouth before he realized what he was admitting.

"Something wrong?"

"Just some disappointed cheaters I would guess."

"Someone broke in?"

"Nothing was taken, but they made a mess searching."

"You think they were looking for answers to your class materials?"

"Likely, I don't keep much of value in there."

"The semester has barely even started."

If he met her eyes, she would know he was hiding something. All Wolfe could manage was a shrug as he made a show of putting his phone away.

"Someone was thinking ahead."

Never's phone buzzed and she lifted it off the table to check it.

"I guess I should get back too."

Whoever sent her the message, he owed them. Wolfe watched her shove a final forkful of lettuce in her mouth before getting up to carry her foam plate to the trash. He wanted to breathe a sigh of relief, but he couldn't chance it. Never would pull the truth from him in a heartbeat. It was hard not blurting out all the problems plaguing him in the last few weeks as he walked her to the door. He had to keep it to himself. This could be too dangerous to tempt her into snooping.

Wolfe pulled her into his arms for a quick hug outside the cafe. For another fleeting moment he wished they could go back home and spend the rest of the afternoon in bed. They hadn't spent a full weekend together in almost a month. He called every night after work, but it wasn't the same as having Never in his arms or drinking coffee with her on the back porch before work.

He was glad she didn't seem cross with his long absences. She was busy at work too. When she wasn't skulking outside Mayor Ball's office looking for signs of corruption, Never was tracking Archibald Gordon. If he were the jealous type he would be irritated by her fascination with Archie, but Wolfe found the whole situation humorous. The idea of her chasing a disabled man around town several nights a week because she was convinced he was hiding something news-worthy gave Wolfe a chuckle. He could picture Archie Gordon in a three legged race before he could see him as a mover and a shaker in Folman underground activities. But he couldn't begrudge Never's instincts. She was a force to be reckoned with when she was chasing down a story. If she thought Archie Gordon had a secret life, who was he to doubt it.

Wolfe pulled her closer as they rounded the side of the building out of view of the windows and gave her a kiss he hoped would make time in her schedule for him in the coming weeks. She smiled up at him as they split; her walking to the parking lot behind the restaurant and him turning in the opposite direction to walk back toward his office in Guthrie Hall.

CHAPTER 33

Folman Tennessee, Present

It seemed Never was forever pouring liquid. Making coffee, pouring coffee, refilling coffee until the machine beeped a final warning and the light flickered out. Her work was constantly interrupted. She hadn't written a good page since the night Wolfe died. Never continued sitting at her empty desk, gazing into the nothingness. Her eyes would shift with the screensaver's movement from time to time, but it was involuntary. It couldn't compete with the thoughts clouding her brain.

She lumbered back and forth to the coffeepot hoping it would fill the void, but not knowing how deep that void goes or if it was even possible. All she had now was the name CHASETE and nagging suspicion all of this was connected to the break-ins around town.

There wasn't any way to prove a connection. Sergeant Henderson didn't trust her enough to entertain the idea she could be right and Wolfe's family in Florida wanted to move on after Wolfe's house sold.

The house, the only avenue of investigation left, was in the hands of new owners.

If Wolfe had proposed that night, she would have expected to move in full time. His house key would have moved onto her main key ring instead of being turned over to the sheriff's department. All her trial-sized bottles would have been replaced with permanent full size shampoos and lotions. Never would have been expected to pick out dish sets and have a say in the renovation project he had planned for the spring. After Wolfe's death, the house was off-limits to her.

She was angry when he shut her out and flabbergasted when the coroner released a statement that the cause of Wolfe's death was drowning, but did not rule it a suicide. So many questions about the last few months of Wolfe's life made her irritated with him.

CHASETE was the crown in his deception. How did he hide his obsession from her? What changed in August? She had the email from the Egret Society. It painted a rosy picture of his life in Folman and his work at Redmond College. It didn't offer any clues into Wolfe's state of mind.

Nothing was adding up. If she were working on a fall foliage puzzle, she would only have contradictory patches of red. Justine had to be wrong when she let it slip that she caught him buying an engagement ring. Why would she be so certain? Never needed to figure it out. Caffeine was slowly replacing her blood cells at this point. A proactive way to cope with things would be a better answer, but she couldn't seem to find one of those.

The papers from his office at the college were a

dead end. Neither Alvin Lucas nor the strange gold mine story led her to anything useful in establishing a trail, and she didn't see any reason to put a trip to Peru on her charge account. The only link she hadn't explored was a set of notes in his planner that mentioned the treasure hunting site he was active in.

Never opened the tab to the website and clicked *new account* to set up her information. It was a long shot. She could charge it to the paper if it didn't pan out. Her brain kept trying to reassure her as she advanced from screen to screen. If she couldn't figure out Wolfe's passwords for the group, maybe she could find him on the message boards. She had copied down a log of every time he visited the site in the last six months. It should be easy for her to find a pattern between his username and the entries in his planner.

An hour after she started, Never thought she had the hang of how the site's message boards worked. She took her time perusing clues and looking through responses for the dates she compiled from Wolfe's notes. She was almost certain that Wolfe was "Quatermain" on the site. It was a reference to a character in one of his favorite books. Never was excited to see that his messages on the board had the same style as some of the texts she still had on her phone. Everything made sense until she came to the last three dates.

"He went to Paris?"

It had to be while I was working on the mayor's mistress story.

"Why wouldn't he tell me?"

Maybe he did tell her. She was so entrenched in getting Jerry the first shimmer of proof that Mayor Ball had a mistress and was using city funds to hide his dalliances that she hardly slept in her apartment or ate meals anywhere other than her car. Citizens of Folman were up in arms about the $60,000 missing from the city's restoration funding, and no one could say how or why it disappeared. The fact that many hours of stakeouts had yielded nothing but an unconfirmed gossip getting fired at city hall still irritated Never.

The story had been shelved. It reminded her of her similar frustration with following Archie Gordon. It had been weeks and she was still striking out. Whoever said men weren't complicated never had to put in the leg work to catch them when they lied.

According to the message board, Wolfe was a superstar when it came to the treasure hunting game. He found every treasure he went after except one. He didn't get credit for solving the clue listed for Paris. That was odd. Why would he go all the way to Paris and come home without his prize? The message had been edited after the date in his planner. Never hadn't noticed that type of change on any of the other clues. She pulled up the chat history and looked through the exchanges.

"He found a wooden box?" bounced off the walls in her office nook as she looked up from her reading.

Realization hit her. That had to be the connection to the break-ins. But where was this box? It wasn't in the house or at the college or whoever was looking for it would have found it by now. He didn't give it to her. Where would he hide it? Where would Wolfe think it would be protected? He had a locker at the gym. Never had found a spare key in his office boxes. Would he have hidden the box there for her to collect later? It all seemed a bit like a movie plot. By this weekend, she would be driving to the next town over, under the cover of darkness, to check lockers at the closest train station. He didn't exactly leave her a map. What other choices did she have?

"You crazy fool," she scolded. "What have you done?"

She was flipping through pages trying to locate another entry when her text alert went off.

911 called to Our Mother Mary's Holy Catholic Church on Spring Street, possible break-in with injuries.

Wasn't that where Justine was headed after work? Never grabbed her purse and shoved her feet into worn sneakers as she struggled out the door.

"Oh, look at you go." Her neighbor's voice caught her off guard as she tried to turn her key in the lock. "I bet there is going to be some breaking news in the *Folman Gazette* tomorrow!"

"Mrs...,"

"Cora, dear, Cora."

"Cora, I really have to go."

"Of course dear." She waved her off. "We can chat all about it when you get back."

"Can't wait," Never muttered under her breath as she ran.

She swerved around every dawdling car and ran every stoplight without oncoming traffic, but the ambulance was already being loaded as she screeched into a spot in the back lot of the church. Justine's car was two spaces over. It was empty. Never got out her phone as she slammed her door. She hit the call icon under Justine's contact before she took off toward the entrance. Never could hear the phone ringtone as she made it to the line of first responders.

"Sorry, Miss Martinez, the building hasn't been cleared yet," a deputy told her as she approached.

"Justine," was garbled, but she managed to get it out between pants for air. "I need to see Justine."

"I think this belongs to one of the victims," called another deputy with a fresh haircut and shiny black shoes as he came down the steps carrying a still ringing cellphone. "It must have been knocked behind the sofa when she was attacked."

"That's Justine's," Never growled as she crowded the man in front of her. "Where is she?"

"Do you really think your newspaper's lawyers can keep you out of any trouble you get into?" a recognizable voice asked from behind her.

Never didn't care how undiplomatic she looked as she rounded on him. "Sergeant Henderson, I have every right to know where my friend is."

"How do you know she's here?"

"That's her car." Never jabbed a finger behind them. "And I just helped your new recruit find her phone."

"You're just chasing radio calls."

"I don't have to chase calls, but I'm proud to say I still made it here before you."

"You probably even saved a few kittens from trees while you were at it."

"Where is Justine?"

"How do you know her?"

"I work with her at the newspaper and we have been friends for the last three years."

"Where does she live?"

"259 Arnes Street," Never bit out. "Where is she?"

"Why would you think she was here?"

"She is getting married here at Christmas. She said something about coming by after work to talk to someone about a change she wanted to make in the service."

The sergeant was not happy about the situation, but Never could tell she made headway when he came closer and admitted, "Miss Martinez, your friend and the priest she went to see were attacked during an attempted robbery."

"Robbery of what?"

The shield when right back up between them.

"I am not able to comment at this time."

"You still haven't told me where she is," Never ground out.

"She is still being stabilized," he admitted in hushed tones. "There is a possibility of a serious back injury."

"Where is she?"

"You'll have to wait until they bring her out."

Never tried to rearrange her thoughts as she paced up and down the lines of the parking lot. Her thoughts kept returning to the box Wolfe wasn't supposed to find. The box she had the barest scraps of information about. Maybe she should try weaseling more out of the sergeant?

"There are an awful lot of attempted burglaries in Robertson County lately."

"Three or four attempted burglaries don't amount to a crime spree."

They were up to three or four attempted burglaries. That was interesting. Why were they so bad at stealing?

"Especially if nothing is taken."

"Are you suggesting that there is a set of incompetent serial burglars that have set their sights on us?"

"I saw what was done to Wolfe's house, and I know what happened at my apartment."

"Those were both widely different cases."

"Was anything taken here Sergeant?"

"I can't confirm anything yet, but this…"

"Is a different case," Never mocked as she watched him.

"We all can't jump to conclusions and start making wild accusations like you do Miss Martinez."

"When are you going to start using reason Sergeant?"

"When you produce evidence that is reasonable."

"How many more people have to get hurt for you to see there's a connection?"

He blew out a breath and regarded her as one would an angry child. "I'm sorry your friend was hurt, but random crime happens, even here."

Never was planning the next crime when her phone sounded in her palm.

"Excuse me, while I explain your ineptitude," she informed him in a tone that would make a man grateful for his jacket as she walked away.

"Hi Rory." Never braced for the question she knew she didn't want to answer.

"Hey Nev, are you with Justine? Her phone is going to voicemail."

"Justine went to the church after work. It's

possible she turned the ringer off to talk to someone about changes."

"Sure, sure, that's probably it." He didn't sound convinced.

"Are you driving home?"

"No, I was calling to tell her I was home."

"I'll head for the church to see if I can speed things along, maybe you should meet us there?"

His soft chuckle was followed by, "In case you need someone to run interference?"

"It couldn't hurt."

"See you in a few," was all she heard before he clicked off.

Never had no doubts that the sports-crazed, bear hugging, giant her best friend was about to marry would be devastated when he found out the whole truth, but she could not bring herself to tell him before he got behind the wheel of a car. His own safety was at stake. She would never forgive herself if Justine lost her happy ending because she failed to protect them from whatever Wolfe had unleashed. Never just wished she felt better about withholding the truth from him.

"You didn't tell him." The sergeant's voice was soft, but it cut through her thoughts before she could collect them.

"According to you I don't know anything yet."

"That's never stopped you before."

"Contrary to what you think about me Sergeant, I don't purposefully put people's lives in danger to help me win an argument."

"Instead you're bringing the argument to me?"

"You won't keep him away for long," Never admitted as she walked closer to watch a group of first responders exiting the building. "I'm just getting him here before he finds out."

"So I'll be distracted."

"So he won't be attempting the things I did to get here faster."

"You like him," Henderson bated. "Are you hoping to console him after this is over?"

"Your inability to use your brain for good is astounding."

"But it doesn't make me wrong."

"It doesn't make you right either."

Sergeant Henderson was called away by someone exiting the building and Never was left to pace while she waited for more answers. Most of the people outside were milling around like she was. The ambulance was still idling by the ramp to the back stairs, but no one was coming out of the building with medical gear. What was the hold-up?

Never was preparing herself for the next round of sparring with the sergeant when the sound of running feet behind her made her turn. Rory in his tan suit and blue soccer tie was speeding toward her in record time for a man wearing loafers. He stumbled at the curb, but kept coming. The police must have blocked off the entrance to the church after her arrival. Never couldn't see his truck. She had no doubt that he parked as close as he could and took off on foot.

Never walked over to meet him as he came charging into the parking lot.

"Nev!" he rasped like a man drowning. "What happened?"

"Rory, do you need some water?"

"No, tell me what happened. Where is Justine?"

"I can't get much out of the sergeant, but there was a burglary attempt. Justine was injured, and they are still prepping her for a trip to the hospital."

"Where is she?"

"She's still inside. They were loading someone else into an ambulance when I got here."

"Do you know how bad it is?"

"The most he would tell me was possible back injuries," Never admitted as she watched him agonize. "But he's not my biggest fan."

"He's the same guy that accused you of killing Wolfe?"

"Yes, and apparently he's never wrong."

"I'll see what I can find out," he said as he gave her a quick side hug and charged into the milling officers like a man confident he would make it to his target untouched.

Never continued to watch the scene and Rory's conversation with Sergeant Henderson as she paced. They should both be with Justine right now. Justine should be on the way to the hospital. What was taking so long? Rory's shoulders were slumped, but he looked relieved when he turned and headed back in Never's direction.

"She's awake, but they said she refuses to leave without her cat."

"Houdini's in there too?"

Never almost laughed. That was what the delay was about. It made sense Houdini was somewhere in the church. Justine had a habit of taking him almost everywhere with her. She would never leave him behind. Never could visualize a group of frazzled first responders calling "here kitty kitty" as they walked hallways and searched under cushions.

"I should have gone with her to look at dogs last week."

"You don't know if that would have done any good."

"I told her she needed protection while I was away for work."

"You're not responsible for what happened."

"It's my church, our wedding plans...I should have been there."

272

"Rory it would rip her apart if something happened to you," Never assured him as she reached out to catch his arm and pull his eyes down to meet her firm russet gaze. "Be grateful you don't have to put her through that kind of pain."

"I'm sorry Nev, I..."

Rory didn't make it to the end of the sentence. Both their heads shot up and zeroed in on the sound of something coming down the hall near the back door of the church. They crowded as close as they could to the back of the ambulance and waited.

Never couldn't make out any scratches or bruises as they wheeled Justine closer. Her hair was tangled and pulled from its usual ponytail. One of her new hot pink acrylic nails was damaged. She had her purse, but had somehow lost her phone. She was clutching Houdini to her chest.

"I'm sorry ma'am, but the kitten can't come to the hospital with you."

"He saved our lives!" Justine wasn't giving in easy.

"If he isn't a service animal, he can't go," the EMT insisted as he positioned her bed to be lifted up into the bay.

"I'm not going without him."

"Justine, honey, you need to go to the hospital," Never heard Rory plead with her.

"He's just as traumatized as I am. He needs to

know I'm here for him."

"He'll be fine at home until you get back."

"The specialist is waiting for you," the EMT interjected again.

Rory was reaching down to give Justine a kiss on the cheek when she thrust the kitten up at him with pleading eyes. He was forced back from her bed with an unhappy feline wiggling in his palms. Justine looked tired and unhappy, but satisfied that Houdini was taken care of. The little creature looked as confused as Rory was by the latest course of events.

"I'll take my godson." Never reached out her arms to scoop Houdini out of his hands. "Rory, we'll be fine while you're at the hospital with Justine."

Never didn't even wince when the kitten climbed up her shirt and stretched his claws into the hair swinging loose around her neck.

"We'll be right behind you," she whispered to Justine as she reached down to pat her shoulder.

Never stepped back and watched the emergency workers load her into the ambulance with Rory on their heels. Never didn't notice the shadow over her shoulder until Houdini let out a spitting sound beneath her hair. As she turned to see what he was upset by, Never noticed Sergeant Henderson standing behind her.

"So you're godmother to Miss Aldridge's hero kitten," he asked as he studied the tail switching in and out of her curls.

"Yes, Houdini came from one of my neighbors."

"That explains his temperament."

Never turned to watch him. "What happened in there?"

"It was a botched robbery attempt, and the kitten caused a diversion that gave Father Andrews enough time to call for help."

"That's it?"

"That's it."

"What were they going to take?"

"I can't comment on that."

"I'll know in a few minutes. Why not give me your opinion on it?"

"My opinion is that you are trying to sell more newspapers with your conspiracy theories."

"Can I quote you on that?" Never yelled as he walked away.

A startled Houdini repositioned himself on her shoulder to meow his displeasure.

"I guess the sergeant isn't a fan of hero kitten stories either," Never told her godson as she reached up to rub his silky coat. "But I'm sure you deserve lots of new toys for your efforts."

Never took Houdini to their favorite burger place and ordered him a plain burger patty and vanilla ice cream for his heroic efforts before they cruised over to the pet store for a fresh new package of catnip mice. It would take a while for Justine to get to a room at the hospital and Rory needed some time alone with her. Never walked over to the park with Houdini on her shoulder. They could both use some sun and watch the children play. They weren't on the pathway long before the shadow of Archie Gordon caught her attention.

Archie was circling the playground as he had for months, looking at equipment children weren't playing with, pushing an empty swing from time to time. She had followed him for weeks and never saw a single thing that would explain it. Was he a drug dealer? She couldn't prove it. Was he into children sexually? She didn't see any proof of that either, but what was he doing every night after work? Why would a single, workaholic male visit the city playground and haunt the streets downtown at night?

"Archie, I need to ask you something," Never blurted out as she walked closer.

Archie looked up from the seesaw he was studying and took a step back.

"What are you doing here every night?"

He straightened to his full height. "I didn't know you were keeping tabs on me Miss Martinez."

"I have watched you for weeks and I can't figure out what you're doing."

"But you're sure that I'm doing something?"

"That's about the size of it."

"Wouldn't it be dangerous for you to ask me while you're alone?"

"I'm not alone." She pointed to the kitten on her shoulder. "And I haven't seen you do anything that makes you seem like a threat."

"I guess I should be thankful for that."

"But what are you doing?"

He motioned to a bench away from the pathway. "Maybe we should have a seat."

Never followed his uneven strides and sat down facing him. She eased Houdini to the ground so he could explore while they talked.

"I assume you've already researched my backstory?"

"I have."

"Then you know that I have had this disability since birth. My father gave me my first and only job out of high school because he knew finding a place in the local job market would be difficult."

"You've worked for the package company since you were eighteen?"

"Sixteen, I answered phones on the weekend."

"How has that led you to walk the park and downtown every night?"

"When I was young, there were a lot of things I couldn't do with the other kids. There were parties I stopped being invited to."

"That's terrible."

"The thing that bothered me that most was not even being able to go to the park and play with the other kids. I couldn't run. I accepted that, but I always thought with modifications I could play on most of the other equipment without diminishing the experience for the other kids."

"So, you spend your nights out here trying to come up with recommendations for ways the city can improve the playground?"

"Not exactly." He seemed to be weighing the idea of telling her the whole truth.

"Go ahead," she encouraged. "What is going on exactly?"

"I want to found a company that designs playground equipment and gym equipment for all physical abilities. I take these walks to work on my ideas and talk to possible investors."

"That's wonderful! But why can't you ask your father for help?"

"My father would be devastated if I told him that I don't want to run the family business. What if he fired me over it? I wouldn't have any income to secure a loan for the prototypes I want to build."

"You already have plans?"

"Yes, several."

"But if your father found out about your side venture you could lose everything."

"That is the scope of it."

"There has to be a solution."

"Have you got a bag of money you would like to invest?"

"It would be yours if I did."

"That's the problem with Folman." Archie shook his head. "I can't ask the few people with money because it will get back to my dad."

"Don't give up yet." Never reached out and squeezed his hand. "Give me some time to do some research and maybe we can form a plan."

"You really think you can help without involving the newspaper?"

"I can't promise anything, but I will protect your secret until I can find a way to help."

"I guess that's the best bargain I can hope for." Archie reached out to shake her hand before he pushed himself off the bench. "I'll look forward to our next talk."

Never nodded and smiled. She was right about Archie Gordon being up to something, but she had been completely wrong about what it was. The idea of a dissatisfied rich kid wanting to strike out on his own without Dad's approval or help was the last thing she would have suspected from him. Archie would be helping thousands of children if his designs were as inventive as Never suspected they were. And she intended to keep his secret until she could find a way to help.

So many secrets swirled around her. Was Archie right? Was it impossible to make a connection with others without sharing a secret with them? Never was beginning to wonder if it was possible to be human without having one.

CHAPTER 34

Folman Tennessee, 29 Days Earlier

Wolfe enjoyed the early morning sun through his kitchen windows as he sipped coffee and gathered his thoughts. Autumn was lending its paintbrush to the woods around his home. He held the open letter from the dean in his hand, rereading it for a fourth time. The "powers that be" at Redmond College had accepted his summer class offering proposal. He would be planning and setting up appointments with local sites for next summer. Never would get her article.

As much as he hated the *Folman Gazette* reprinting the article from the college newspaper, he was happy to have Never's help drumming up support for his project. Much of his time in the spring would be spent asking Robertson County residents to suggest and give him access to local areas of interest. He would need volunteers and supply donations. He had lists and plans to make for the college's approval.

Things were looking up for the first time in

weeks. Never came by late last night to help him celebrate the news that his summer class had been accepted, and after an early shower this morning she was already on her way to work to pitch the idea to her boss. His office break-in concluded with a police report and new security measures for the hallways and outside of Guthrie Hall where his classrooms and office reside. There were still no new notes.

Wolfe didn't want to ruin his morning with those thoughts. There were only going to be a few more weeks like this in Folman. He didn't want to sit inside worrying about notes and statues. He wanted to gather his paper and leaf through it on the back porch before heading to Redmond. He left the front door unlocked as he walked down the steps to the drive. His loafers crunched leaves and tiny branches carried by the wind. It was a crisp, beautiful day that even the cottage witch would have trouble finding fault with.

He had to pay his yard service more than his neighbors to maintain his long driveway and front yard, but he loved the walk to the mailbox on the main road. It did wonders to organize his thoughts and clear his head at the start of his day. There was nothing like this in the small subdivision he grew up in on the west side of Atlanta.

When Wolfe first accepted the position at Redmond College and moved into faculty housing near campus, the hushed nature of his surroundings made him question his latest change. He switched on radios and added social events to his calendar that didn't interest him in the slightest just to counter the silence.

Now, in his new place, he loved to sit on the porch or walk the driveway and listen.

Chasing Wolfe

"Next thing you know you'll be reading Whitman."

The thought made him let out a chuckle followed by a snort. Being in his twenties in Atlanta was fun. He had all the nightlife and baseball games he could ever hope to choose from. He would be in a very different place if he had grown up in Folman. Maybe he would have followed his family to Florida for a life of sunshine and tiki-themed bars.

But fate landed him at Redmond College. He was offered positions in Chicago and North Dakota as well as an internship in Italy. Redmond College was the only one offering a full-time professor position.

The first night when he unlocked and looked around the worn faculty housing, Wolfe thought he would be there for a year, tops. He saw it as a launching pad for his career. Redmond was the first step in the staircase he intended to build of his professional life. There would be bigger names courting him, book deals, and speaking tours. He was sure of it.

For the first semester, his companion was a small radio that picked up news from Nashville when he angled it just right on top of a stack of unpacked boxes. It was hard to hold back his resentment when he began receiving emails from his classmates about the cities they moved to and the adventures they were having. Even his Mom's postcards of sunny Florida beaches turned his expression sour.

Now, he was content. He had a community of his own. He had support at the college, a beautiful house, and teammates from his cycleball league. And he had Never.

Wolfe stooped to retrieve his paper from the concrete. When he straightened up he noticed the lip of his mailbox was open. He was sure he closed it last night before he pulled up the drive. Maybe one of the neighbors left him a stray piece of mail? It happened from time to time. He reached in from the side and swiped the piece of paper out. It didn't feel very substantial beneath his fingers. Probably another circular, he thought as he held it up.

It wasn't junk mail. It wasn't mail at all. He stood looking at a photo of his house. Never's car was parked by the porch and she was coming down the stairs. Wolfe used both hands to flip it over.

You can't protect everyone.

Everything in his arms was forgotten as he turned and took off in a run toward the house. Whoever was after him hadn't stopped. His plans and coffee forgotten, Wolfe banged through the front door. He registered the thump of it hitting the wall as he sped past. He needed to get out as fast as he could. There wasn't time to finish getting ready for the office. He shoved all his work clothes into a bag with the hangers still in place. Grabbing socks and underwear, he plopped them on top of the rest without ceremony. Packing them down with one hand, he worked the zipper with the other. The loafers under his desk at work would have to do. He didn't take the time to change. He had toiletries stashed in his locker at the gym. Rob had added a new deadbolt to his office door after the break-in. Wolfe had gone to the local hardware store to purchase extra window locks and a safety bar for the door when he was working late. New locks and the added security presence at the college would make it a safe place to sleep.

It was all connected to Marcy's trip to the *Folman Gazette*. He could thank her for this. Everything went off the rails after she took that damn picture. He had hoped there was a way to ensure Never wasn't in danger of getting dragged into this. Coming by last night, as much as he had wanted it, put her in the sights of his stalker. It was hard to accept he wasn't even safe in his house, but there wasn't any use to take chances. Wolfe lurched back through the front door. He wasn't looking forward to spending the night on his office couch.

Never would let him stay with her, but he would have to explain why. He couldn't compromise her safety by leading a stalker to her door. Then it hit him. The house! Never, she practically lived with him. She had her own key, came and went at will. She wouldn't be scared away if he didn't level with her. Even if he did, Never would still be a target.

How could he protect her?

"I have to stop her from coming back here," he decided as he cranked the Jeep and headed back down his long driveway.

CHAPTER 35

Folman Tennessee, Present

Never hit snooze on her normal morning alarm and fell into bed fully clothed. The next sound she was aware of was a heavy pounding from the hallway. Never didn't know where she was, whose breathe smelled vile, or why there were sounds of construction in her building all of the sudden, but she covered her head and rolled to the far side of the bed to ignore it. The pounding continued in a rhythmic pattern as it grew louder. The noise outside was soon accompanied by the jingle of her ringtone on the nightstand. Hadn't anyone ever heard of a day off? Never opened a drawer and pushed her phone off into the void before closing it and reapplying the pillow over her face. Maybe she should have a "Do Not Disturb" mat printed up to put outside the front door for days like today. She needed one to deal with Cora anyway.

Never tried to sleep, but it was just no use. She could still hear her phone in the drawer and the banging outside was echoing. How was it echoing? Was it bouncing around inside her skull? She threw the pillow off and pulled her t-shirt back down to her waist. She wanted to scream at someone as her phone launched into a jingle again. Never sat up and dug in her drawer to do just that when she realized it was Justine's name that appeared on the screen for the eighth time in the past half hour. Never said a few curse words she wished she could have shouted at a telemarketer and stumbled down the hall in her socked feet to open the front door.

It took her a minute to convince her brain how to work the lock. When she finally got the right combination of turns, she flung it open with a bang against the wall.

Justine still had her cane held out, ready for an encore.

"Justine, what are you doing here?"

"I thought I would stop by and bring you lunch." She held up a bag of takeout from one of their favorite sandwich shops and Houdini's head popped out of the bag over her shoulder to sniff the air.

Her best friend was still leaning heavily on her new cane when she walked, but she seemed in high spirits. Her hair was brushed back into her normal ponytail and her cheeks were rosy. Rory's pampering must be doing her worlds of good. Never couldn't believe he would let her out of his sight long enough to make a solo trip across town while she was still recovering.

"How did you talk Rory into this?" she eyed her with suspicion.

"He had a special meeting he couldn't miss, and I didn't have time to mention my plans."

Never just shook her head and ushered her into the kitchen. Justine had been out of the hospital for three days and was already ignoring doctor's orders for bed rest. Rory was going to have a hurricane on his hands when she was back to full strength. There would be tux fittings, house showings, new pets, and children running everywhere to distract them both. How would he handle further distraction when he couldn't even keep Justine in bed with an injury?

Never helped Justine ease herself into one of the chairs in the kitchen and rummaged through the cabinets to find tea bags to go with their takeout from Mambo's.

"You really shouldn't be pushing yourself like this."

"The doctor said nothing was broken."

"There's a wide area between broken and fine."

"Says the woman who won't even swallow a pain pill," Justine rebutted.

"I really don't like the idea of you driving or climbing stairs alone."

"I wasn't alone." She motioned to Houdini disappearing around the corner and into the living room.

"Yes, I see you have your fierce warrior kitten with you."

"You sound just like Rory."

"He is probably blaming himself for being away and not going with you."

"He feels guilty," Justine agreed. "But I hope he will get over it."

A loud crash followed by a *thunk, thunk, swoosh* grabbed both their attentions before Never could respond. They both stopped and turned in the direction of the hallway.

"What was that?"

"I don't know."

"Help me up?" Justine asked as she tried to push herself out of the chair.

"It's probably just your warrior cat destroying my apartment."

"It sounded pretty loud for Houdini."

The *thunk, thunk, swooshing* sounds continued as they peered around the corner.

Houdini was stalking something in the hallway. He hid behind one bag and reached out a paw then he rounded another and jumped in the air like something had stung him. *Was there a mouse?* Neither of them could see anything. All they could hear was the strange pattern of sounds from before.

"Why don't you take a seat on the sofa while I figure out what he is going on about?"

Never didn't give Justine much time to think about it. She just headed for the living room. Helping her friend lower herself to the cushion, Never turned to inspect the hallway.

Houdini had tousled several bags and knocked over a pottery crock from Wolfe's house. The side was chipped and Never couldn't see the lid anywhere. Houdini bounded up beside her chasing after his prize. Never could tell he had found something among the piles that he enjoyed very much, but what on earth was it? He slapped it again and it zipped by her before she could get a good look. All she could make out was the kitten's swishing tail as he scampered off behind it. Never wished he would slow down long enough for her to see it. After a few seconds of quiet, he came walking up to her issuing a mournful sound and sat down at her feet.

"Did you get tired of it already?"

He cocked his head to the side as if she said something that didn't compute and made his sad sound again.

"Unless you can show me what you want, I can't help."

She continued to look around for the crock lid and the missing piece. Houdini ambled off and a new scraping sound emerged behind Never. *Was the thing he was chasing alive?* Never walked toward her bedroom and found the kitten hunched behind one of the bags lining the hallway. He was determined in his stance as he continued clawing to get at something underneath. When she squatted down, the kitten looked up at her and gave another mournful meow before going back to his fight with the unprotected bag.

"Okay, wait a minute and I will pick it up."

She grabbed the side of the bag and angled her body as far away as possible. If a mouse or any other living creature came screeching out onto the floor, Never wanted plenty of room to flee before it scampered up her leg. Her mind projected mice, rats, snakes, and large bugs as her newest acquaintance, but was caught off-guard when a little red box with a diamond fabric pattern and small silver beads emerged.

Houdini gave out a yowl of protest when she picked up the box and didn't return it to him.

"This is curious," Never called out as she carried it to the living room.

"What did he find?"

"It's a box."

She sat down on the sofa and placed it in the palm of her hand so Justine could see it too.

"This was in the stuff Carrie gave you back from Wolfe's house?"

Never nodded. "I cleaned the boxes and bags out of the rental car."

"Something like this and you weren't even curious?"

"I started with the boxes. I hadn't gotten to the stuff in the hallway."

"Houdini sure seems to like it."

"If it's like the rest of the junk I inherited from Wolfe, Houdini might get to keep it."

"Let's see what's inside."

Never pulled the decorative cover off the top and looked inside. There was another box. This one was light blue. "I guess he picked up a set of nesting boxes somewhere."

"Keep going," Justine urged as she angled closer.

Never opened the second box to reveal a black velvet jewelry box. She felt a sinking feeling make its way to her gut. Was this the box he found in Paris? It didn't look wooden to her. Maybe he moved it to a new box to hide it? If it was the treasure everyone seemed to be after, she might just hand it back to Houdini and keep high hopes that it would disappear.

It was such a small box. Was this what people were searching for at Wolfe's house? If it was linked to Wolfe's death, she didn't want it anywhere near her.

Never could feel Justine shift beside her. "You don't have to open it."

"I won't stop wondering until I do."

Justine grabbed her hand and squeezed. *Should I hope that it's empty?* Never held her breath as she flipped it open. Justine gasped beside her. The box wasn't empty. It was a large round diamond circled by smaller diamonds and ringed on the outside edge with small rubies. It was unlike anything she had ever seen before. It reminded her of a rose. The egg-shaped diamonds on the sides flanked the main setting like leaves of a flower and the metal had a pink hue to it. It was beyond beautiful. It was perfect.

This couldn't be real. Why would Carrie send it home with her? It had to be a mistake. It should have been sold after Wolfe's death. Never let out the breath she was holding and closed her eyes. When she reopened them the ring was still there waiting for her to examine it.

"I thought all of Carmen's boxes were blue."

"Maybe he didn't buy it from there?"

"Where else would he go? I caught him with a Carmen's bag at the festival."

Never shrugged as she continued to study the gems.

"This has to be a fake."

"Why?"

"Because Carrie wouldn't give me this if it was at Wolfe's house."

"Maybe she thought it was yours since it's for a woman."

Never had her doubts but she stayed silent as she pulled the ring from its enclosure and noticed the small clear stones continuing around the band. It was beautiful. A fake or not, she couldn't take her eyes off it.

"Why would Wolfe have a fake ring made and

box it up like that?"

"Maybe he was planning a treasure hunt?"

"Never be serious."

"I am."

"You think that Wolfe had this made for a treasure hunting prize?"

"Why not?"

"Let me see it."

Never passed the ring to her friend and busied herself with the ring box. She couldn't find a name on the inside, just an artistic shape near the corner. It was strange. Most jewelry stores printed their name on the inside of every box, but this one was blank. The ring was stunning. It had to be a specialty design. Why would someone not include a brand name or a plug for their business?

"Never." She felt Justine grab her arm. "You should look at this."

"Why?"

"Just look at the inside of the band," Justine instructed as she forced the ring under her nose.

"Okay, okay..."

Never steadied the band between her fingers and focused. It was engraved! But it couldn't be. Why would Wolfe have a fake ring engraved?

"Flip it over silly."

Never did and the letters made less sense. They spelled out "Never Strickland" with a heart in the middle.

"It has my name on it."

"I guess that explains why Carrie sent it to you."

"That's the only thing it explains."

"He intended to marry you Nev."

"Then why didn't he?"

"I don't know." Justine reached over to hug her. "But a man doesn't order a ring like that if he is unsure."

Never kept the small velvet ring box in her lap and threw the bigger red one in the floor for the waiting Houdini.

"Let me help you back to the kitchen."

Their tea was still hot, but the takeout sandwiches they had abandoned were not. Never got plates from the cabinet and shifted them over for a spin in the microwave. The ring box felt bulky in her jean pocket so she took it out and set it on the table between them.

"You want to talk about it?"

What was there to say? Wolfe bought her a ring and hid it in his house. She couldn't ask him about it and she didn't know where he had it made. Everyone involved was keeping Wolfe's secret. Now she would be the one holding a ring he talked himself out of giving her.

"There's no jeweler's name in the box. Isn't that a bit odd for a custom piece like this?"

"Why does it matter?"

"I just wish I could find out when he had it made. Then I would know how to feel about it."

"You think that he was saving it?"

"I don't know what to think or where to start."

"Maybe it's tiny."

"I think I have a magnifying glass around here somewhere," she muttered as she searched through a drawer.

"Most jewelers print their name in the dome. Why don't we flip it upside down and take a look?"

Never moved the magnifying glass over the small space as Justine held the box in place. There was no name. Just clean white paper taped to the dome.

"It doesn't look like fabric."

"Is it a name?"

"No, I think paper has been taped over it."

"Tape, why would anyone do that?"

"I don't know, but I am going to need tweezers to

get it free."

Never rushed back down the hallway dodging Houdini's playful attacks as a she went. She flipped the bathroom switch and pilfered through the medicine cabinet until she came up with a pair of tweezers. Clutching them like they would wiggle between her fingers and escape if she didn't, Never raced back to the kitchen.

Justine wiped her hands and held up the box for Never to poke at with the narrow metal clamps.

"Man this is worse than trying to get a splinter."

They both tried angle-after-angle until Never felt a corner begin to give. The small folded piece of paper came out and "Gupmann's Jewelers" in flowing silver type came into view.

"Was he worried you would know he didn't buy it in Folman?"

"I don't know."

"Why did I see him with a blue bag from Carmen's?"

Never didn't have an answer for Wolfe's strange behavior. There weren't many things that were adding up. This ring shouldn't exist, and Never had no idea why there was paper taped over the jeweler's logo. She put the paper down and got out a pad of notes from her bag. She added Gupmann's Jewelers to her list of questions to look into.

"I think there's writing on it."

Justine's soft voice directed her back to the table.

"Where?"

"On the paper you pulled out."

Justine picked up the tweezers and removed the remaining piece of tape from the edge of the small strip of paper. It took some effort to unfurl it without ripping it.

"Some look at love like a noose, others seek it to put down roots."

It was in Wolfe's handwriting, the same determined perfection as in his planner. But why would he include it? It didn't belong to any writer she was familiar with. It wasn't exactly romantic either.

"Why would he cover up the jeweler's name with that odd note?"

"Why would he buy a ring like this for me if he was going to dump me?"

"None of this seems right."

"That's what I have been saying for weeks."

She had been dumped, then Wolfe died, her car was tampered with, her apartment was searched, Wolfe's house was trashed, Justine was attacked, Never found a message about a mystery box on the treasure hunting sight Wolfe frequented, and now there was an engagement ring. Nothing on that list made any sense, but her gut said they were connected in some way. How was she going to link them based on limited planner entries and cryptic love notes?

CHAPTER 36

Folman Tennessee, 17 Days Earlier

Wolfe wanted to talk to Justine. Winter break at Redmond College was in two weeks. If he could keep Never away from his house that long he could buy himself time to disappear from the person trailing him. He needed Justine's help if he was going to accomplish that without arousing suspicion. As her best friend, Justine would be the perfect foil to keep Never distracted. He just had to make it look like he bumped into her as a chance encounter. If she worked somewhere other than the newspaper, he could stake out her favorite coffee or lunch spots. Since Justine and Never were also close co-workers, Wolfe needed to steer clear of their usual routine. He needed to find an unusual event that would give him access when Never was busy elsewhere. The trouble was that he wasn't staying in Folman, and he hadn't been to Folman in the last week unless he had a cycleball practice.

After his stalker threatened Never, Wolfe abandoned his home and settled for long chats with her at night from his office. Instead of his comfortable bed and full-sized bathroom, Wolfe had to adjust to sleeping on the uncomfortable couch in his office and using the restroom down the hall. He wasn't happy about the new arrangements, but it was the best he could come up with at the moment. He wasn't sure of his safety on his own property. He could install security equipment, but knew he wouldn't be able to sleep in the house under the current circumstances. On the bright side, his commute to work was the shortest of any of his colleagues. Grooming in the small restroom down the hall had its challenges, but the fall semester students who looked like they had just rolled out of bed weren't judging him.

Never mentioned a festival happening this afternoon in Folman when they talked last night. She couldn't go because she was watching for a break in another story. It sounded like the best chance he would get to see Justine alone. He was satisfied that if he created a rumor that he was hiding an engagement ring for Never at his house, Justine would help him keep her away while he was sleeping in his office. He needed to find Justine, persuade her of his intentions, and enlist her as his confidant. He had to convince Justine not to spoil the surprise. She was enough of a romantic that Wolfe knew she would help him if he played his part with gusto. He just needed to bump into her. It was his best chance at keeping Never's suspicions at bay. Wolfe was hoping Justine would give her friend enough hints that she would think she knew his secret.

Wolfe wasn't sure if he should involve the police again. Redmond only had a Forest Ranger who doubled as local law enforcement for the area. Larry kept the ranger's presence at the college to a minimum, but Wolfe would have no excuse or smokescreen to hide behind if the Robertson County Sheriff's Department were called to his home as well. Reporters would be monitoring police scanners, his neighbors would worry, and Wolfe didn't think there was enough evidence to do anything about it. If Never found out that way, he would have no excuse. He would have to come clean about the mess he had created.

To get through this, Wolfe had to play his part well. He ran by the barbershop near campus and had a frail, white-haired man in a red apron trim his hair as well as his beard. He had a bag from Carmen's Jewelry, who was participating in the holiday bazaar crowding downtown Folman this afternoon. The bag had contained a small brooch purchased weeks ago for his mother's birthday. Wolfe stumbled across the empty bag when he was cleaning up his office last week and thought it would improve his chances of securing Justine's help.

Everyone in town knew the light blue gift bags. They were a tradition at Carmen's. Since the early 1900s, Carmen's Jewelry had served as Folman's only boutique jewelry store. Everyone in town expected major life events to start with a little blue bag from Carmen's. In the locals' mindset, it was a tradition he couldn't afford to ignore if he wanted to launch his happily-ever-after on the right foot. Locals were permitted to go to other jewelers for birthdays or crushes, but if it was real love, the ring had to come from Carmen's.

Wolfe was whistling as he drove the winding road across the mountain. His plan was simple. He wanted to use the bag to give Justine the impression she caught him red-handed buying Never a ring. If she jumped to her own conclusion, he could look crestfallen and admit to the plans. She would be happy to have early notice of the event, and help him conceal it. He just needed to search out Justine and convince her he had a secret without making her suspicious for other reasons.

As he stepped out of the Jeep in the festival parking area, Wolfe took in a multitude of sights, sounds, and smells. The streets were crowded with holiday shoppers and tents. Country music was blaring from a radio station promotional van down the street, and Wolfe could smell funnel cakes and turkey legs cooking in vats of grease. Strands of lights twinkled on and off as he moved under the wide arches covering Main Street. Couples strolled hand in hand, stopping from time to time at random booths or to talk with friends. Children raced past with caramel apples and half-eaten bags of salt-water taffy. Main Street had an infusion of vitality that failed to make an appearance the rest of the year.

Observing it now made him think of Never and their determination to outdo each other at balloon darts the first year they dated. She ended up with a large bear and he gave her the smaller one he had won. They always had fun at these types of things when she had to cover it for the paper. It would be easy to smile and enjoy himself with the rest of the crowd if his task were not so important.

Wolfe had to get into tracking mode and find Justine before she found him unaware. Where would she be tonight? She had to be here taking photos and helping out at the newspaper booth. He had spent many date nights with Never, strolling the street during this festival or that festival, while she covered it for work. She was moving up in her career. She would be chasing after bigger fish tonight, but Justine would be here with her camera snapping photos for the social media page. She would be by the booth with popular children's games or the stage for the chili cook off. He just had to pretend he was trying to sneak by her.

As he ducked into an alley behind the booths lining the street to think of ways to make their chance meeting seem natural, Justine came bursting around the corner with a plate of nachos in her hands and ran right into him. The bag fell, the nachos slammed up against his chest and warm cheese splashed onto the front of Wolfe's green dress shirt. A startled Justine bounced back and hit the brick wall beside him.

"Wolfe!" whooshed out as she regained her balance.

"Is this how you share dinner?" he asked as he gestured to the fusion of meat and cheese oozing to the ground between them.

"Sorry about your shirt," she tried to console as she reached to swat at a thick clump of meat clinging to his belt buckle. "I was trying to take a quick break."

"Good thing I was going home anyway."

"Send me the dry cleaning bill."

"It will probably wash out," he said as he reached to pick up his bag.

"You've been to Carmen's?" she asked as she eyed the blue gift bag.

Wolfe tried his best to look pained, but he was

overjoyed she took the bait.

He put it behind his back and leaned in to speak in hushed tones, "Look...you weren't supposed to see this."

"See what?" she was teasing him now.

He tried to look even more irritated.

"Did you buy Never a surprise?"

Did he ever.

Wolfe shifted his feet and looked over his shoulder for anyone who might come to his rescue, but there was no one nearby he could distract her with.

"Please, don't tell her," he pretended to give in. "And keep her away from my house until I can set everything up. I'll need a month."

She studied him with serious eyes before replying in her sternest best friend voice, "You've got two weeks."

"Thank you, thank you so much Justine." The relief in his voice was as real as her giggles and the nasty smell wafting from the front of his shirt.

"Make it memorable or you'll answer to me," she instructed as she watched him squirm. "I will have more than hot cheese with me next time."

"I don't doubt it."

"Get out of here before someone else sees you."

She didn't have to tell him twice. Wolfe turned and headed for his Jeep. Several children made faces and pointed to the orange and brown splotched mess on his shirt, but Wolfe didn't notice. He was elated his plan had worked. He wanted to smile and dance his way back to the parking lot, but he had to restrain himself to a brisk walk. Justine's reaction was better than he could have hoped. Nacho cheese aside, he was pleased by the result. If he could keep Never away from his house, she would be safe. He could visualize her exasperation when she pressured the truth out of him, but an expensive set of earrings might convince her Justine was mistaken about his intentions after he was covered in nachos. Worst case scenario, he would buy her an actual engagement ring in two weeks.

Wolfe wasn't sure if his skin itched from the thought of marriage or the hot cheese drying. He unbuttoned the dress shirt and wiped away what he could before wadding it into a ball and throwing it in an open trash can as he passed. It was chilly in just the thin, white undershirt, but it smelled better than his ruined dress shirt.

Mission accomplished, Wolfe needed to get back to Redmond before Never noticed his presence. He had sacrificed one of his best dress shirts, but it was worth the prize. Two weeks, he had bought himself. Unlocking the Jeep, Wolfe slid in and cranked the engine. He had to get out of town. The worst thing he could do now was slip up and squander the small amount of good fortune he had left.

CHAPTER 37

Folman Tennessee, Present

Never made note of the week Wolfe found the box in Paris and looked through the entries in his planner with new eyes. She found two weekend entries that sparked her curiosity.

Out late exploring possible local history site, the Saturday entry stated.

Slept late, missed cycleball practice, was his only entry for Sunday.

She put down the planner and thought for a moment. Never had never seen Wolfe skip practice on purpose. As the league's creator, Wolfe was always adamant about adhering to the attendance guidelines to set a good example for new members. He argued with her one time when he had the flu that the physical activity would be good for him.

What kind of information would he be looking for at a historic site after dark? What would be so important that he stayed out late and missed practice? She flipped back a few pages. It was after he found the box in Paris. He had a lunch date with her earlier in the week. Never remembered the letter he was waiting to open. It was also the day she told him that the story ran in the *Folman Gazette* and he seemed upset by the news. He had a strange message at the end of lunch about replacing the locks on his office. Had the break-ins started at Redmond College's campus and spread to Folman?

Wolfe said something about letting Justine retake the photo in the reprint. What would the original tell her? Was there something in the photo that could explain his odd behavior and the strange events leading to and continuing after his death? Maybe it was the piece that would bring everything together. Never needed to find a copy of that article.

It was after nine, but the security guard at the front desk of the *Folman Gazette* let Never in without much of a fuss. Most of the daytime workers were gone for the day. Jerry's light was on, but his office door was closed. Never suspected he was down in the press room. She headed the opposite way to archives and hoped she could find the back issue she was searching for without Mable's help.

During the day, Mable Ayers ruled the archives. Nothing got in or out without approval and notes added to her clipboard. Never always mused that Jerry and Mable would make a solid couple, if they weren't already devoted to their work. Jerry was always barking for things and Mable always knew where to find them. One couldn't ask for better qualities in a companion than that.

Never just hoped she could find what she needed. She wanted to see the original photo from the reprint of Wolfe's summer class proposal. There had to be something in the photograph. Never would bet it had to do with the box. She just needed to see the photograph to prove it.

Never rifled through filing cabinets and bundles of papers under the long work table. She sorted and moved bundle after bundle until she stumbled across the date she was looking for. Bumping her head in her haste to bring it up to the table top, she spread the newspaper out under the hanging lamps. She flipped through the issue's content until she came to the reprint of Wolfe's article.

The photograph was of Wolfe sitting behind his desk. It was just like she remembered. He looked every bit the college professor in his tweed jacket and evergreen tie. Compared to its usual disheveled look, his work space was spotless for the interview photo. Wolfe must have cleared away the lingering stacks of newspapers and open books littering his desktop before the reporter arrived.

"What did he want to hide?" Never whispered as she searched the photograph.

Everything he was wearing looked like attire she had seen him wear before. The desktop was clean. There weren't any strange reflections in the window. What was she looking for?

Then Never spotted a small statue over his right shoulder she had never seen in his office before.

"Is that it?"

The statue would be small enough to hide in the slit that was cut in her coat. She pulled a large magnifying glass over and looked closer before she picked up her phone and tried to search for photos of statues. Thirty minutes of scrolling rewarded her with a clear image of the statue behind Wolfe in the photograph and a link to the original article connected with it.

As she read, Never realized she unearthed the relationship between Wolfe and the strange article on stolen Peruvian art in his box of papers. The article told of a priest who met his end in a churchyard high in the Andes Mountains. The priest suffered over twenty stab wounds, had broken fingers, and bled to death from his injuries. The statue and several other religious artifacts were taken in the robbery. The local police acknowledged it could be tied to organized crime.

This whole time she thought the article in Wolfe's papers was an outlier with no connection at all, but it was the focal point. She had been through the boxes Susan and Paul had dropped off from his office. The statue wasn't hidden there. The ring was the only small surprise she found in the boxes and bags that Carrie gave her from his home. Where did it go after the photo was taken? Who was looking for it?

"No wonder you didn't want to tell me."

Never left everything where she found it and ran back upstairs. She pulled out Sergeant Henderson's card, took a few deep breaths, and punched in the numbers. It rang three times and went to voicemail. Never gave a passing thought to him avoiding her calls, and left him a brief message to meet her at the *Folman Gazette* to talk about new information in the Wolfe

Strickland case.

She made copies and waited by the front door for twenty minutes before his patrol car came into view. He would be in his uniform tonight. Thick utility belt and sand-colored material defined his status as she swung open the door for him to follow her back to her cubical.

"So what made you so eager to see me tonight, Miss Martinez?"

She pulled the small scrap of paper from the top of the pile on her desk and held it out to him.

"I found this taped into a ring box that came back to me from Wolfe's house."

He took the small piece of paper reluctantly and squinted at Wolfe's handwriting.

"What does a badly written love note have to do with the case?"

"Wolfe used to tell me local stories while we sat on his back porch at night. One was about the tallest tree on the ridge behind his house. The story goes that there were three Confederate soldiers, likely deserters, who came upon a free black man named Albert Gunner working on a nearby farm. The soldiers were drunk from a barrel of whiskey they acquired. The sight of Albert in clean clothes and new boots set them off. They had shoes that were barely serviceable and were down to their worn undershirts and uniform trousers. They attacked Albert Gunner, stripped him naked, and hung him from the tree on the ridge. Wolfe said it was more likely that Albert's spirit haunted the ridge than the Folman Witch. He called it the Hanging Tree whenever he referred to it. I believe Wolfe wanted me to know that the statue he found is buried at the base of the Hanging Tree on Widow Jenkins' property."

"What statue would that be?"

"Wolfe went to Paris on a treasure hunt. The clues were wrong and he ended up digging up a statue that wasn't part of the treasure hunt. He brought it home with him."

"What does that have to do with his death?"

"I believe that someone killed Wolfe because he wouldn't give them their statue back."

"That is quiet a leap, Miss Martinez."

"I have been through his planner, I have articles about the statue, photos of the statue in the *Folman Gazette*. The statue is at the heart of Wolfe's final days. There were break-ins in his office at Redmond College, security said there was stalking involved. The statue didn't reappear in the boxes I received from his office and house. It vanished. I found entries in his planner for the night I think he buried it. He missed cycleball practice that next day because of it. He would never do that."

"That's it? You have a vague note and a theory?"

"Yes, but Widow Jenkins' has given her okay to search the property. You can go with me and prove it is buried there."

"And do what exactly?"

"Return it to Peru, and get it out of our town.

Find out if someone killed Wolfe."

"You're still a suspect with ample opportunity to plant anything anywhere you wanted around the property. Weren't you caught coming out of Wolfe's house the morning after he died? His body wasn't even dry from being fished out of the lake."

"But the note is in his handwriting."

"Which you interpreted." Henderson pointed a finger in her direction before continuing, "None of it makes sense to anyone but you."

"Why would I bother to track all of this down?"

"I think you're throwing out distractions because you need a cover for Wolfe Strickland's death."

"Why is that?"

"You were the last one to see him alive. A third party would come in handy for your defense."

"Handy or not, the statue exists."

"So it exists, it doesn't prove who put it there."

"If you would go and check, you could fingerprint it."

"You think it will have your boyfriend's prints on it?"

"Wouldn't it be worth checking?"

"If I do this, I give you what you need to confuse a jury. Why don't you get it yourself?"

"I knew you wouldn't believe me if I showed up at your desk with the statue."

"More like you thought I would give your story credibility."

Never knew it was useless, but she tried again to sway him as she thrust a stack of papers into his hands.

"I have the articles, the research, his planner notes, the information from the treasure hunting site, and copies of the break-in reports from Redmond College campus security. Please, at the very least, read through them."

"You have nothing to prove a threat exists. Are you trying for an insanity defense?"

"You're impossible!"

"Miss Martinez, Wolfe Strickland met a tragic end and the last known person to see him was you. I suggest you spend more time with your lawyer mapping out a useful defense if this goes to trial."

"All of this is connected. The break-ins, my car, all of it. Why would he write *noose* in a message to the woman he intended to marry?""

"I could think of some reasons." Sergeant Henderson shrugged as he turned and headed for the door. "Goodnight Miss Martinez."

Never followed him. She watched through the glass door as he threw her stack of papers into the seat beside him and shifted his frame into the driver's seat. Locking the door between them, she let her disappointment consume her. How was she ever going to save anyone, or expose a crime when she couldn't even convince one hard-headed man she was telling him the truth?

CHAPTER 38

Folman Tennessee,
Two Hours before Planned Meeting at the Lake

It was approaching the two week limit Justine had given when Wolfe drove back to his house for the mail and a few changes of clothing. He found a note with today's date clipped to a stack of photos in his mailbox when he turned up the drive.

> *Meet me tonight. I will kill them all if you don't.*

He should have turned around and driven straight back to the college, but he was tired of hiding in his office and living like a refugee. Wolfe continued up the drive and parked by the porch. He would spend the afternoon in his own house and enjoy a real shower that didn't take place in a gym facility.

Showered and dressed, Wolfe headed to the desk in his office. He looked at the photos for a long time. There was another photo of Rebecca on campus. Never and Justine were featured in one leaving the *Folman Gazette* together on a rainy afternoon. One was a grainy photo of him in the Paris airport. The last photo, had instructions written on the back. It was where he would be forced to meet his stalker. Wolfe knew the place. It wasn't far from the beach at the lake where he planned to meet Never tonight to propose.

The terror of the last few weeks was linked to the statue. Nothing he could do now would put things back the way they were, but he was determined not to return the statue. If his stalker could find it without his help, Wolfe would be dead already. He was sure of that. Keeping it would endanger them all. Most important, Never would be in danger forever if he continued to hide it from the world and from her. She would never forgive him for his blunder when she found out. Wolfe knew he could take it to the police and turn it in, but approaching the police with the crazy story he had to tell would increase his chances of going to prison. Wolfe didn't like either of those options. That only left one other option. He could run.

Nothing had changed since he brought it home. The statue was a curse. Wolfe took the ring box he planned to give Never down from the crock on the shelf in his study and flipped open the box lid. The diamond shone from the center and when he tilted it the rubies ringing the edge started to sparkle. Smaller diamonds raced up the side of the band to support the larger one above. It was stunning. When he asked the shopkeeper to engrave it for Never, he knew it would look amazing on her. Wolfe found the place in the rose gold band where he had her name added. He was beyond confident in her response when he asked the jeweler to personalize it. What a fool he had been thinking she would ever get to see it. Wolfe flipped the lid shut and held it for a while.

He hadn't intended to marry anyone this year, but he was convinced he could pacify Justine and Never with a ring and press for a long engagement. He could always call the engagement off later. If things went the way Wolfe expected, he might have to permanently relocate. What a mess he had made. Everything in his life had changed because of a mistake posted on the treasure hunting site. The statue would cost him everything he held dear to keep it safe and hidden, but he couldn't give it back to a killer. He had no guarantee that the person threatening him wouldn't murder everyone involved regardless of the outcome. Never, Rebecca, Justine, or anyone else could disappear without warning. He had no way of telling.

Wolfe pulled out the bottle of scotch from his file cabinet and filled his mug. He spent what was left of the afternoon with a drink in one hand. He rotated his activities from flipping through the photos, staring at the ring box, and getting up to pace the floor. With his mug empty, he studied everything around him one last time. Wolfe put the ring away in the crock and picked up each photograph to rip them to shreds. He had come to a decision.

He couldn't save anyone if they knew his plans. They would try to help him despite his warnings. There was only one way to keep everyone out of harm's way. Never needed to be angry at him. She needed to be furious with the results of the meeting he invited her to, and Wolfe was sure he knew just the way to provoke her. He knew Justine had to let the staged jewelry store meeting slip by now. She was a hopeless romantic with her own wedding on her mind. She wouldn't keep his secret for long. Never hadn't suggested coming by in the past few nights. She must know about the jewelry store bag by now and understand she should stay away until he asked her over to pop the question.

She was cheerful when he called to invite her to the lake at sunset. Wolfe hated the idea of deceiving her, but it had to be done. Never was expecting a grand event ending with a proposal planned out over the last two weeks. He could give her that, but to skip town without her suspicion, he had to dump her. Not just that, he had to make her believe he was unfaithful. She had to believe he was cheap and thoughtless. He had to treat her like her feelings were an afterthought. It would kill him. She would cut him down at the ankles with her fiery temper and he would have to take every bit of it. If he disappeared, the ring would stay hidden and so would the statue. She would leave the lake tonight hating him and wishing him dead. But it might just be the only way to save her life.

CHAPTER 39

Folman Tennessee, Present

Drowning or Murder
By Never Martinez

Information that has come to light in the weeks after Wolfe Strickland's death has lead me to believe he was murdered. I have found the elusive Chasity he referred to that night and it is not a person, as I was led to believe. CHASETE (Chasity), College Historians Aggressively Searching Everywhere Treasure Exists, is an online treasure hunting group composed of people enthusiastic about treasure hunting activities. It is similar to geocaching in its goals and the prizes are not of any monetary value. Finds are instead exchanged for bragging rights and rankings that get a player into exclusive clue groups.

What does this discovery have to do with his death? The meticulously kept notes in Wolfe Strickland's planner, contained many references to "CHASETE". Message boards and chat room conversations indicate that, Wolfe Strickland found his last treasure following a clue in Paris. The messages between him and the clue provider show that Wolfe would not get credit for the find because it was from the wrong location. The find was referred to as "the box" in the conversation between them. I have reason to conclude from research papers in his office at the time of his death that the box contained a stolen statue from Peru that he displayed on the shelf in his office for a brief time.

Somehow, Mr. Strickland became aware of the statue's origins, but not before the *Redmond Recorder*, the campus newspaper, photographed him with the statue. The same article was later reprinted in this paper as a regional interest piece.

I have confirmed with the head of the Redmond College campus security, Larry Harden, that Wolfe reported a stalking incident and a break-in after the articles were run in both newspapers. I was present when someone in maintenance at the college texted Wolfe's cellphone to tell him that his new door locks had been installed. At the time, he played off the break-in as students looking to score test answers.

Paired with other information from that time period, I now believe it was an organized crime ring trying to retrieve their property. What is more concerning is that I don't think these occurrences stopped when they dissipated on the Redmond College campus. I believe the people stalking Wolfe Strickland followed him home to Folman. Several occurrences in Folman over the past few weeks can and should be linked to the box Wolfe Strickland carried home from Paris. Aside from Wolfe's untimely death, my car was tampered with, my apartment was searched, Wolfe's home was torn apart, and a friend was assaulted. Nothing was found to be missing after any of these break-ins.

Robertson County Sheriff's Department Sergeant David Henderson stated on the record that none of these events are connected or related. I am to believe that it is a series of random interrupted burglaries without one thing being stolen from the properties in question.

There is one more thing that I found during this journey. I discovered a ring that Wolfe Strickland had engraved with the name "Never Strickland". I believe that before he realized he was in danger Wolfe Strickland intended to propose that night by the lake.

The jewelry box contained a small note with a strange message about love.

Now that I have decoded the message, I believe it was meant to lead me to the statue if I ever needed protection from the men that killed Wolfe. Due to Wolfe's actions to cover up his find and save me from the problems brought on by the statue's presence, the Robertson County Sheriff's Department is dubious of my conclusions. It is up to the citizens of Folman to protect the statue and its people from the crime ring hiding in our town. I am revealing its location to you. I believe the statue that caused Wolfe's death is buried near the witch's cottage. We need to protect Widow Jenkins and her property until the statue can be returned to the people of Peru.

Never spent all night putting the pieces together on paper. She kept going over the timeline and rereading it. She knew she couldn't do it any other way. Everyone would stay in danger until the statue was found. Widow Jenkins' had agreed to let her search the property, but Sergeant Henderson refused to help her recover the statue. He would be the first one to call it a hoax if she did it alone. She needed to be safe and keep the statue from leaving the woods. The only way to do that was to get the police involved whether they liked it or not. They would have to monitor a large gathering of good-old boys with guns patrolling Widow Jenkins' property. Never had already called ahead and asked her to approve the intrusion.

She had every reason to believe that not only would Sergeant Henderson refuse to help her in her efforts, but he would be determined to charge her with something as well. He would be by to collect her as soon as he started receiving calls. Never was sure her article would cause the results she was looking for. She just had to persuade Jerry to print it. She brushed her teeth while the new pages were printing and grabbed them as she headed out the door.

"Jerry I need this article to get me arrested," Never explained as she barged into his office and pushed the copy of her article across the desk.

"What the hell Never!"

"It is the only way I will be protected from what will come," she insisted.

"What about our readers?"

"I believe they will want to help, and I know it to be the only way to prove my case."

"What exactly is your case," Jerry asked as he pulled out the bottle of antacids from his desk drawer.

"I have evidence reprinted in our paper that leads me to believe that Wolfe was murdered over a Peruvian statue from the 1500s that he brought back from Paris by mistake."

"You think your professor boyfriend was whacked, because he went on a treasure hunt in France?"

"Yes."

"Jesus, Never! What kinda TV soap opera defense is that?"

"The one Wolfe left me a trail of clues to."

"You can prove the facts in this article?"

"Yes, I have copies of our article, statements from security at the college, police reports from all four break-ins, and screen shots from the website message board conversations between Wolfe and another treasure hunter talking about the box."

"But you don't know for certain where he has hidden it?"

"I don't have proof of where, but I do have planner notes that allude to the when and a note in my ring box that is a clue to the where."

"I'll have to run it as an opinion piece with a newspaper disclaimer on it," he said before popping some chalky disks into his mouth.

"I just need to make sure everyone sees it."

"What if you can't get yourself out of this Never?"

"I will live with my decision and you will get a series of articles."

"You've really thought about this?"

"All night long." Never's nod was solemn but her eyes were bold as they met his. "It is the only way the sheriff's department will follow my findings to the illogical conclusion that Wolfe put in place."

Jerry picked up the printed pages and read for a few minutes as he munched on more antacids. Never didn't know where to go or what to say if he rejected her. She had to hope he would see the merit in publishing it for the loyal readers of the *Folman Gazette*. The fingertips she had shoved under her thighs to keep herself from fidgeting were pinching her skin as his silence lengthened. Never almost jumped to her feet when she heard him blow out a short sigh and lay the papers down between them.

"Give me until five to talk to our lawyers and decide."

Never didn't chance speaking. She just nodded and walked back out to her desk.

"What was that about?" Justine asked as she limped up to the wall beside Never's cubical with

Houdini in her shoulder bag.

"A meeting about my next article," Never answered. "What are you two doing here?"

"It's Wednesday."

Wednesday, what was on Wednesday? Never looked at her best friend hoping she would fill in the rest.

"The three of us have a date to sample cakes."

"Right, right, I'll grab my bag."

"Are you sure the chat with Jerry was just about your next article?"

"Yes," she insisted as she shooed them to the door.

Never didn't want to lie to her best friend, but she didn't want her to know any more than necessary. It would be hard to deal with the fallout from her next article, but her friend wasn't in any shape to join her in a cell. Never didn't want Justine to call off her wedding because she was in jail trying to protect her. As much as she was tempted, Never couldn't share this secret before the paper came out. She just hoped Justine would understand.

They exchanged their usual chitchat as they drove to Cindi's Sweets, and Houdini played on Never's lap. If she hadn't already disappointed Justine by forgetting their appointment, Never would have begged her to reschedule. She wasn't really up to giving her opinion on cake samples. Jerry's non-committal answer about her article had her stomach tied in knots. She expected the introduction of food would make it feel like someone was using her midsection as a trampoline for a kid's birthday party.

Never knew she needed to take the chance and say something while they were alone. As Justine pulled into a parking spot, Never put a hand on her arm to stop her from getting out.

"What's going on?" Justine looked up in surprise.

"There is something I want you to promise me."

Justine gave her a curious look. "What would that be?"

"Whatever happens after my next article comes out, don't try to get me out of it."

"What exactly are you getting into?"

"I can't tell you that, but I need you to promise you will let me go through it my own way."

"That's a promise I don't know if I can keep."

"I know that, and I wouldn't be asking this of you if it wasn't important."

"Your next article is going to trigger a reaction?"

"Hopefully," Never hedged as she scratched Houdini behind the ears.

"Good or bad?"

Never remained silent. She could feel Justine's eyes on her, but she refused to look up. She stroked the kitten's back as if it would grant wishes and hoped Justine wouldn't continue to push her for more information.

"I hope you're more descriptive during this cake testing," came from the driver's seat as Justine opened the door. "I'm going to need more than 'it tastes like cake' if I am going to finalize cake orders today."

Never knew her companion was irritated, but Justine was taking it with as much grace as she could. She just hoped her best friend wouldn't get in the way if Jerry published her article. She could be in jail for any length of time. Never was prepared to accept the consequences if it would rebalance the scales. Nothing would be right again until she was able to interrupt the course Wolfe created. If things went according to plan, Folman would be protected. That was all she could ask for at the moment. She didn't want to play the hero or have someone ride in to rescue her. Never just wanted to expose and clip the strings the puppet master put into play.

She might lose her job, her home, and her freedom in the bargain, but she was willing to try. Wolfe's find had lost him his life and she wanted to get the statue back to its original owners before it cost anyone else theirs. She just needed to be firm with herself when it came to Justine. It was hard to see her best friend struggle to walk, knowing that Wolfe put this entire situation in motion. Adding her own deception to the mix to stop further damage was even harder. It made her wonder how Wolfe carried his burden those final days. If Justine had been the one he was hiding his secret from, it would have been much more difficult.

"Let's go eat cake Houdini," Never muttered as she opened her door and scooped him into his mesh shoulder bag.

Never always felt like a child when she walked into Cindi's Sweets. The white tile on the floor shined and reflected the soft yellow walls covered with dancing pastel cupcakes. Clear glass cases filled with every confection imaginable made an l-shaped design on the left side of the room and white café tables lined the right side near the wide windows overlooking Lundy Park.

"Hello Never!" Cindi greeted when she noticed her stalled approach. "Grab a cookie and come join us."

Cindi Newsom was a petite woman with short blond hair and a bubbly personality that made Never wonder if she snorted pure sugar when no one was looking. She managed her shop with a small staff of loyal workers that graduated from Folman High not long after Cindi went into business twenty-five years ago. She gave everyone a well-practiced smile and a cookie when they walked into her shop. No detail was too much for Cindi. She called the bakery her dream job and didn't stop working when her husband decided to retire from teaching ten years ago. Upon entering her shop patrons could hear her humming as she cleaned dishes and restocked trays. Cindi was the type of mother Never always imagined when she was little. She envied her close-knit family filled with grandkids eager and old enough to help behind the counter on the weekends.

The place always smelled like spices and lemon

cleaner. A wave of warmth washed through her when she entered here. Maybe it was the free cookies or the smell of flour and chocolate, but Never always imagined if she could bottle what a home should smell like, it would be like walking into Cindi's Sweets.

"We're set up back here," Justine's voice carried none of its usual warmth.

"We're coming."

Justine still wasn't happy about secrets being kept from her. The tension remained in the lines on her face when she turned away to talk to Cindi. She was the one person Never could go to with everything, like a favorite sister. She never failed to show her loyalty and honesty. It was painful to lose her support right now.

Never felt the distance grow between them as they sat down in the back of Cindi's Sweets at a small table with several small plates arranged in a circular pattern. Houdini wasn't happy being confined to the bag, but after a few meows of complaint and being given his favorite toy he settled down for a nap. Never tried her hardest to be helpful, but she couldn't get really excited about any of their options.

Between them sat several different versions of buttercream icing on top of cake made from chocolate, spice cake, peppermint, and simple yellow cake. There were seasonal offerings like eggnog and sugared pecan. For the adventurous and those without a critical mother-in-law in the making there were chai cakes, alcohol-laced Nutella cakes covered in dried fruits, and cakes dripping with a multitude of colors and flavors. Never did her best to ask helpful questions about each cake and compliment one aspect of each to give Justine some feedback in her decision. By the third sample, Justine was smiling and chattering.

Though Justine loved the idea of a red velvet cake for a Christmas wedding, she thought the dark icing would be too much of a diversion from her idea of a traditional white wedding cake. They both liked the spiced carrot cake and it could be made with white chocolate buttercream icing to give Justine the chocolate she was craving without the added color. They picked out red berry stems and white gardenias to grace the top and sides of the three layers. It seemed unreal to Never that she was waiting to learn if she was going to jail in the next twenty-four hours and she was tasting cakes and planning events. A worry always persisted that she could miss the wedding. She didn't want to miss her best friend's wedding for any reason, but Never had to make sure she wasn't a target first.

If Jerry refused to publish the article, things could get much worse. She didn't think that the people looking for the statue would back off, and she was no closer to unmasking them than she was to designing her own wedding cake. Being in jail would be awful, but life would still go on. Releasing her article was the only path forward, as much as she disliked walking it.

"Earth to Never," came careening through her thoughts and she looked up to see Justine's agitated look from before.

"What?"

"Do you think the spices in the carrot cake and the cinnamon icing will be too much flavor for the guests?"

"I thought you just decided on chocolate."

"Yes, but for Rory's groom's cake."

Never looked over at her and shrugged. She had no idea what was going on at their small table while she was mulling over her future. Thank goodness Cindi had worked with difficult and confused clients for years and she handled ill tempers with ease.

"Why don't I mix up a small sample while you look through the design book for something that suits your groom's interests, and we'll compare notes when I get back?"

Cindi got up from the table and disappeared through the swinging doors into the back. Never was left to contend with the irritated and confused Justine alone.

Justine leaned closer with a sigh and commented, "I know you don't want to tell me what's going on, but you're worrying me."

"I'm sorry." Never held her hands up in surrender. "I will try to pay attention."

"There are a lot of things up in the air right now."

Never knew Justine was referring to her therapy and the wedding plans, but the comments described her situation as well. They both had things hanging over their heads, and Never felt helpless to do anything productive about her own situation. It felt strange to be thinking about trivial things like cake and icing combinations on a day like today, but it was one problem she could work on.

"I guess we need to check these cakes off your list then," she encouraged as she tried to give her best friend a smile.

They formed a pact to focus on the current situation. They tackled the design book first. Justine knew Rory would want a sports-themed cake. That was the easy part. They decided on a large sheet cake design with one layer and soldiered through tiny plate after tiny plate of offerings until Justine tried a snickerdoodle cake sample she thought Rory would love. They had just eased back from the table to give their taste buds a rest when Cindi came back through the swinging doors carrying small paper containers with tiny wooden spoons. She placed one beside each of them.

"This can be altered to a fuller flavored cinnamon or a lighter version if it is too much for you," she assured them as she settled back in the seat across from them to watch their reactions.

"This is wonderful!"

"I think this is the one," Never agreed through the bite of snickerdoodle cake she added it to. "Your other guests may not get any."

"He is going to love it," Justine agreed as she turned her wide smile and the design book around to show Cindi. "Can we do something like this one?"

Their heads bent together over the book and Cindi brought out a tablet to take notes on. Justine requested the snickerdoodle sheet cake with cinnamon cream cheese icing for Rory's groom's cake. Cindi offered to personalize it by adding snickerdoodle footballs, baseballs, and basketballs around the base and piled high in the center of the cake. Rory and his co-workers should be delighted by it. Never could see the love poured into every detail of Justine's present to her future husband. She couldn't help but feel a stab of jealousy. Never thought about the ring she had taken to the bank for safekeeping. If things had turned out the way she had expected by the lake, Justine would be helping her plan another, much smaller, wedding after she returned from her honeymoon. As it stood now, Never didn't know where she would be after the new year.

As they said their goodbyes to Cindi, Never hoisted the straps of the bag carrying the sleeping Houdini onto her shoulder and followed Justine to the door. She meandered through the parking lot and looked at her watch as she waited for Justine to unlock the car doors. She would make it back to the office sooner than she expected. She just hoped Jerry had good news.

CHAPTER 40

Folman Gazette, Folman Tennessee, Present

It was early the next morning when Never approached her desk. She was too nervous to sleep through the night. She had dreamt that the presses had broken down and killers were loose in the building. The images were so vivid she had to get up and check for herself.

The building was quiet. Jerry was in his office with the door closed. She suspected he was on the phone with the higher-ups justifying the shock they would have when they read what was picked up by paper delivery people in the early morning hours.

Never didn't have anything productive to do. She made coffee and picked at a stale bagel from the breakroom before grabbing a copy of today's paper. Her co-workers were trickling into the maze of cubicles as phones began to ring. When she first arrived at the paper years ago she loved the sound of the room waking up with chatter and buzzing phone extensions, but today she set her desk phone to "voicemail only" and scooted back into the interior corner of her small office space to avoid visitors.

Never read through her published article twice, folded the paper back into place, and started emptying her pockets when she heard the first signs of a scuffle in the reception area. She had been on the clock all of fifteen minutes before she saw the figure she expected come marching toward her down the hallway. Sergeant Henderson trudged past every block in his path without acknowledging the receptionist or the other co-workers lining the halls of the building. It was obvious her words had the intended effect on her readership and the Robertson County Sheriff's Department had as many complaints as she had expected.

When he reached her desk, he didn't pause or offer pleasantries, he went straight into his accusations.

"Men are walking around the woods with rifles on Widow Jenkins' property scaring the crap out of the people who just moved into Wolfe Strickland's old house."

It pleased Never to know the townspeople had taken up her cause, but she shifted the conversation back to him.

"Is there any other reason you're here?"

"You've got people complaining to my office that we don't care about widows and orphans."

Never couldn't contain the smirk creeping onto her lips. She hid it behind her hand, pondering if Justine had called him. There were very few people in town who knew of her orphaned childhood. Paired with the Widow Jenkins' current situation, someone found the one time that particular phrase rang true and used it to her advantage.

"I'm sorry for the inconvenience Sergeant."

"It's more than an inconvenience."

"What do you suggest we do about it?"

"I am here to arrest you for tampering with evidence, inducing a panic, and trespassing."

"Collecting evidence is tampering?" Never argued as she let him cuff her in front of her shocked co-workers and ramble through her rights before addressing her again.

"You aren't capable of guilt are you?"

"According to your department, I am capable of several things."

Jerry opened his door and watched in silence with everyone else. When she sent him a weak smile, he nodded. In their meeting yesterday afternoon, he ran over a list of things with her. The newspaper would defend her actions and their own for printing her work, but she had to stay on a tight leash while all this played out. The pushback would be swift. He promised a lawyer would be provided by the paper until her trial and that her position at the paper would be retained until then. After that, her future was unprotected.

"The mayor is up in arms about your article," Sergeant Henderson rambled on. "He is convinced you are a public safety threat."

"The same mayor who knows we are investigating his office for fraud?"

"You're going to get an innocent person shot over your obsession and you don't care do you?"

It was hard for Never to bite her tongue and hear his assessment of her actions without defending herself, but she swallowed hard and clamped her mouth shut as he walked her out of the building. Never didn't speak again until they were outside in his unmarked cruiser.

"It's good to see the people of Folman are finally being protected," she told him as he pulled out of the parking lot.

"You're going to get a front row seat to our vigilance."

Never hoped he was right. It might be the only thing that would save her life after the article found her target audience. Whoever was after that statue would stop at nothing to get it back. Giving the citizens of Robertson County a clear path and hoping they would protect the statue's location would be the only way to keep Wolfe's killers from finding it first. Never just hoped no one else would die in the process. She had a hard time betting on the police to save her own life, but she was hopeful they would prevail in saving Widow Jenkins and her new neighbors. All Never could do now was perform her part in the waiting game and pray she was strong enough to see the conclusion.

CHAPTER 41

Hickory Lake, Robertson County, Tennessee

Wolfe didn't leave the lake after he heard Never's car rumble out of the parking lot. Everything had worked out just as he had planned. The look on her face, the reaction to the cheap flowers, everything was perfect. And it was killing him inside.

Wolfe just wished that one day he could explain everything to her. Let her know there were caring thoughts, tortured thoughts, behind his actions. He just didn't seem to be pulling the strings of his own life since that damn article appeared.

The sight of his Jeep just feet away confused his thoughts. He couldn't stay on the pier worrying about her any longer. He needed his wits about him. The note said half-an-hour from now. He should be headed for the airport. His footsteps crunched gravel as he headed for the parking lot.

Wolfe didn't know anyone had walked up behind him until he heard a voice in his ear, "You gave me the perfect cover mate."

The fact that the shadow behind him wasn't exceptional in size was worth figuring into his plans. Wolfe acted like his arrival was of no consequence.

Wolfe turned his head without much interest before informing him, "None of this was for you."

"I hope for your sake you have something for me. We had plenty of time to check your Jeep while you got rid of that nosey reporter girlfriend of yours."

Wolfe could see two more shadows emerge from the darkness cutting him off from the path to his Jeep. His stalker hadn't come alone after all. Three to one made a much stronger impression as Wolfe studied his latest predicament.

"How did you..." he trailed off as they came closer.

"My men have very useful skillsets."

"I'm sure they do."

"Funny thing is...they didn't see a statue box in your suitcase."

"You think I would just walk in here with it?"

"I think you were going to run again Professor. And that won't work with my plans. Start walking."

"Where should I go?"

"Head for our meeting spot. It's time you started following my rules."

The stalker stayed in the shadows, but Wolfe saw the knife without any problem.

Wolfe considered his options as he walked. He didn't have much of a chance getting to his Jeep. He encountered a few bicyclists with flashing headlamps earlier in the evening, but the majority of the space was empty this time of night. He wished he could signal someone to help. There was no one present to witness his distress as his captor motioned him to turn around and head for a path around the eastern side of the lake. Insect noises, the random call of a night bird, and the soft lapping of the water kept him company as he watched lights come on in the elaborate homes along the western side of the lake.

The men followed him at a distance until he was ordered to stop along the section of beach in the photo and lean against a large boulder.

"Search him," the leader commanded and one of the shadows behind him came forward to do his bidding.

"Cell, keys, and a wallet boss," the other man related in a matter-of-fact tone after he rummaged through Wolfe's pockets like a kid searching for candy.

"Where's my statue Professor?"

"You mean Peru's statue?"

The punch to the gut was so swift Wolfe didn't even see the other man give the order before he fell to his knees.

"Why don't you stick to simple answers from

now on," his captor instructed as he paced. "Where is my statue?"

Wolfe remained quiet, trying to catch his breath.

"So you're only going to talk if you can be funny?"

He pulled his knife from his belt and slid the blade under Wolfe's chin. The angry citrine eyes of a panther glowered back at him across the blade. "I would enjoy slicing you apart, but my friend's skills are more efficient for my plans."

Wolfe watched pieces of hair from his beard along the blade's path flake off and fall as it retreated. The friend he was talking about was built like a mountain range and Wolfe had no doubt the man would serve his boss as he grabbed Wolfe around the neck and pulled him from his kneeling position to a standing one in a swift jerk.

"It's time for a cruise."

Wolfe wasn't sure if he was walking or being propelled forward in front of the giant who put him on his feet. They were on some sort of a trail, but it didn't seem well maintained. Brush scratched his cheeks and reached to snare his feet. He stumbled once and a large hand lifted him by the back of his coat to steady him. Dealing with the mountain walking behind him, Wolfe barely had a shot of slipping away, but there was another man lurking. Three against one athletic, middle-aged professor would still be no contest. He had no weapons. He hadn't even worn a belt. Wolfe must have slowed his pace while he was lost in thought. A wide hand came from behind him and shoved.

"Keep moving," a low, gruff voice demanded as he stumbled forward.

Stars were coming into view through the openings in the canopy above. The air was crisp, but not cold. It would have been a lovely night for the engagement photos Wolfe knew Never had expected. She looked exquisite in his favorite red dress with her dark curls twisting playfully in the wind. It took everything in him not to reach out and pull her to him when she walked out onto the pier. He wanted to kiss those red lips one more time. That was the damnable problem of it all. No matter what he did, how long he thought, Wolfe couldn't devise a scenario that would work without hurting her. In a last-ditch effort before leaving the house tonight, he taped a small piece of paper with a clue to the statue's position in the ring box he wanted to give to Never. If she ever saw it, she would see it as a justification for his disappearance. Maybe, in some small way, Wolfe was hoping it would help her forgive him for the scene he created to hurt her earlier. Maybe one day, she could forgive him for abandoning her in the midst of all his troubles.

His thoughts were spinning and the pain from the punch he took to his midsection was a distraction to his already splintering thoughts. As he moved through the darkness, Wolfe was losing hope that he would ever be able to explain any of the events of tonight in person. These thugs clustered around him may be the last people he ever spoke to. The thought wasn't soothing.

As they crested a hill, Wolfe could make out the shape of a midsized cruiser anchored in an inlet off the trail. The white lines were crisp as the main part of the hull met blue stripes near the waterline. The craft looked ready to catch fish or shrimp off the coast of the

Carolinas or host a weekend full of girls clad in string bikinis. Wolfe knew after his trek through the woods that he wouldn't be invited to any events as pleasant as those.

He tried to dodge to the right and into some undergrowth, but a firm arm grabbed him as he attempted to flee. He heard a grunt from the mountain behind him before he was given a shove. The ground came rushing up to meet him as he went rolling down the hill.

Muffled laughter followed Wolfe as he rolled to a stop on his back staring up at the side of a slate gray motorboat. It was thin and sleek. The color would be almost undetectable on the water at night.

The third man came down to the beach beside Wolfe and untied something from a tree before pushing the craft into the water. He didn't haul Wolfe to his feet or speak. He just stood and waited.

A chuckle came from somewhere above him.

"Is that any way to treat our guest?"

Wolfe could see shadows making their way toward him. It was his last chance to escape, but the third man lingered within a few feet of his inactive body. Once he rolled to his feet the two other men were behind him again.

"Give him the front seat," his captor instructed as the colossus picked him up and deposited him on the small wooden board as though he weighed no more than a sleeping baby.

"I want our guest to have the best view."

If anyone saw them from the shoreline, it would look like a group of guys heading out to their boat for a round of drinks or a weekend of fishing. Maybe the few who remembered seeing them would recount the tale of the guy in the front of the boat with envy. They would imagine him heading out to party the night away on a luxury boat with his friends. No one would know that Wolfe was caught in the middle of what most people would consider their worst nightmare. His captors hadn't produced guns that would be detectable in the moonlight. If he tried to jump now, he had no doubt the Titan behind him would yank him back before he hit the water. If he caused too much of an altercation, the leader still could reconsider slicing him apart to sink to the bottom undetected. Wolfe couldn't see the knife from his position, but he knew it was there. He wasn't sure he could endure watching his own limbs drift away without him. And what would it buy him?

He had to keep reminding himself that the men behind him were capable of crimes beyond his reasoning. He had read what they did to acquire the statue in the first place. Dispatching him would be trivial to them.

They were cold and business-like as they talked about his life. They wanted their product and they wouldn't stop looking for it unless there was nowhere else to go. They had resources and time on their side. He had to make them sure that he was the only one left that knew about the statue's location and that he was keeping his secret. It left Wolfe with only one card to play. He went to Paris alone and he hid the statue alone. The others knew nothing.

They pulled up along the side of the bigger boat within minutes. A small silver ladder swayed as Wolfe was prodded to a standing position to grab the closest rung. His captor was already out and on board. The mountain and the third man in charge of the craft were left to sandwich Wolfe as he climbed the swaying ladder. They led him to an open door at the back of the boat and pushed him inside. The floor was lined with glossy wooden planks. Fluffy white and blue sofa benches flanked the outside walls. A built-in wooden cabinet housed an entertainment station with mounted television and electronic equipment in the far wall. The cruiser had a classic look any avid fisherman and his persnickety wife could agree on.

Wolfe came to a stop beside a table made of oak or cherry. The mountain behind him had stopped shoving at his back. Wolfe wasn't sure if he should move farther into the room. He was blocked from the doors he just came through. He scanned for another exit, and his eyes strayed to the three shiny silver-plated steps where his captor lounged.

"I am hoping a change of scenery will help your memory."

Wolfe kept silent as he awaited the next set of attacks. He hoped he could hold his silence under their continued physical pressure. Wolfe had never pressed his body to its limits. He had incurred sprains and strains before, but he would be naive to think that anyone in attendance was more of a novice to the trappings of torture than he was.

"Why don't you tell us where my statue is Mr. Strickland?" the younger man encouraged as he came closer to sprawl on one of the blue and white benches.

"We are all riveted to hear what you're going to say."

Wolfe stayed where he was. He made eye contact to convey his defiance.

"Without me you'll never find it."

"Nothing obvious," his captor instructed as the behemoth and the other man came closer. "See if anything makes him feel like cooperating."

The first round of punches caught him in the ribs. There was a yank on his shoulder, and Wolfe cried out. They pushed and pulled at the dangling arm.

"Where is my statue?"

When Wolfe didn't answer they pulled him down on the gleaming wood floor and put a boot into his stretched tendons.

"Where is my property?"

Wolfe spit out the bile rising in his throat.

"Let me go and I will get it for you."

It went on for what seemed like hours in his addled brain before Wolfe saw the leader give a grim smile and slight nod. The mountain shoved his shoulder back in place and Wolfe thought the other man had ripped off his arm instead of repairing it. Blood ran from his lip where he had penetrated the flesh in an attempt not to cry out. He didn't have time to wipe the blood and spit away before the mountain grabbed him by the neck and hoisted him to his feet. Wolfe speculated about their next attack before he realized he wasn't on his feet. He was dangling between the big guy's massive arms and the squeezing had intensified.

"Last chance to tell me what I need to know."

Wolfe struggled to reach up and hit at the giant hands constricting his airway, but the third man had circled him and held Wolfe's arms behind his back in a firm grasp. It felt like minutes before he heard the leader speak again.

"No one will think twice in the morning when your body comes floating in," he said as he walked past Wolfe to stand outside by the railing.

The mountain turned him to follow the direction of his captor's words. The pressure on his neck increased. Wolfe attempted to stall with some small detail, but could only produce panting sounds. As hard as he tried, he couldn't turn them into discernible speech.

Wolfe focused on the dark curly head of hair and designer suit jacket covering the other man's turned back. He gasped for air as he watched the man by the railing pull a lighter from his pocket and reach up to light a cigar. Hints of leather and spices filled his airways. The last images running though his mind were of nights on his back porch smoking a Petit Robust and holding Never's hand as they stared out into darkness.

CHAPTER 42

Robertson County Correctional Facility,
Robertson County Tennessee, Present

On day three of her stay, Never was settling in to the reality of her situation at the Robertson County jail. The outfits were tan and scratchy against her skin, and their quality matched the pink flip-flops she had to trade for her sneakers. She was given a towel, one pillow, and one set of sheets to carry to her cell when she first arrived. The chemical smell of the new gray paint on the walls greeted her as she entered. It wouldn't dissipate and induced a headache the first night she tried to sleep on the flat, water-protected, twin-sized mattress.

Justine had forgiven her silence before the article and had been by twice to visit. She carried in a set of office supplies on her first visit and brought an extra container of copy paper for Never to have while she was here. On her second visit, she brought a bag of newspapers and reading materials. It was a sweet gesture, but the lighting was limited when Never wasn't in the common rooms for visitation. Besides, she had plenty of reading in her cell. Readers were sending letters by care of the "Robertson County jail" and the post office was delivering them. She had stacks in the small cubby beside her bed that doubled as a desk.

Never had already written one article about her arrival at the jail and her accommodations to reassure her readers she was okay. There would still be many meetings between herself and Howard Copland, the attorney the *Folman Gazette* had provided for her, before she saw a judge. She still had her job until the trial was over. That assurance made the situation tolerable for the moment. Never could still produce meaningful content while she was here and her readers wouldn't forget about her efforts if she kept her name in print. She had time and support to continue writing while she waited. She just needed to remember to ask Justine or Mr. Copland for more stamps on their next visit. Her articles would do no good if she couldn't continue to mail them.

Never was grateful Justine brought her news of the efforts on Widow Jenkins' property. Her warning had worked as she had anticipated. The townspeople patrolled the area around the ridge by the witch's cottage in shifts, but no one had showed up to challenge their boundary. The sheriff's department was forced to have a car patrolling the area. So far, everything had been peaceful. Never was grateful no one lost their heads and shot at innocent people trying to help, but she also wondered what was taking so long. She gave the location and whoever it was had no qualms about going after it before. What was the holdup? Did they have trouble figuring out where the witch's cottage was, or would they wait for the distraction of her trial to steal it?

By day five, Never was getting stir-crazy. She didn't have much else to report on in here. The cornbread wasn't name brand and the milk came in powder form, but that wasn't going to get anyone excited. There were people she felt sorry for and people she needed to avoid, but nothing she thought her readers would find interesting. She felt like she existed on the sidelines of time. Nothing was accomplished and nothing was lost. Every day since she entered the cell block was the same boring routine.

In a strange way, she felt like a life in foster care had prepared her for this. The constant inspections, limited possessions, and small sleeping space didn't seem much different. She ate what was offered without complaint and did the chores they assigned her. Bathroom time was seldom private and shower time was short with falling water temperatures. Never didn't enjoy her current situation, but she could cope while she was here. The only nicety she was provided was a cell without a roommate. Robertson County crime was low this month. As the domestic disturbances and occurrences of DUI increased closer to the holiday season she might get company, but Never hoped to be out by then. Mr. Copland seemed certain that the judge would lean toward community service. He seemed to think there would be a stronger argument to get the case thrown out if the statue or the thieves were found before she went to trial. Never just hoped they would act soon and no one would get hurt in the process.

It was later that night during her shift as cook in the small cafeteria that warning bells and lights came on along the walls.

"What is that?" she asked one of the other women turning off stoves and removing things from ovens.

"That's the sound of us losing out on dinner," one woman grumbled.

Never was still trying to figure out what that meant when two guards came in issuing orders to return to their cells.

"What's going on?" she tried to ask, but was shoved toward the door for her efforts.

"Everyone needs to return to your cells. Your dinners will be delivered there later."

Never followed an older woman named Betty and tried to keep up in her ill-fitting flip-flops. In the main hallway they shared with the police station, patrolmen were not shuffling paperwork around on their desks like they were before she went to the dining hall. Coffee cups were forgotten and Sergeant Henderson shot Never a look through his office window that was meant to freeze the blood in her system. She wanted to shout at him. *What have I done?*

Since she had been here, Never had tried to be the model inmate. Whatever he was mad about couldn't be linked to her behavior behind bars. Her first article was very favorable to the way she was treated. She didn't owe the sergeant any more admiration than that.

She was still angry and confused as he turned away from the window to speak into his cell phone. Maybe the mayor was irritated she still had a voice in jail, or he was still getting phone calls complaining about her arrest. Something was wrong, Never just wished she understood what was going on.

She was almost to the corner that led to the women's block when she heard, "911 call at Jenkins and Bradley isn't responding to dispatch" coming from the radio on the shoulder of an officer as he passed.

Oh, my God! It is happening. They're going after the statue.

Never fought the urge to run for the door with all she had in her. Her first instincts were that she should be out there helping and getting that story. If she made a move, she would be laying on the floor still twitching from the Taser shock by the time the crisis was over. The commotion at the station was caused by Wolfe's statue, and she couldn't even make a phone call to warn or help anyone.

She tried one more time by turning her head to ask one of the guards herding them down the hallway, "What is going on?"

"It's none of your business," the chubby blond guard informed her before poking her in the back. "Keep moving."

Never's fingers twitched. Her natural instinct was to be the first in line to see what was going to be tomorrow's headline. Tonight, by her own design, she was stuck watching and waiting for others to give her the news. She hated it.

But this is what you wanted.

Her brain kept trying to reason with her, but she still felt trapped. It was the first time since she handed over her clothes and walked to her cell that she felt like things were spinning out of her control. When the cell door closed behind her, she went straight to her desk. Dinner was forgotten as she began writing tonight's story from her unique perspective.

It was late that night when Sergeant Henderson came to stand outside her cell. Never was close to dozing off when she heard his heavy footfalls. She waited until he slowed to a stop outside before she rose up from under her sheet to look at him.

It wasn't the same angry man she saw earlier through the window in his office. His curls were tousled, dirt and other substances ran from his pant legs to the cuffs of his dress shirt, and his utility belt was missing. Never couldn't smell it from where she sat, but she bet the sweet smell of dried sweat was following him. As bedraggled as he was, Never envied him. She knew without asking that he had been to the Hanging Tree. She wanted to shout questions she had been holding for hours, but she couldn't will her vocal cords to cooperate with her wishes. She wanted to know what he found. Instead, she gawked at the man standing before her hoping he would explain his visit.

"Conner Bradley was thirty-five with a child on the way, and they snapped his neck like a twig," was hurled at her like a throwing star when he managed to speak.

"Oh dear Lord!"

"If I find as much as a five second phone call between you and any of the people we rounded up tonight, you could be charged as an accessory."

Never wasn't surprised by his words, but they stung her all the same. When she found her voice the questions came tumbling out.

"Is anyone else hurt?"

"One of the bad guys Ancel Reyes is headed to the morgue and Mr. Bernard took a shot to the shoulder."

"Did they find the statue?"

"Is that all you care about?"

"If the statue still exists in your county, they will be back for it," Never informed him as she got to her feet and came closer. "I didn't want anyone to die over it, but you said my theory was crazy."

"It was crazy."

"Two men were dead before I brought it to you."

"And now there are two more."

Things grew quiet between them.

"Why are you standing outside my cell?"

"It seems the mayor's 'mistress' was a cocaine addiction. One of the guys we caught tonight admitted to giving him all the free rides he wanted as long as he found a way to approve any building permits they needed. The mayor went to high school with the Folman zoning and permits department head, Trey Emery. "

She was right about the mayor? "And you're telling me...?"

"The mayor forced our hand on arresting you to help his buddy."

"I don't understand."

"They didn't want to expose themselves. Mayor Ball's new friends were making lots of money in town. Trey Emery at the city zoning and permits department was giving out business permits like Marti Gras beads, and a branch of a Dominican crime family was set to put down roots here. The family does business in several of the surrounding states. Running across the statue in the local paper was a surprise to everyone involved. Reyes thought it was safely buried in the churchyard in Paris. The statue was a personal issue of his, from before he joined the family. He buried it in the churchyard for leverage if he ever got fingered for illegal activity. Called it his retirement plan. The family wanted the statue issue settled quietly. After they tracked Wolfe down, he wouldn't cooperate. Neither would you. When they lost the bid on Wolfe's house through a straw buyer out of Chicago, they had to resort to a different strategy. They thought you were too close to the truth, and they wanted you out of their way."

"Does that mean you're here to finish the job?"

He glared at her like he was considering it before he continued, "I came to tell you that your lawyer will be taking you home in the morning."

"And the statue?"

"The box is being guarded by members of our SWAT team until it leaves here," he bit out before turning to go.

"Thank God!"

Never just prayed their vigilance would be enough. She wanted to know more, but he was already fading from view at the end of the hallway. There was no way she could go back to bed. She walked over to turn on a desk light Justine had given her on her last visit and started to write. Folman would lose a mayor and its zoning department head by breakfast tomorrow in a way she never expected, but they would all be safer for it. Never gave up her freedom, a citizen was injured, a child lost a father, a wife lost her husband, and the people of Robertson County lost a public servant dedicated to protecting their future. It wasn't the article Never wanted to write, but it contained the facts she was given. She worked late into the night. Crumpled pieces of paper littered the floor beneath her unyielding chair and words were blurring together. When the last nightshift guard made her rounds, she found Never's light still shining. Her hair cascaded down over the side of the cluttered desk and her fingers clutched a pencil.

With the first specks of morning light came Mr. Copland. Never was relieved to find him waiting in a visitation room with fresh coffee when she was herded in to greet him. After gathering her possessions and sitting through meetings, Never walked out of the Robertson County jail in her own clothes and shoes.

Her lawyer said she had a good case to sue the city over the mayor's abuse of power, but Never waved him off. Hearing the recount of the drug-abusing mayor being rousted from his bed and stripped of his privilege was enough for her state of mind. She didn't want to see anyone punished but him. She didn't need the money or the notoriety. Never was just grateful he played into her plan so well.

Mr. Copland was surprised by her easy-going demeanor, but he didn't push her decision. He picked up take-out from her favorite cafe and wanted to drive her straight home, but Never insisted on going back to work. She wanted to hand-deliver the article she wrote last night to Jerry before she did anything else, she wanted her co-workers to know she was back, and she needed to collect the belongings she left behind at her desk the morning she was taken into custody.

A smile lit up her face when she saw Aurora sitting in the parking lot waiting for her. Her co-workers had washed her car and filled it with balloons before writing, "Welcome Back Never!" on the rear window for everyone to see.

"Never, Jerry said to send you straight to him when you arrived," Ally, the receptionist, chirped as Never pushed through the glass doors of the paper.

She wasn't surprised Jerry expected to see her this morning. She tossed her bags on her desk as she passed and marched to the Editor-in-Chief's door with her story rolled in her hand. She reached up to knock as the door flew open.

"Never! Get in here," came barreling at her as a firm hand grabbed her elbow and the door slammed behind her. "Tell me you got something from last night."

She handed him the pages curled in her palm and slumped down in a seat.

"I would have preferred to go running out the door to report on it myself, but I think I had an interesting perspective on the situation."

"Readership went up 10% after you were arrested."

"I'm glad I could give them more to read about than off-brand kitchen staples."

"You're welcome to a few days off."

"I had a few days off," Never assured him. "Now I want to talk to Widow Jenkins."

"She said you're the only reporter she'll speak to."

"I guess I better get moving then," she said as she got up to leave.

"Never, you might want to swing by home and take a shower first."

She looked down at the clothes she was wearing when Sergeant Henderson arrested her.

"There will be lots of other reporters with cameras camped out on her lawn."

"And I shouldn't give them any more photos of me with bad hair and pale skin?"

"Our readers should see you looking vindicated, and you smell like mothballs."

"I'll get Justine right on that."

"I'm glad I didn't have to reassign your desk Martinez."

"I know how you hate unnecessary paperwork

sir." Never grinned as she closed the door between them.

She heard a gruff laugh and the shuffling of papers as she walked away. Things in her life might finally get back to normal. She gathered her keys and the remains of her lunch from her desk and marched out to the parking lot. Justine was waiting beside her car with Houdini.

"I knew you would come here first." She reached out to give her a hug.

"Can you follow me back to the apartment?" Never asked as she released her. "Jerry said I need to look vindicated and not smell like mothballs when I visit the Jenkins' farm."

"You're going today?"

"I want to know everything I missed last night and Mrs. Jenkins is the best place to start," Never told her as she fought to gain entry into her car through the layers of balloons.

"If you drive your car like that, the sheriff's department will stop you again."

"Are you offering to drive?" Never asked as she slammed the door closed causing a loud pop.

"Get in." Justine motioned. "We need to un-jailhouse rock you before you see anyone."

Never didn't know why everyone was so upset about her appearance all-of-the sudden, but she climbed into Justine's balloon-free car and took the kitten onto her lap. It would be nice to use her bathroom and shampoo without someone watching her. She doubted she could get a brush through her curls at this point. After a week of being deprived of her normal routine, her long, shiny curls were dull and frizzy.

Never didn't care much about her appearance. The mothball smell was a turnoff, but not the worst thing she had suffered through in pursuit of a story. If it was just her, Never would drive straight to Mrs. Jenkins' door and conduct the interview as she was, but Jerry had gone to bat for her. He wanted Never to convey to the public she was professional enough to warrant such special treatment, and Never hoped Justine would know which one of the outfits in her closet would communicate that point. A gray suit with a set of red heels or a plaid sweater with a pencil black skirt and loafers might do the trick. Neither seemed like the right outfit for a visit to a farm turned crime scene. She smiled as she watched the loose hairs fall from Houdini's back as she stroked it. Bad hair, no make-up, and a week without underwear would lead most women to a hysterical breakdown. Maybe in another week she would have pulled out her hair and sold her soul for a container of cheap lip gloss from the overpriced commissary, but driving home today she felt peaceful. Never was sure Justine would do her best to make the rest of her presentable.

"Stop a few blocks away," Never ordered as they turned into traffic. "There are probably people waiting in front of my building again."

"I'm sure Cora already told them everything they want to know." Justine chuckled. "She is probably acting as your unofficial tour guide by now."

"She is my biggest fan."

Justine pulled into a space behind a favorite neighborhood Mexican restaurant and cut the engine.

"I guess we are on foot from here."

Never eased Houdini into his shoulder bag and walked around to give Justine her cane. She hated the cane, but it was good to see Justine making progress. Never noticed a change in the way her best friend carried herself and the length of her strides. Justine was more in control this week. The cane might still be present at the wedding, but she was making improvements in physical therapy to limit its use. As she walked along beside her, Never was grateful for the changes.

"What's the plan?"

"You and Houdini through the front," Never instructed. "I will climb up the back stairs while you distract them with tales of seeing me at the newspaper office."

"Why would I be here?"

"To drop off clean clothes and check on my apartment while I am at work."

"I don't have any clothes."

"They may think Houdini's bag is clothes."

"If they don't?"

"Say you forgot them." Never shrugged. "Keep it simple or they will smell a rat."

"You'll be lucky if they don't smell your mothballs."

"I guess I will have to move fast," Never told her as she passed Houdini to her and headed for the alleyway behind the building.

Never watched Justine as she stuck to the sidewalk that would lead her to the front of the building. She wasn't crazy about the idea of crawling through underbrush or hiding behind dumpsters, but Never would do what she had to do to get into the building unseen. The back entrance was known to others but it required a key to get in. If someone came through the front door, reporters and cameramen would flock to see who it was. Never just hoped Justine was already in place.

She need not have gone to the trouble of hiking through the filth behind her apartment building. There was no one smoking beside the building or hanging around the back door. Never craned her neck until it hurt, but she didn't see any cameras or news vans parked out front. She didn't see or hear the presence of reporters or curiosity-seekers. She stayed low behind a fence until she caught Justine's voice talking to Houdini. Using the chatter as her cue to run from her cover, Never inserted her key and flung open the door to the stairs.

She was almost inside her apartment when she heard the intimate squeak of a door and a voice behind her, "Never, dear, you've had several messages while you were away."

"Thank you, Cora." She turned and took the stack of small pastel squares from her.

"You're not on any type of registry you have to tell us about are you?"

"Nope, not bridal, baby, or otherwise registered."

"That's good dear." Cora chuckled as she turned away.

"Everything is clear out front," Justine called out as she came down the hallway to meet them.

"Justine, it is good to see you too." Mrs. Basket pulled her into a hug. "Will you be by Saturday for cards?"

She nodded. "I can bring some potato salad appetizers."

"That would be wonderful." Cora smiled as she stepped away. "I will see you then."

"Thank you for your help," Never called after she watched the strange exchange.

"You should look into charity work for your next story," her nosey neighbor called back as she retreated. "People love to see prisoners give back to the community."

"I'll get right on that," Never muttered against the wood frame and heard Justine snicker behind her.

"She means well."

"Why are you having dinner with her?"

"Houdini misses his mom sometimes."

"So, you're co-parenting now?"

"Just socializing with a bored old lady." She giggled.

Never just looked at her and shook her head.

Mail was piled up on her table. Justine had been collecting it and taking care of things while she was away. Never owed her for more than her daily trips to the jail visitation room. It would have been much harder to get through this week without her best friend's help. There were bills to catch up on and boxes of Wolfe's stuff still sitting around every surface of her living room, but Never didn't want to think about any of that. She headed straight for the shower, discarding shoes and clothing as she went.

"I'll look through your closet," she heard Justine promise.

It felt nice to have warm water on her skin. Never lathered and rinsed her hair twice before weaving conditioner through her curls. She could shave with a decent razor and revive her spirits with her tangerine body wash. If Mrs. Jenkins and the reporters outside her house smelled mothballs, it wasn't coming from her anymore.

When she opened the bathroom door, steam flowed out behind her and Houdini flew by the doorway chasing a toy.

"I laid out a couple of options on your bed," Justine called from the kitchen.

There was a blue sweater with a pair of tan slacks

and brown boots and a coral shirt paired with a blue suit and tan pumps. Both were nice, but she would have passed them both for her comfortable jeans and a pair of rain boots.

Never opted for the blue sweater and tan slacks because of the boots. She remembered the look of Sergeant Henderson's clothes when he came to talk to her last night. She didn't want to ruin her best interview suit or get her tan heels stuck in the mud. It felt luxurious to look through her underwear drawer again. It wasn't filled with silk and lace, but it still felt like a treasure as she pulled out a clean set and began to dress.

"Never, you really should read this article from the *Howler* before you go."

"Why are you reading our competition?"

"Rory knows the sports columnist," she explained. "Just read it."

"Okay, okay, I will read it on the way."

"You can't be photographed holding that."

"Okay, hand it over," Never demanded as she finished lacing her boots. "I don't know what the big deal is."

Never spread the paper out over the table in front of her. The whole room crackled with energy, but no one uttered a word until Never looked up.

"Marcel was a middleman for a crime family?"

"It says his real name was Ancel Reyes."

"Fifteen different identities," Justine mumbled as she looked at the photographs accompanying the story.

"Sergeant Henderson told me that a Dominican crime family was behind this. I didn't recognize the name Ancel Reyes when he told me last night."

"You think Marcel...I mean Ancel, had something to do with Wolfe's death?"

Never nodded and discarded the rival paper. "I think he was responsible."

"I guess we need to get to Widow Jenkins'," Justine prompted as she gathered up Houdini and turned off the kitchen light.

Never couldn't disagree with her. It was good to see her apartment, but she wanted to spend the rest of the week looking for information. She gathered her work bag and followed Justine out into the hallway. She promised Jerry an interview with Mrs. Jenkins and she was going to get it. When she was done, Never hoped she would be able to connect the rest of the dots.

She grabbed her old notes on the mayor's office fraud case and eyewitness accounts of what happened on the ridge last night. Now that Marcel/Ancel was dead and linked to two city officials, Never could snoop through documents and permits related to the court filings. The available resources were close to endless compared to what she started with. She could feed her obsession to uncover every detail of the web she was drawn into.

Never called Mrs. Jenkins as they walked to

Justine's car. The older woman insisted she would be granted access to the property and an interview with those involved last night. She would be waiting for Never to arrive at the farmhouse.

It was fifteen minutes of feverish note-making while Justine drove out to the Jenkins' farm. Turning onto the lane, they were greeted by men with shotguns, but were ushered through the crowd of reporters lining the road. The widow made it clear she wanted to see Never as soon as she arrived.

Justine drove on without incident, and passed a sheriff's cruiser farther up the road. Never studied the lone car wondering if there were more officers on the other side of the ridge. She could make out muddy ruts marring the grass where wheels and men had left the road.

As Justine edged closer to the small white farmhouse, Never looked at the tracks and damaged soil that used-to-be a yard. Four large trucks were parked to the side of the house making Never wonder who would be joining them. Justine pulled close to the porch to avoid most of the mud, and took Houdini from Never's lap.

"We'll wait in the car until you are finished," Justine told her as she handed her a lint roller from the console.

"Don't you want to come in?"

"And give a random photographer a shot of me with this cane." Justine shook her head. "No thanks."

"I'll be back as soon as I can."

"Head up, curls behind your shoulder," Justine instructed as she gave her a supportive smile.

"This is it," Never muttered and she stepped out of the car and made her way up the five wooden steps to the peeling white door.

Her fingers barely brushed the wooden panel when it edged open and a male voice ushered her inside.

"We've gathered in the kitchen to speak with you Miss Martinez," a man she recognized as Mr. Bernard informed her as he lead her down the hall.

The pine table in Mrs. Jenkins' kitchen was crowded with men and coffee cups. Cornbread graced the middle of the table in a linin-lined basket, but no one was eating when she walked in. Never studied the faces gathered around the table. She only recognized a few. They had to be a small portion of the group branded "the protectors of the ridge" that saved the statue from being taken last night.

Never was grateful to see them. She had a hard time believing the civilians involved in the battle over the statue made it out alive. Mr. Bernard had on a sling, but the rest of the men sported only an odd bruise or two on their exposed skin.

"I'm grateful to see everyone," she greeted.

"Please take a seat," Mrs. Jenkins invited. "I think we are about ready to start."

Laying out her notebook and recorder in front of her, Never slid into the last remaining seat. Mrs.

Jenkins gave her a nod and they were all walking back through the hours of last night together.

A man named Lenny Aikens began the conversation with, "As near as I can figure it, they started from Wolfe's old house."

"Why do you think that?"

"The scouts on the ridge said that there were lights on at strange hours the night before. They didn't think it was that big of a deal until they heard shooting."

"You think that they were watching from Wolfe's house?"

Mrs. Jenkins nodded. "Mr. and Mrs. Henry were still tied up in their kitchen when the deputies found them."

"What about the 911 call?"

"I didn't make it," Mrs. Jenkins admitted.

"The call didn't come from here?"

"I didn't know what was happening until Bernard showed up at the door with blood on his shirt."

"How long was it between Mr. Bernard coming to the door and the sheriff's department response?"

"Ten minutes, the boys had to fight them off from the tree stands to have a shot at winning," Clay responded as he looked into his mug.

"What do you mean by 'fought them off'? What

happened?"

"There were these three men."

"Two men and an ox would be a better description. The muscles on that man were beyond human," Mr. Bernard chimed in and all the other men nodded.

"What happened after they left the Henry's house?"

"Bernard thinks they killed the deputy in the car on the subdivision road first. Then they came up the hill toward the tree line while everyone was switching out for dinner breaks."

"What happened when they were spotted?"

"It was like they expected the men to scatter. Two of the men walked straight into camp and pulled their guns," Clay spoke up again.

"They were betting that the townspeople protecting the ridge would run when they were threatened?"

"It seemed that way."

"Where did the third man go?"

"He went for the Hanging Tree, and Bernard came across him searching around the base."

"Is that how he got shot?"

"No, the man by the tree had a blade. He was young and fast. He disappeared before Bernard could capture him," Lenny explained.

"Did this man find the statue?"

"No, he came back with one of the others," Bernard explained as he shifted in his seat.

"What happened then?"

Clay pointed to the young man with dark curly hair beside him. "Jimmy had gotten away from the camp, called 911, and snuck back to help Bernard at the tree. I heard shots."

"Then Bernard showed up at the door with blood on his shirt," Mrs. Jenkins concluded.

"How did the rest of the night go?"

"Lights were everywhere. The sheriff's department made a camp in my yard and another in the subdivision on the other side. There were men running everywhere."

"That sounds terrifying."

"It was four hours before I got word that all three were captured."

"What did you do until then?"

"I sat in my rocking chair and prayed."

"I'm sorry to make you relive it," Never comforted as she squeezed the older woman's hand.

"If it wasn't for you, I might not be around to tell it."

"I'm sorry everyone was dragged into this. I couldn't find any other way to stop what Wolfe set in motion. I put us all in danger."

Mrs. Jenkins looked around to all the people gathered at her table before she spoke.

"A mistake made out of love is easier to forgive."

"I hope you're right."

They all sat sipping their coffee for a moment.

"To Never Martinez and the Folman Witch for protecting us once again." Mrs. Jenkins raised her mug and the men gathered at her table followed suit.

Never was surprised by their support, but she couldn't keep a genuine smile from her face. There were so many reasons this could have turned into a tragic mess. Never was amazed that people could forgive so easily. It would take her more time to accept the things she had been through in the past few weeks, but she had to give Wolfe credit for the bond growing between herself and the people in her adopted home. The faces looking back at her around this table had all experienced something they would never forget, and they had survived it together.

CHAPTER 43

Hickory Lake, Robertson County Tennessee,
Three Weeks Later

Never stood on the same platform she had the night she last saw Wolfe, clutching a bundle of flowers. She fidgeted with the engagement ring as she looked across the frigid expanse of Lake Hickory. Her eyes landed on a spot she had seen in the news coverage of the day they pulled Wolfe's body from the water. She was furious the last time they were here together, heart-broken in the visits that followed, but today she wanted to say goodbye to the man who would have made her his family. After all he put her through, it seemed right to be on the pier remembering him.

She would never be a Strickland in the same way she had never been a Martinez. Never shook her head. She shouldn't think about that now. The universe had a strange way of teasing her.

Wolfe did every crazy thing he did to protect them, to protect her. He wanted their love to have roots.

He had already written it in his heart that she was worth saving. Maybe her parents had similar thoughts on the fateful day they took her to the church. Never wished she could find them and figure out if they deserved a chance at redemption as well.

It was so strange to think what a difference time made. Never had seen it over and over again when she talked to sources for her stories. There was a limited time to find answers for her profession, victims needed time to heal before they spoke, and it was up to individuals to decide when to forgive. Everyone had their own timetable.

She had worked for the last few weeks trying to put her thoughts in order. Thoughts that would never make it to any pages other than the journal she kept in her bedside table. Once the final article about Wolfe was written, she had the option of tending to her grief. It took her many nights of pouring herself out on the pages like a spluttering geyser before she had control again. She was accustomed to providing facts on the page, but the garbled flow of emotions coming forward in her entries felt foreign and unnerving.

Never always thought her life's story would be a simple one. The girl who sprang from nowhere would work her way to a normal life and retire to obscurity. But it hadn't turned out that way. Wolfe's deception thrust her into a life she didn't recognize.

The town of Folman was on the map in a big way now that the articles she co-wrote with Landon were receiving national attention. Jerry beamed when he told her earlier this week that the series of articles surrounding Wolfe's death would be up for awards. After her discussion with Mrs. Jenkins, Never had been to several interviews at the Robertson County Sherriff's Department about her date with Ancel Reyes AKA Marcel Weaver. With Justine's testimony and other evidence collaborating her story, Sergeant Henderson and the FBI agent looking into the crime family connections found nothing linking her actions directly to Ancel's quest to reacquire the statue or his unforeseen death. With her final association in Wolfe's story concluded, the pressure accumulating since his death was beginning to ease.

Authorities from the Preservation of Peruvian Art and History had contacted her in person to thank her for the recovery of their property and to tell her there would be a ceremony later in the month to commemorate the transition of the statue back to their country. Never was still processing that bit of information when someone from New Jersey called about the possibility of a book deal. It was flattering, but she gave them an "I'll think about it" before she hung up the phone.

Never had always wanted to write a book, but she expected it would be about someone else's life. Maybe she should give the idea serious consideration after Justine's wedding. Final wedding prep and interviews about her involvement in solving Wolfe's death would fill most of her free time from now until Christmas.

During all the confessions, it was confirmed that the incident at the church was an attempt to abduct Justine and use her kidnaping to get Never to cooperate. They were all lucky that Houdini saved the day with his diversion. It hurt Never to think that Justine might not be able to stand without a cane at her wedding, but they were all dealing the best they could with the unusual circumstances.

Never was even warming to the idea of including
Houdini in the celebration. If Justine had to be helped
down the aisle, Houdini could walk with her instead of
in a wagon with the flower girl. The church organist
would have to double the time of the wedding march so
Justine could make it to the front of the church, but she
wouldn't hear of delaying or postponing her Christmas
wedding plans and neither would Rory. They wanted to
start adding to their family as soon as possible,
beginning next week with a dog. Never would not be
surprised by a baby announcement from them this
spring. Justine and Rory seemed dead set on having the
big family they dreamed of in record time after their
wedding. Maybe when they settled into the suburbs in a
cute little house, Never could commission Archie
Gordon to build them one of the finest kid's
playgrounds in the county. After all, what else would a
cool godmother do?

"I guess everything worked out the way you
wanted," Never whispered as she looked out across the
water.

"That's a strange way of looking at things."

Never didn't need to turn to identify the voice,
but she swiveled to glare her displeasure at Sergeant
Henderson's decision to join her.

"Aren't you a little far from the station,
Sergeant?"

"Things are quiet since you single-handedly
wiped out all the crime in the area."

"So you're going fishing?" she suggested with wide, innocent eyes.

"I ran out of excuses to find you and apologize."

"Hold on...let me call a medic," Never made a show of pulling out her phone. "I think your own venom has finally poisoned you."

Never wasn't expecting the low, rolling rumble of laughter before he spoke, "I didn't expect you to make this easy."

"It is well established that your judgment is lacking."

"Yes, and what I am trying to say is that I was wrong about you."

"That I'm not a murderous, black-hearted woman, with revenge on my mind?"

"You can be overdramatic when you want to be."

"You might want to practice your apologies longer," she told him as she turned back toward the water.

"I was wrong, I admire you, and I could see how anyone would want to strangle you, but not the other way around."

The direction of his thoughts caught her unsuspecting. He had a strong and honest tone she had never heard him use before. Never turned and saw that he had lost the bravado she saw at the sheriff's office. He wasn't here to intimidate her, wasn't wearing his uniform, or his shield. His dark hair was fighting with the wind to cover his eyes and the plaid shirt he had on was sporting a rip near the breast pocket. His jeans were clean and worn, but there was a change in him that ran deeper than his wardrobe. She could feel it as clear as the breeze coming off the lake. He had the air of a man searching for something instead of a man confident he held all the answers. Had Sergeant Henderson taken the last few days to come to grips with his misconceptions as she had?

Never would have to draft a new abstract of David Henderson's character with this information. She couldn't help but thaw to his efforts as if he were a stray dog ambling by. Never didn't know if she trusted him not to bite without warning, but she would give him a chance and see how he behaved. Maybe one day they could find common ground.

"Please believe me when I tell you I am truly sorry."

Never let the silence stretch between them. She didn't want to give his actions over the past few weeks a full pardon, but she had to acknowledge his unusual effort to make amends.

"How about you volunteer to be my escort for Justine's wedding and we call it even?"

He gave her an odd look that included a cocked brow, but it faded into a smile.

"Charity work to absolve me of my crimes?"

"Repairing a bond with the community is never easy." She smiled up at him as he leaned against the railing beside her. "I'm sure with hard work and humility you will make progress."

He seemed apprehensive of their shaky truce, but he made no move to leave. Never was sure he wanted to ask her a string of questions long enough to catch a trout, but he tried to act casual as he feigned interest in the sunset. She felt his eyes on her when he thought she wasn't looking, but the reserve between them grew as she removed the flowers from their packaging. She didn't begrudge him remaining by the railing, one boot propped up on the lowest rung redistributing mud and sand, but Never strived to block out Henderson's presence as she started her ritual.

Picking up the first rose, she tore the rich, red petals off one at a time leaving the thorns and stem behind. Once she had a handful of petals she opened her hand to watch the breeze as it pulled them free of her palm and scattered them. She repeated the pattern over and over again until there was only one long-stemmed rose left. For the twelfth and final rose, she pruned off the bruised outer petals to feed to the breeze as before, but left the perfectly formed bud unspoiled. Never twisted it free from its stem, recited Wolfe's final message, and launched the flower's burgundy heart out into the darkness beyond the pier.

About the Author

JESSICA P. MORGAN is a native of East Tennessee and a Graduate of Tusculum University. This is her fifth novel. She currently lives in Knoxville, Tennessee with her husband and son. She is a proud member of the Knoxville Writers' Guild and the Knoxville Chapter of Sisters in Crime.

For news on upcoming appearances and publications go to facebook.com/jessicapmorganbooks or contact the author at jessicapmorganbooks@gmail.com

Made in the USA
Columbia, SC
09 September 2020